"What happened to your face?"

"Makeup party." Kitty tried to smile. "My niece was the makeup artist today. Don't I look pretty?" Instead of waiting for an answer, she hurried to the front door. With a deep breath, she pulled the door wide.

Oh, no. No no no. She couldn't breathe. Her heart stuttered to a stop, then picked up at triple speed.

That always happened when Tyson Ellis showed up.

Like now.

He stood on the doorstep, staring off into the distance, looking as handsome as ever. He was wearing his tan felt cowboy hat—one of Kitty's favorites. Even though he wore a quilted coat to stave off the chill, his cheeks were red. And when he turned to look at her, the shock on his face was almost comical.

Almost.

Why him? Why now?

But when it came to Tyson, she'd always had terrible luck. So, in an odd way, it made sense that he would show up when she looked this way...

Dear Reader,

Spring is in the air and love is in bloom. Or it might be, thanks to the Fiftieth Sweetheart's Rodeo and Valentine's Festival in my fictional town of Garrison, Texas.

Kitty Crawley has loved Tyson Ellis forever, but he knows nothing about her feelings for him and she's fine keeping it that way. He's handsome, world-weary and no-nonsense, not to mention her brother's best friend. When Tyson's two young nieces come to stay with him, Kitty offers to help occupy the girls. Horseback rides, costume fittings, Valentine's parties and more pass the time. It's all fun and games until it's not.

Being with Tyson makes her heart ache for what she's too afraid to ask for. Tyson's never thought of Kitty as anything other than...Kitty. She deserves a man who'll cherish and respect her. And while his track record with women is littered with lies, betrayal and desertion, his battered heart is oddly tempted to try again—with Kitty.

This book made me smile and giggle a lot while I was writing it. I hope it does the same for you!

I'll see you back in Garrison soon!

Xoxo,

Sasha Summers

HER COWBOY CUPID

SASHA SUMMERS

HEARTWARMING

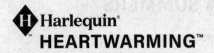

Harlequin®
HEARTWARMING™

Recycling programs
for this product may
not exist in your area.

ISBN-13: 978-1-335-05137-0

Her Cowboy Cupid

 Harlequin Enterprises ULC
22 Adelaide St. West, 41st Floor
Toronto, Ontario M5H 4E3, Canada
www.Harlequin.com

Printed in Lithuania

MIX
Paper | Supporting
responsible forestry
FSC® C021394

USA TODAY bestselling author **Sasha Summers** writes stories that celebrate the ups and downs, loves and losses, and ordinary and extraordinary occurrences of life. Sasha pens fiction in multiple genres and hopes each and every book will draw readers in and set them on an emotional and rewarding journey. With a puppy on her lap and her favorite Thor mug full of coffee, Sasha is currently working on her next release. She adores hearing from fans and invites you to visit her online.

Books by Sasha Summers

Harlequin Heartwarming

The Cowboys of Garrison, Texas

The Rebel Cowboy's Baby
The Wrong Cowboy
To Trust a Cowboy
Home to Her Cowboy

Harlequin Special Edition

Texas Cowboys & K-9s

The Rancher's Forever Family
Their Rancher Protector
The Rancher's Baby Surprise
The Rancher's Full House
A Snowbound Christmas Cowboy
Love Letters from Her Cowboy

Visit the Author Profile page
at Harlequin.com for more titles.

Dedicated to Dr. Aaron King. Thanks for keeping me alive for the past couple of years. My T1 diabetes journey has been a lot, I know. Thank you so much for continuing to cheer me on!

CHAPTER ONE

"THAT'S A VERY bright shade of pink." Kitty Crawley eyed the tube of lipstick her six-year-old niece, Samantha, held at the ready. It was an alarmingly bright shade of pink. Definitely not something Kitty would have worn well...ever.

Samantha was not deterred. Instead, she puckered her lips, her eyes narrowing as she coated Kitty's mouth in what could only be described as neon pink. Once done, she sat back, a satisfied smile on her adorable face. "Pink is *so* pretty."

"Is it, though?" Kitty's sister, Twyla, sat opposite them—her over-the-top makeover already complete. "I hope, when you look back at your childhood, you remember just how much we love you, kiddo."

Samantha Sundays had been a tradition since her niece was a baby. Now she was six, but it was still just Kitty, Twyla, and Samantha—doing whatever sounded most fun. Tea parties. Story time. Pillow forts. Dress-up. That sort of thing. This Sunday, it was makeovers.

For the first time, Samantha requested to do their makeup. Considering Twyla had taken one look at her reflection and sighed, it was likely this would be the one and only time her niece would be playing makeup artist.

"You're silly, Aunt Twyla." Samantha giggled. "You love me *so* much."

"Am I done?" Kitty asked, smoothing one of the braids from her shoulder.

While Twyla's hair was pinned up high on her head with a number of different-colored clips. Kitty's head was covered in a mix of braids and ponytails secured by ribbons.

"Uh-huh. You can look now." Samantha clasped her hands in front of her, beaming with pride.

"Oh my," Twyla murmured when she caught sight of Kitty. She clapped her mouth shut and pressed her lips together—but it didn't wholly stop her from laughing. Instead, it sounded like a series of coughing wheezes.

Samantha nodded. "You look so *so* pretty, Aunt Kitty."

A snort-cough escaped from Twyla.

"I'm sure I do." Kitty braced herself as she turned to look in the vanity mirror. *Oh my, was right.* "Well… I am…colorful."

Aqua blue eye shadow—with glitter—covered her entire eyelid. Samantha's attempt at liquid eyeliner resembled an inkblot test. The liner swept up on the left eye and down on the right. Not to mention how thick and wobbly both lines were. The mascara… Well, her lashes stuck together when she blinked. And that was just her eyes.

Dark red circles sat dead center of either of her cheeks. Similar to the center of a dartboard or hunting target. The pale white foundation only made the contrast that much more startling. All that plus the appallingly glossy and bold lipstick. How all the colors, together, produced an overall jaundicing effect to her skin tone was a mystery. But she did, in fact, have an oddly yellow cast to her face.

"As pretty as a doll." Twyla cleared her throat. "That's been left in the attic to traumatize unsuspecting visitors."

"A princess doll." Samantha nodded, too young to understand Twyla's not-so-veiled insult. "I used all my pretties in your hair."

All. Kitty felt certain Samantha had used every single one of her clips, sparkly rubber bands, and hair ties on Kitty's sandy brown hair. And a bejeweled headband, too. It sat right before the two crooked ponytails atop her head. With all the accoutrements, her hair was as equally appalling as her makeup. But, she only said, "You did a good job on the ponytails." They stuck up, like antennae, on the top of her head—there was no missing them.

"Yay. All done." Samantha clapped her hands together. "Sewing time now?"

"Yes, indeed." Kitty stood. "Mr. Abernathy needs some more cuddle blankets for all his foster animals."

"Yay!" Samantha jumped up and down. "I can make those."

"And you make them very well, too." Kitty smiled down at her beloved niece.

"I like helping all the old kitties and puppies." Samantha sighed. "Poor li'l things." She paused and turned to Twyla, who held a makeup wipe in her hand. "Aunt Twyla! You can't wash it off, yet. I want Daddy and Mabel to see. *Please please please.*"

"Fine." Twyla nodded but she wasn't happy about it.

With any luck, their brother, Jensen, and his fiancée, Mabel, would be home soon and she and Twyla could both scrub their faces clean. Until then, best to find something useful to do. Kitty led the way from Samantha's pink, princess-themed bedroom to the sewing room at the other end of the hall.

"Don't use the good stuff." Twyla followed, leveling her sister with a steely look. "It's not like we're getting paid for these things, Kitty. And money doesn't—"

"Grow on trees." Kitty and Samantha finished the expression in unison, then smiled at one another.

"Grampa says that lots." Samantha sat at the table.

Twyla nodded. "And it's true. Your aunt Kitty means well, being charitable and all, but sometimes she winds up doing and giving too much."

Kitty pulled out the bin of fabric bits and set it on the table beside Samantha's "work" station. "Making blankets out of scraps isn't doing too much."

As the co-owners of the Calico Pig boutique on Main Street, Kitty and Twyla were very careful with their money—as was reflected by their bank account. Not only did they have the largest fabric inventory in a fifty-mile radius, they sold patterns, sewing machines, thread, and any sewing-related notions a person could think of. Kitty also taught quilting classes, did alterations, and occasionally made custom clothing for customers. Recently, they'd started carrying knitting supplies, too. Twyla had grumbled about the initial investment but they'd recouped that investment, plus some, within six months. Donating a few blankets to a local animal rescue and relocation center was the least they could do—in Kitty's eyes, at least.

"Here we go." She'd already cut several twenty-four-inch squares from the fleece fabric for her niece. All Samantha had to do was stack two of the squares together and tie together the cut fringes all the way around. It was an easy no-sew project that kept her niece busy. "All set?"

Samantha nodded, reaching for the top square. "I like this one. Ladybugs."

Kitty was about to sit at the sewing machine when she heard her father. "Someone is at the door." His voice echoed down the hall.

"You go." Twyla didn't look up from her sewing machine. "I'm not facing anyone like this." Where Kitty's face was pink and blue, Twyla's color palette was green and red—like Christmas, Samantha had said.

"But you look pretty, Aunt Twyla." Samantha was all sincerity. "Like princesses."

"Mmm-hmm. And if a real-life prince charming is ringing the doorbell, I *bet* he will fall in love with your aunt Kitty." Twyla glanced at Kitty, her smile all mischief. "Go on."

Kitty hesitated. She knew full well how ridiculous she looked.

But her father's second bellow sounded more agitated than the first. "Would someone answer the dad-gum door?" He wouldn't. He said the only people he wanted to see wouldn't need to knock or ring the bell, they'd come right in.

"Coming," she answered, hurrying down the hall to the great room.

"Land sakes, Katherine Ann." Her father's eyes widened at the sight of her. "What happened to you? To your face?"

"Makeup party." Kitty tried to smile. "Samantha was the makeup artist today."

"Samantha did that?" He scratched his head. "On purpose?"

"Don't I look pretty?" Instead of waiting for an answer, she hurried to the front door. With a deep breath, she pulled the door wide.

Oh no. No no no. She couldn't breathe. Her heart stuttered to a stop, then picked up at triple speed. That was what happened whenever Tyson Ellis showed up.

Like now.

He stood, staring off into the distance, looking as handsome as ever. He was wearing his tan felt cowboy hat—one of Kitty's favorites. Even though he wore a black-and-red quilted coat to stave off the chill in the air, his cheeks were red. And when he turned to look at her, the alarm on his face was almost comical.

Almost.

Why him? Why now?

But, when it came to Tyson, she'd always had

terrible luck. So, in an odd way, it made sense that he would show up when she looked this way. The memory of her reflection had her wincing. The urge to cover her face and flee was almost too much to resist. Instead, she stepped behind the door and peered around it, trying her best to hide.

"Kitty?" He tipped his hat back and scratched his temple.

"Hi." She leaned around the door just enough to see him. "Are you… Is Jensen expecting you?"

"Um…" He blinked, moving closer just enough to see her better.

"Who's there?" Her father yelled. "If they're selling something, tell them to get off my property."

She was so nervous, she blurted out, "Are you selling something?"

"What?" He had yet to stop studying her face. "No. No, of course not." The corner of his mouth quirked up then.

Mercy, but he is a fine-looking man. Kitty's toes curled.

"I was hoping to talk to your dad." He tucked his thumbs into his belt loops. "If now is okay?"

Now was *not* okay. Not when she looked like this. Not when he was wearing that crooked smile. He should stop that so she could breathe normally. But, really, she didn't want him to stop smiling. He had a lovely smile. And, considering he didn't do it all that often, she'd bear it—even if her cheeks were going hot. "Well…" She swallowed. "It's hard to say if it's okay. You know my dad." She gave him a one-shouldered shrug—the shoulder he could see.

"I do." He no longer appeared alarmed so much as confused.

There was no help for it. She'd have to let him in *and* play hostess. Her mother had been a firm believer in gracious hospitality. It didn't matter that she resembled a deranged Muppet. With a deep breath, she said, "Come in out of the cold."

"Thank you." He stepped inside, his gaze never leaving her face.

She reached up to smooth her hair—and wound up patting the bejeweled headband instead. The hair. The makeup. She hurried to explain. "Trying out a new look." Her laugh was forced. "You see, Samantha—"

"Who is it, Kitty?" her father interrupted. "Do I need to get myself up out of this chair and chase them off?"

"It's Tyson, Dad." *Who is staring at me like I've grown a second head.* She waved Tyson to follow her, ignoring the mortification curdling her stomach, and headed back to the great room. While her father would never admit it, he was hard of hearing. So, to play it safe, Kitty repeated herself. "Tyson Ellis is here."

"He is?" Her father set aside his newspaper. With age, her father's face had become permanently embedded with his scowl lines. Now, even if he wasn't in a temper, he looked like he was. "This is a surprise. What's brought you out this way, son?"

A surprise, indeed. Kitty risked another glance Tyson's way. Her sister had been teasing her earlier—she'd no idea that it would be Tyson at the door. But the truth of the matter was, Tyson Ellis *was* Kitty's Prince Charming. A Prince Charming whose attention, in all these years, she'd never managed to catch.

Thanks to Samantha's handiwork, she definitely had his attention now, though in the worst possible way. She'd be all too happy for the floor to open up and swallow her whole.

IT WASN'T TYSON'S place to point out that, perhaps, this new look of Kitty's was not…good. At all. The makeup. The hair. He wasn't sure what look she was going for, but if it was slightly unhinged and a little bit scary, she'd nailed it. Surely, Twyla or Jensen or even her curmudgeon of a father would kindly steer her in the right direction: toward some soap and water.

It took effort to tear his gaze from Kitty, but Tyson managed to do it. Instead of puzzling over her appearance, he needed to focus on why he was here. Business negotiations with Dwight Crawley were never fun. The man loved to hear himself talk and assert his power whenever possible. But, after playing phone tag, Tyson figured coming out to the Crawley ranch was the only way to get things firmed up. If old man Crawley changed his mind, Tyson still had plenty of time to find other options.

"Afternoon, Mr. Crawley." He took off his hat. "I figured I'd stop by and follow up with you. About those calves."

"What calves?" Dwight Crawley sat back in his leather recliner and glowered up at him. "Kitty, how about some refreshments for our guest." He didn't bother to look at his daughter as he spoke.

"I'm fine, thank you." He made the mistake of glancing Kitty's way but—seeing the state she was in was just as jarring the second time. "I don't want to cause any bother."

"It's a little late for that. You're here, aren't you?" Dwight Crawley sighed.

Tyson didn't take offense to the older man's words. Over the years, Tyson had come to accept Mr. Crawley's inability to be civil. It wasn't personal, it was simply his way.

"Dad. Be nice." Kitty's tone was gentle. "It's no bother at all, Tyson." She almost ran from the room, her ponytails streaming out behind her.

"Sit." Dwight nodded at the couch. "How's your pa? I haven't had a chat with Earl in a bit. He still alive and kickin'?"

Tyson sat. "Yes, sir. Getting excited about rodeo season, of course." His father had been a part of the pro rodeo circuit when Tyson was younger. When his body got too banged up and he'd had too many concussions to be cleared, he'd moved on to be a rodeo announcer for Garrison and most of the surrounding rodeos.

"'Course he is." Dwight nodded. "You ever miss it? I know you weren't an all-around like your father, but you weren't too shabby at bronc riding back in the day. I never understood why you gave it up." His gaze narrowed as he spoke. "It's a real shame. Rodeo's in the blood. I bet you would have made your pa proud."

Tyson liked to think he made his father proud even though he didn't participate in the rodeo events. He'd seen the long-term toll years of bull riding had taken on his father's body and mind and still chosen to try his luck at bronc riding. And he had been good at it, too. But after having his leg broken in four places and needing several pins and rods to piece it back together, he'd called it. Not only had he lost his career, he'd also lost his wife. It'd taken a while to heal, but now he was more than content to serve as a pick-up rider during the rodeo—doing his part to keep everyone safe. "Guess I outgrew it."

"Hmm." Mr. Crawley shook his head. "What's this about calves, now?"

"You'd offered to give us the calves for the calf scramble back in October. I just wanted to make sure that was still the plan? For the fiftieth Sweethearts Rodeo? During the Valentine's Festival?" He'd had this conversation with Mr. Crawley two times before. Both times, the old man had acted like it was the first he was hearing about it.

Jensen Crawley, Dwight's son and Tyson's good friend, said his father liked to maintain control. Was the old man trying to keep the upper hand, here? Or did he really not remember the discussion they'd had about this? Correction, several conversations they'd had about this.

"Hmm." Dwight's brows knitted together and he shook his head. "I do not recall such a thing."

Tyson took a deep breath and kept his irritation in check. Getting the older man on the defensive would only make things that much more difficult. "I know, in the past, your family has provided the calves for the calf scramble. I didn't want to assume that would be the case this year." He honestly didn't care one way or the other where the calves came from, but he didn't want to get on Dwight Crawley's bad side, either. That's why he was here, doing his best to keep feathers from getting ruffled, while trying to do his job.

Presently, the most important part of his job was making sure the Sweethearts Rodeo went off without a hitch. It brought in tourists, put heads in beds, and gave Garrison's economy a little boost so the whole town got involved. And while Crawley Ranch normally sponsored the event, so far, he hadn't heard a peep from Dwight or Jensen.

"Here you go." Kitty reappeared, carrying a tray. "You like peanut butter cookies, don't you?" Sure enough, there was a plate of peanut butter cookies and two tall glasses of iced tea.

They were his favorite. "I do." He nodded his thanks. "Thank you."

Dwight took the glass of tea Kitty offered him, his expression shifting to full disapproval when he saw his daughter. He didn't hear what the old man mumbled but, from the red creeping into Kitty's cheeks, it wasn't good.

As much as he'd wanted someone to say something to Kitty, chances were her father wasn't all that tactful about it.

Kitty reached up to pat her hair, and her face went even redder.

"This year is important." He jumped back in, hoping to redirect the conversation. "The Garrison Ladies Guild have big plans for the Valentine's Festival and the rodeo, too—as you've probably heard. They want to pull out all the stops for the fiftieth. Especially Miss Martha. She's invested quite a bit of her own time and money into it."

"That woman." Dwight's tone was razor-sharp. "Throwing her money around, acting important and all. It's *her* personal mission to make sure the whole world knows Garrison is the best little town in all the Hill Country, not mine."

"Fifty years is an awful big deal, Daddy. Definitely something worth celebrating." Kitty offered the plate of cookies to her father, then held it out to Tyson—smiling.

He tried not to stare, he did, but man, her face was even more startling up close. The bright red cheeks. Her eyelids were covered with aqua. Was there glitter in her eyelashes? He did his best to stop staring and took a big bite of the cookie he'd taken.

"That may be." Dwight shrugged. "Whatever that *woman* does has nothing to do with me. Not all of us have the extra time or money to dump into a two-day event that'll get me nothing." Mr. Crawley took another sip of his tea. "If she thought you coming out here name-dropping would get me to start writing checks, she's got another think coming."

This had backfired—terribly. Weren't Dwight and Martha dating? He'd hoped hearing Martha Zeigler's interest would be enough to get Dwight to settle on a deal for these calves. Instead, the old man seemed less inclined to help. "No, sir. She doesn't know I'm here."

But Mr. Crawley didn't look convinced.

"Did…did something happen between you and Miss Martha?" Kitty's question was pure concern.

"What are you talking about?" Dwight glared at his daughter. "Nothing has ever happened between the two of us. Never will, either."

What now? Tyson did his best to keep his surprise in check.

It wasn't every day two of the wealthiest, crankiest, most opinionated people became a couple so, of course, the whole town knew about it. It was big news. But, from the sounds of it, the couple must have hit a rough patch. Now he'd gone and made things worse by kicking up a hornet's nest. It was almost a relief when his phone started ringing.

"Go on." Dwight stood, gripping the handle of his cane. "You young people and your phones. Always on them. Always calling and texting and in each other's business. It seems to me things like respect don't seem important to your generation."

Actually, he agreed with Dwight Crawley on most of what he said. Phones were all too often the reason for a lack of attention or, ironically, miscommunication. But it was his father calling—which he'd only do if it was an emergency. If it was anyone else, he'd let the call go to voicemail. "Excuse me for a moment?"

"Go on and take your call on the way out the door." Dwight Crawley shot him a narrow-eyed glare and pointed at the door with his cane before heading across the great room in the opposite direction.

"Dad." Kitty stood.

Tyson put his hat on his head. "I'm sorry for the inconvenience. Mr. Crawley. Kitty." He touched the brim of his hat and headed for the front door. "Hello?" he answered the call the moment he'd stepped outside. "Dad? What's going on?"

"I just got off the phone with your cousin, Margaret." His father sighed. "You headed home?"

"On my way now." Tyson was down the porch steps and across the lawn to where his truck was parked. "Everything okay?"

"Nothing life or death—don't worry too much. But, come on home and we'll talk when you get here." And his father disconnected.

He stared at his phone. It was good to know whatever was happening wasn't too serious, but his father had called him home—so something was up. He climbed into his truck and started the engine but paused when he saw Kitty running down the steps, a brown paper bag in one hand. In the sunlight, her makeup was more psychedelic than ever.

He rolled down the window of his truck. "I forget something?"

She shook her head, the ribbons blowing in the wind. "I just…here." She handed him the brown paper bag. "The peanut butter cookies. Dad is not supposed to have sugar but he'll find a way to sneak them, so you're helping me out by taking them with you."

He took the bag. "Happy to help."

"And try not to worry about the calf situation. Daddy is in a snit about something, but I'll talk to Jensen and we'll get it taken care of." She smiled and stepped away from the truck. "Take care."

"I appreciate that." And he meant it. Kitty had always been thoughtful. She was sweet—unaffected. In his experience, those were rare qualities. Why she felt the need to start caking herself up with makeup he didn't know. With a parting nod, he backed up the truck, then headed down the driveway.

He turned onto the highway that led back into town, hoping his cousin's circumstances weren't too dire. With the upcoming rodeo and festival, his plate was already full.

CHAPTER TWO

"SOUNDS LIKE YOU'RE doing well." Kitty held the door open for her father but didn't offer him her arm. That would turn his partial bad mood into a full-on bad mood—and she'd rather that didn't happen. He wouldn't take her offer of help as a sign of caring—he'd take it to mean she didn't think he was able to care for himself. Or, worse, that he was weak. Her father couldn't abide weakness in a man. So, as hard as it was, she kept her arm pressed to her side as he, with the aid of his cane, took the steps from the clinic front door to the sidewalk. "Doc Johnson said your cholesterol is down and your blood pressure is, too."

"I know. I was sitting right there, wasn't I?" Her father huffed. "A man my age doesn't have a whole lot left to look forward to. Now he wants me to give up bacon?" He shook his head, scowling. "That's not going to happen."

She wasn't going to argue about this. Arguing with her father was an exercise in futility. Instead, she'd try changing out his regular bacon with turkey bacon and hope he wouldn't notice.

"Good thing you came with me." He glanced her way and shook his head. "Eye infection. I told you there was something wrong. Did you look in the mirror this morning?"

Yes, she had. And, yes, she'd known that what she'd thought was a bad reaction to the eye shadow from her makeover had, indeed, turned into something more serious. Her eye ached, was swollen and was an alarming shade of red. "I'll be fine soon." Thanks to the prescription drops Doc Johnson had given her. Instead of harping on about her eye, she went back to praising her father. "I'm proud of you, Dad."

He made a noncommittal snort.

"Seems like those dance classes with Miss Martha are helping, too." She'd spent the last couple of days trying to figure out what, exactly, had happened between her father and Martha. So far, she'd learned nothing.

"That had nothing to do with it," he snapped back. "And I'm not going to be dragged around by that woman any longer. That's enough of that."

His angry words made Kitty sad. After being a widower for twentysomething years, her father had finally found companionship in Martha Zeigler. That the woman was even more ornery and stubborn than her father was likely the reason they got along so well. Neither one of them could be intimidated by the other. *A match made in heaven.* Or so it had seemed.

Instead of pushing for answers now, she'd try again later—when and if her father was in a better mood. "Twyla is meeting us for lunch." Now that they were on the sidewalk, she could hook arms with her father without fear of retribution.

"I don't see the point in spending money in town when we've got plenty of food at the house." But her father headed toward the Buttermilk Pie Café, anyway.

"It's a Wednesday, so there should be lemon meringue pie." Which was the reason her father wasn't putting up more of a fuss. Lemon meringue pie was his favorite.

"Hmph."

Kitty patted his arm, keeping her pace slow to match his. She didn't mind it, though. She loved strolling the Main Street of her little town. From the big picture windows of all the shops to the old-fashioned street lamps that bordered the sidewalks, Garrison Main Street was charming.

Outside of the florist shop sat several oversize pots of brightly colored pansies. The delicate flowers were swaying cheerfully in the breeze, as if in greeting. Her pleasure was dampened by the sandpaper-like feel of the breeze on her eye.

The stinging and tearing had her digging a tissue from her pocket.

"Katherine Ann." But there was equal parts sympathy and censure to her father's tone. "I don't know what you were thinking."

"I was thinking about how happy Samantha was." She smiled up at her father, blotting the tears from her eye. "You love seeing her smile as much as I do, so don't make a fuss."

"Afternoon," the café owner, Lorraine, called out in greeting. "Twyla's at a table in the back. I'll be over to take your order in a sec."

"She's already here?" her father asked, waiting to reach the table before speaking again. "There's plenty of tables, it's so dad-gum early. Don't you two have a business to run?"

"We do, Dad." Twyla crossed her arms over her chest and sighed. "And we can close for lunch every now and then—if we want to." She glanced at Kitty. "What's the news from the doctor? And did he fix…that?" She pointed at Kitty's eye. "I hope? You're going to scare the customers."

Kitty filled her sister in on everything Doc Johnson said. The two of them tried to share the caregiving of their father. Since Kitty had more patience, she went to all his doctor's appointments. Twyla, ever practical and no-nonsense, made sure he took his daily medication.

"Are we done talking about my health now?

You're not getting rid of me yet." Her father scowled at them across the table.

"Dad." Kitty frowned back at him. Her father was prickly and impatient and sometimes irrational, but she loved him dearly. She had lost her mother in middle school and that hole in her heart had never healed. She couldn't bear the thought of losing her father, too. "Don't say things like that."

"Oh, come on, Kitty. It's not like I'm going to live forever." Her father shook his head.

"But you are going to live?" Twyla rolled her eyes. "For now, anyway."

"Seems like it." Their father chuckled.

"Which is a good thing, too, since you have plans with Miss Martha tomorrow night. She wouldn't take kindly to you messing that up." Like Kitty, Twyla was just as curious to discover why their father was all but frothing at the mouth whenever Martha Zeigler's name was mentioned. So far, her sister's efforts had been just as fruitless as her own.

Still, she held her breath as she waited for her father's response.

"I don't know what you're talking about." He glared at the menu he was holding.

She exchanged a look with her sister. Neither of them was a fan of Martha Zeigler, but there was no denying the effect the woman had on their father. He'd scowled less, laughed more, and gotten out of his recliner to go out and do things. But the past week he'd been back to his grumpy old homebody self, so something had happened.

"And you're not going to lose your eye?" Twyla leaned closer to her for a further inspection. "That looks miserable."

"Stop making me feel worse about it, please." Kitty gently pushed her sister back.

"I did get an email from Martha—the Garrison Ladies Guild want help with costumes for the kids' dance showcase." Twyla shook her head. "I can't believe they waited so long to reach out. It's only four weeks until the Sweethearts Rodeo and Valentine's festival. Kitty can't be up, sewing, round the clock."

"No?" Their father glanced between the two of them. "You're not doing anything else. If you were trying to get yourselves a husband, that'd be one thing. You're not. Might as well do something useful with all the free time you've got on your hands."

"Dad," Twyla snapped. "It's not the nineteen forties. Your daughters' current goals might not include getting married and having a bunch of babies."

"Hmph." He shook his head. "That's selfish. I'd like to be alive to meet my grandchildren."

"Let's try to have a nice family lunch, please."

Kitty blotted her watering eye with a tissue and blinked. Over the years, she'd accepted her position as family peacekeeper. It was a thankless, exhausting job, but someone had to do it. "I'll reach out to her when I get back to the shop."

"Reach out to who?" Their brother, Jensen, came to stand beside the table. "Good morning—" He broke off, frowning at the sight of her. "Kitty. What happened? Are you okay?"

"I'm…" She stumbled to a stop when she saw her brother wasn't alone. It wasn't Mike or Rusty Woodard that bothered her. It was Tyson. She really, *really* couldn't catch a break. "I'm fine."

"You don't look fine." Jensen stooped. "Your eye… You have pink eye? Samantha had it once and it looked just like that."

And now everyone was staring at her.

Thank you so much for drawing attention to it. First the makeup, now the monster-movie eye. Kitty propped her elbow on the table and covered the side of her face with one hand. "I'm fine, Jensen."

"Who'd you get into a fight with?" Rusty Woodard teased. "Want us to settle the score?"

"Funny," she murmured before picking up her menu to use as a shield.

"Doc Johnson gave her something to clear up the infection," her father said. "Are you three joining us?" It wasn't an invitation.

"No, sir," Mikey answered. "Just walked over together."

Kitty glanced over the menu to find she was no longer the center of attention. Tyson...well, he wasn't looking at her at all. Everything was back to normal. She breathed a sigh of relief and set the menu aside.

"Wanted to be neighborly and say hello, is all." Rusty clapped her brother on the shoulder. "Give us a call when you're headed back into town, Jensen. Been a while."

"Will do." Jensen pulled back the remaining chair at the table. "And Tyson, I'll bring some stuff by later on this week. If that works?"

Stuff? What stuff?

Tyson nodded. "I appreciate it."

"You've got this." Jensen offered up one of his encouraging smiles.

"Easy for you to say." From the looks of it, Tyson didn't agree.

Kitty watched the exchange with mounting curiosity. What was happening with Tyson?

"You can't let a couple of little girls scare you." Rusty nudged Tyson with his shoulder.

"I can't?" Tyson ran a hand along the back of his neck. "Guess we'll see."

Little girls? Kitty was beyond curious now.

"You going to sit or go with them?" Her father crossed his arms over his chest and stared up at Jensen.

"We'll go." Mikey Woodard chuckled. "You have yourselves a good day."

"Good to see you all." Rusty touched the brim of his hat.

"Take care of that eye, Kitty." Tyson's warm brown gaze landed on her.

"I…" She swallowed. "Yep." She stared at the table, her face going hot.

Seconds later, they were gone, Jensen was sitting at the table, and her embarrassment was beginning to wane. It was silly, really. Why did Tyson's offhand comment leave her so flustered? After all these years, she should be past the red-cheeked, fawning stage, surely? But no. It wasn't his comment so much as…him. If he was in her presence, she was flustered.

I'm pathetic.

"Everything okay with Tyson?" Twyla asked, glancing her way—because her sister knew how besotted she was. "He seemed worried about something."

"Family stuff." Jensen grinned.

"So it doesn't have anything to do with my cattle?" their father grumbled.

"No, sir." Jensen glanced between them. "Why would it? What am I missing?"

"Nothing." Her father sighed. "Are we going to

order or sit here and starve to death?" He glanced around.

Jensen smiled, then turned to Kitty. "Your eye like that because of the makeup?" He shook his head. "Sorry, Kitty-cat. Looks like it hurts."

"You know how impossible it is to tell Samantha no. Besides, there was no way of knowing I'd have a reaction to the eye shadow." She shrugged. "It's a pain, but I'll be fine in no time."

"Will your pride recover, too?" Twyla murmured so their father wouldn't hear her. Her sister had found it hilarious that Tyson had been the one at the door on Sunday—Kitty, not so much.

Did it sting that Tyson only saw her when she was in a state? Yes. But there was no help for it. She'd resigned herself to the fact that, to him, she wasn't a woman, she was Jensen's little sister. And while her love life was a blank page, she'd watched plenty of love stories write themselves. The one thing they all had in common? There was no denying or forcing the heart to feel. She couldn't control her feelings for him. Just as he couldn't control his lack of feelings for her.

TYSON STOOD IN the middle of the guest room, beyond overwhelmed. This weekend, two little girls would be moving in. It wasn't that he hadn't seen them in person for almost a year or that he'd be responsible for them so much as *two little girls* would be living here for six to eight weeks. The Air Force was shipping his cousin, Margaret, to Germany. She wanted to go ahead, find a place, and turn it into a home before bringing her daughters over. Her husband, who was off doing something classified somewhere else, would be meeting them there.

Since Margaret had no other family, and her husband's family "wasn't suitable to care for the girls," there was no way Tyson or his father would say no. He and his father had been video calling with the girls since they were little, so they called his dad Grampa Earl and he was Uncle Tyson. But that didn't make him feel confident about this arrangement… What did he know about kids? He'd barely been one or had much of a childhood, thanks to his mother. His mother had left when he'd been eight. She'd popped up every few years, needing help with something or other, but then she'd take off without a word. It had been seven years since she'd last made contact and, for his father's sake, he hoped she'd stay gone. He knew not to trust the woman that had birthed him, but his father continued to give her chances—only to have his heart shredded anew. Between his mother and his short-lived marriage, he was wary of the opposite sex. Very wary. It was sad that, somehow, he and his father were the best option for Margaret's girls: June and July.

"You look like a deer in the headlights. What are you doing?" His father stood in the doorway. "You going to cut tail and run?"

"Have I ever?" He put his hands on his hips and faced his father.

His father chuckled. "There's a first time for everything."

"I'll never walk away from my responsibilities." If there was one thing he'd learned from his mother, it was the true meaning of family. Family helped one another out. Family could count on one another. Family stayed with you, no matter what. So helping his cousin out was the right thing to do. He ran his fingers through his hair.

"I know that, son. You've never shirked your responsibilities." His father leaned against the door frame. "Looks clean enough, I'd think."

He glanced at his phone, a text from Jensen scrolling across his screen. "And Jensen's here."

"Good. Nice of him to let us use some of Samantha's old stuff." His father trailed after him down the hall. "I figured the first time this room was made over it'd be when you made me a grandfather." His father chuckled.

"Sorry, I guess."

"No need. There's still time."

He made a noncommittal noise and hoped

his father would drop it. After his mother took off, his father had never recovered enough to try again. If his loving, gentle father couldn't find a loyal partner, who could?

At one time, he'd pictured having a family of his own, but the one time he let his guard down and tried to commit, his worst fears had come true. His accident had been a wake-up call for him and, in a way, for Iris, too. She'd said she'd married a rodeo cowboy not a small-town family business owner. His decision to give up bronc riding had been the first step toward the end. She told him she'd turned to another man because he'd been too busy. But the man she'd turned to happened to be a good-looking all-around rodeo champion with big potential. For him, cheating was it. Iris hadn't put up a fight when he'd suggested divorce. But, in time, he realized he hadn't made time for her—prioritized her the way a husband should prioritize a wife.

He'd spent the last six years questioning whether he'd be able to do that. His faith had been shaken, and the walls he'd put up to protect himself were tall and thick. As a man of habit, he'd become used to the status quo. Other than his father, he had no one to answer to. Any involvement he had with a woman was temporary—he let her know from the start he wasn't interested in anything serious. So far, he'd never been tempted to change that.

He felt bad knowing he might never give his father the grandchildren he was so eager for.

"Evening." Jensen took the steps up onto their front porch. "I brought some reinforcements." He nodded at the truck.

Kitty and Mabel, Jensen's fiancée, climbed out—each holding plastic bins and looking excited.

"Looks to me like you brought some sunshine with you, Jensen." His father was all smiles. "Miss Kitty. Miss Mabel. Awfully nice of you to come give us a hand."

"Of course." Mabel Briscoe shifted the tub to her hip. "Two little girls. Samantha's age, too. We'll have to get them together for a playdate."

Tyson swallowed. Because playdates would now become a part of his life.

"Don't panic," Kitty whispered, peering up at him.

Kitty. Back to her old self—mostly. Her eye was still a little swollen but it was a vast improvement from the technicolor nightmare he'd witnessed on Sunday. He was also pleased to see her without the ribbons and ponytails and glittery lashes. "Trying not to."

"I've got the trundle bed in the truck bed." Jensen gestured behind him. "Give me a hand?"

"I'll take you ladies to the bedroom and see what you think." His father kept on talking as he led Mabel and Kitty inside.

"Your dad seems fine with it." Jensen tugged the wrought iron headboard to the end of the truck bed.

"He is fine. He says it'll give him training for his eventual grandpa duties." He grabbed the other end and, between the two of them, they lifted the frame off the truck.

Once they had all the pieces out of the truck bed Jensen asked, "You're not?"

"I'm supposed to say yes, but…" He shook his head. "Do I have any idea what to do with a four- and six-year-old? Little girls, at that?"

"You might not. But we do." Kitty came walking up. "Mabel and Jensen are raising the most adorable little girl on the planet, so you know they're doing something right. Not to mention Twyla and I are the best aunts in the world." She smiled. "Well, in Garrison anyway. We can help. And if you let the Garrison Ladies Guild know—"

"No." Tyson held up his hand. "If I let them know, they'd be here, underfoot, all the time. Getting into my business." If he gave that nosy bunch of gossips the slightest indication he needed help, they'd give it to him. Not just where the girls were concerned, either. They liked to think of themselves as some sort of Garrison matchmaking service and, being a longtime bachelor now, he'd be a great challenge for them.

Jensen chuckled. "Let's spare him that *help*, Kitty."

"But I appreciate the concern." And he did, too.

"Of course." Kitty leaned into the back seat of the truck and pulled out another box . "All I meant was you've got plenty of backup." She gave him another smile and headed back into the house.

Her assurance eased some of the tension from his shoulders. She was right. He wasn't alone. "Your sister is something else, Jensen."

"She is selfless. Caring. Positive. Gentle." Jensen paused, then added, "And pretty."

"I was going to say *kind* but that works, too." When he faced his friend, Jensen's expression gave him pause. "What?"

His friend's inspection was a little too intent. "You think my sister is pretty?"

"She is." What sort of question was that? Wasn't it obvious? Anyone with eyes would say as much. So why did he feel like he'd said something wrong? "Is this a trick question?"

Jensen shook his head and hefted one end of the bed frame. "Let's get all this inside so we can put it together."

Tyson was impressed by what they managed to accomplish in a couple of hours. It was no longer an oversize storage room stacked high with broken furniture, steamer trunks, and cardboard boxes. Now it was a proper bedroom—a girlie-girl bedroom at that.

"Samantha's favorite color has always been pink." Mabel pointed around the room. "As you can tell."

Sure enough, the wrought-iron daybed was draped with a pink, purple, and white comforter and an array of pillows. Two large framed prints of pink-tutu-wearing ballerinas dancing amongst the clouds hung on either side of the room's large window. On the back wall sat a mini white vanity table, mirror, and pink-poof-topped stool. A bookcase, with books, and two bean bags sat in the corner.

"I can't thank you enough for all this." Tyson shook his head. If he and his father had been left to outfit this room… Well, he didn't want to think about how it would have turned out.

"It's all hand-me-downs or things in storage." Mabel slipped her arm through Jensen's and smiled up at her fiancé. "Samantha wanted to come but it's a school night."

"And she'd probably have been too helpful." Jensen dropped a kiss on Mabel's temple.

Tyson didn't mind the affection. If anything,

Jensen and Mabel had earned the right to express themselves so openly. Their two families had been feuding for generations—and that feud had almost kept them apart. But love had won out and the two had found their soulmates. He might be too jaded for such things, but he was happy for his friends all the same.

"The trundle bed is easy." Kitty crouched by the bed, lifted the bed skirt, and grabbed the handle. "Pull it out like this." She did. "Flip this forward and it can be a regular bed or leave it closer to the ground, as it is." She smoothed her hand over the pink coverlet. "It's made up and ready to use." She glanced up at him. "When do they get here?"

"Saturday." And there was still plenty to do between now and then.

"How about you bring your whole family over for dinner on Sunday?" Tyson's father asked. "I'll cook up some brisket and we can let the girls play some? I'm sure June and July would like having someone their own age to play with."

"June and July?" Kitty lit up. "Those are their names? How precious."

"They are. Watched them grow up on the computer through video chat or the like." His father went on. "They're cute as buttons, both of them. They call me Grampa Earl and him Uncle Tyson, since they've got no other family."

Tyson had no illusions—they were going to have their hands full. Once again, he was grateful for his friends. As much as he prided himself on his independence, this was one time he wasn't going to hesitate to ask for help.

"I can't wait to meet them." Kitty paused. "And I can't wait for your brisket. Don't tell my dad but yours is way better."

Which had his father chuckling—and beaming with pride.

"Sunday? What about Samantha Sundays?" Mabel wrinkled up her nose.

Before he could ask what Samantha Sundays were, Jensen cut in.

"I'm sure she'll be fine with it." Jensen gave Mabel's shoulder a squeeze. "You know Samantha—she loves making new friends."

"Is there anything else we can help with?" Mabel asked, spinning slowly to assess the room.

"You all have done so much." His father glanced at him. "Tyson?"

"Thank you. All of you." He let out a deep breath. "Now they won't be sleeping on the floor in sleeping bags." He was only sort of kidding.

"Then we'll head home." Jensen took Mabel's hand. "You ready, Kitty?"

That's when he realized Kitty Crawley was staring at him. Her light brown eyes seemed honest-to-goodness glued to him. Was there something on his face, maybe? A dusky pink was creeping into her cheeks. He waited, expecting her to say something. Surely, she was going to say something. But she didn't. The longer she stayed quiet, the more awkward things became.

"Kitty." Mabel grabbed Kitty's arm and gave it a gentle yank. "Let's go."

Kitty blinked several times, then pressed her eyes shut. "Right. Bye," she murmured, her face scarlet as she spun on her heel and headed for the door.

What was that all about? He watched her—watched as each step got faster and faster until she was practically running down the hall. The resounding thump of the front door signaled her departure.

"Oh." Mabel's voice dragged his attention back to the other people in the room. "We should go, Jensen."

Jensen, he noticed, was trying not to laugh, but Mabel hurried after Kitty.

"What did I do?" Tyson glanced from his father to Jensen.

"Nothing." Jensen was laughing then. "I should go before they decide to leave me."

Which didn't clear up a thing. "Okay." He shook his friend's hand. "Thank you, again." Long after the Crawleys had gone home, Tyson was pondering Kitty's reaction. He liked to think he knew her well. He and Jensen had grown up together—making Kitty a fixture in his life. If he'd done something to bother her, he should fix it. Chances are, he'd be relying on her while the girls were in town and, besides, he didn't want things awkward between them. Knowing Kitty, it wouldn't take much to sort things out. Something else he'd always appreciated about her: how uncomplicated she was. No secrets. No subterfuge. Just Kitty. He liked the fact that he always knew where things stood with her.

CHAPTER THREE

KITTY SNEEZED—AGAIN—then blew her nose with the tissue in her hand.

"Four," Samantha announced. "Bless you."

"Is it just four?" Twyla tapped her chin with a knitting needle. "I think that was five."

"Okay. Five." Samantha had a box of tissues at the ready. "Need another tissue, Aunt Kitty?"

She shook her head. "I'm good." At least, she hoped so. Her nose was getting sore. "The allergy medicine should kick in any minute." *Please, please kick in.* If she hadn't forgotten to take her medicine this morning, she wouldn't be in this state. Well, at least not this bad, anyway.

While the high rainfall had turned the countryside lovely shades of green and peppered the hillsides with early wildflowers, it had also caused an uptick in mold spores—and the need for allergy medicine and tissues. In a couple of months, the worst would be behind her.

"Poor thing." Dorris Kaye sat opposite her, one of the regulars for their scheduled Friday knitting session. "All that sneezing has to give you a headache?"

"You might not get a headache but, if I have to put up with this for another fifty years, I might get one. Maybe this will be the year you give in and stop being stubborn? Start those allergy shots?" Twyla set aside the knitting she was working on. "It would put an end to all your suffering… And your Rudolph the Red-nosed Reindeer look."

Samantha cocked her head to one side. "You *do* have a red nose Aunt Kitty."

"Just like Rudolph." Twyla sighed. "But you wouldn't, if you get shots."

"You putting pressure on your sister isn't going to help a thing, Twyla." Barbara Eldridge, another Friday regular, kept right on knitting. "You do what's right for you, Kitty. Only you know what that is."

"She's right." Dorris laughed. "Everyone's got an opinion, even well-meaning sisters, but you can't let that influence you. I admit, the older you get, the easier this is."

Kitty smiled her thanks. While there was a strong stubbornness streak in the Crawley family, that had nothing to do with it. Fear did. She'd had a needle phobia since she was a child. If it was someone else, she was fine. But herself? She got light-headed and flushed and went into a full-blown panic attack. She was supposed to willingly inflict that sort of torture on herself once a month?

"What if your nose explodes? Like Daddy said." Samantha's concern had Kitty patting her hand.

Everyone else was laughing.

"I think your daddy was teasing, little miss." Dorris winked at the little girl.

"Your auntie's nose will be fine." Barbara nodded. "A little raw, maybe. But fine."

"Don't you worry." Kitty's attempt at reassurance was derailed as she sneezed four times in rapid succession.

"Nine." Samantha held the tissue box out for her. "That's lots of sneezes."

"Bless you." Twyla, peered up from the pattern she'd been working on. "Times infinity."

"Thank—" She sneezed with such vigor, the loose bun on top of her head started to slip free. "Thank you."

Considering how rotten she felt, Kitty was grateful Friday afternoons at the Calico Pig were quiet. She and Twyla had finished inventory earlier in the day, she'd emailed a reminder for next weeks' quilting class, and taken in a dance costume for repairs. Twyla had gone to pick up Samantha after school, and the three of them had set up for the knitting group's arrival.

Normally the entire Garrison Ladies Guild was here, so Kitty had hoped she'd have a chance to talk to Miss Martha about the upcoming Valentine's Festival. Instead, it was only Barbara and Dorris—so she'd have to call Miss Martha later than evening.

"Looks like we've got a customer." Twyla put a hand on Kitty's shoulder. "You stay put. Nurse Samantha will take care of you. She brought her doctor bag just for you."

"A good nurse is always prepared." Barbara nodded.

"If you decide you don't want to be a princess when you grow up, Samantha, you could be a nurse." Dorris chuckled. "That way you can take care of your daddy or aunties when they get to be my age."

"Can I be a princess nurse?" Samantha unwound a long strand of sparkly pink yarn into her lap.

"I don't see why not." Kitty gave her a hug.

Samantha slipped off of her chair, set the box of tissues she'd been holding on the floor beside her chair, and dug through the "doctor" bag she'd put together. "No Band-Aids… Want a cool pack?" She looked up at Kitty, her gaze considering as she asked, "Do you have a temp-ture?" When Kitty shook her head, she offered her a princess cup full of water. "Here's water. Gotta stay hy-brated."

"I do need to stay hydrated." Considering she was working on her second box of tissues, water would probably do some good. "How is your knitting coming?"

Samantha held up her knitting needle. "It's got some knots."

In fact, it appeared to be mostly knots hanging off of the little girl's knitting needle but Kitty gave her an encouraging smile anyway. "It's a start."

"The more practice the better. Let me show you how to do this loop…" Barbara set her knitting needles aside.

"Okay." Samantha handed over her knitting and squished into the oversize armchair beside Barbara.

"Um, Kitty." Twyla cleared her throat. "Someone would like to see you."

"Okay?" Kitty stood and saw RJ Malloy.

In all the years she and Twyla had run the Calico Pig, she was confident RJ Malloy had never stepped foot inside the shop. He wasn't a quilter. Or a knitter. He was more of an all-around troublemaker—everyone in Garrison knew as much. If it wasn't for his friendship with her brother, she'd likely go out of her way to avoid the man.

So why was he here? Why was he asking to

see her when Twyla was just as capable of helping him with store business?

Twyla was, at that moment, beckoning her over with one finger—her gaze darting to the left and right. It took a minute for Kitty to understand but, once she did, she hurried to the front of the store, where RJ waited. She liked Barbara Eldridge very much, but Dorris Kaye was a bit of a gossip and, from Twyla's reaction, whatever was happening might be worthy of gossip.

"Miss Kitty." RJ stood, his hat in his hands.

"RJ." She smiled, then sneezed. "Sorry." She sneezed again.

"Bless you." He pulled a handkerchief from his pocket and offered it to her. "It's clean. Pulled it out of the dryer before I headed this way. Looks like allergies got a hold of you?"

"Thank you." She took the handkerchief. The soft cotton was a vast improvement to the tissues. "You could say that." Was it her imagination or had RJ shaved? And ironed his shirt? He looked—neat. Very unlike RJ Malloy, to be sure.

"I was hoping you'd help me find something for my momma's birthday. Audy thought you might be able to help."

Audy? Audy Briscoe? She looked to Twyla, who only shrugged. "I can try."

"I'd appreciate that." He was turning his hat in his hands. "You know I've put my poor momma through a lot. Everyone knows, don't they?" His grin was quick. "I figure, I should get her something special. To thank her." He cleared his throat. "Audy says Brooke says you have a real strong…feminine intuition… If you have time?"

Audy and Brooke sent him to her to help him buy a present. "A birthday present for your mother?" Now it sort of made sense why he was here for her help—specifically.

"Yes, ma'am. Something nice?" He cleared his throat again, then smoothed his starched shirt-front. "I mean… That's part of it… Or… If it's better, I could come back later?" He tugged at his collar. "Buy you dinner?"

She was now staring, openmouthed, at the man. "Dinner?" Surely she hadn't heard that correctly. "You're asking me to dinner?"

"No… I mean, yes, ma'am. I messed up already." He sighed. "I wasn't supposed to ask you about dinner straightaways like that."

"Weren't supposed to ask?" she repeated, more confused than ever now. "Says who?"

RJ opened his mouth, his gaze bouncing to the back of the store for the first time. His mouth clapped shut and he headed for the door. "I… I've got something to do." He pushed out the door and slammed into the person coming in. "Sorry," he grumbled before disappearing.

"What was that all about?" Twyla shook her

head, tugging on one earlobe, then the other. "Were my ears malfunctioning just then or did RJ Malloy ask you out?"

"I *think* so." She'd known RJ for years and he'd never expressed any interest. Ever. Truth be told, she couldn't remember the two of them exchanging more than a handful of words at a time—and nothing intimate enough to warrant a date.

"Was that RJ?" *Tyson?* Tyson was the person RJ had slammed into on his way out.

Because of course he'd show up today. First the makeup, followed by the eye infection, then being caught staring at him at his place, and now the Rudolph nose. It seemed like the cosmos was sending her a message when it came to Tyson Ellis. And it wasn't an encouraging sort of message, either. But that didn't stop the surge of pleasure flooding her chest or the delighted smile the sight of him put on her lips or wishing, for a split second, that Tyson Ellis had been the one to ask her to dinner.

Tyson hadn't expected RJ Malloy to come barreling out of the Calico Pig and almost knock him on his rear—but that's what happened. RJ had been so distracted he'd seemed just as surprised as Tyson by the impact.

"It was RJ." Twyla headed to one of the large picture windows, craning her neck to look one way—then the other. "Today certainly got interesting." She giggled. "Very interesting."

"I'll say." Dorris Kaye marched to the front of the store, her eyes wide and alert. "I can't believe what I heard."

Tyson rolled his shoulder. "Why is that?" Twyla and Dorris were both peering out the window now, so he turned to Kitty for an answer.

Kitty shrugged. "Nothing, really—"

"Aunt Kitty got asked on a date." Samantha skipped to Kitty and grabbed her hand. "He asked, didn't he, Aunt Kitty?"

RJ had what now? He watched as red flooded Kitty's cheeks. RJ and Kitty? Now that was a couple he couldn't picture. Not that she appeared all that thrilled over the prospect.

"He cleaned up for you, Kitty." Twyla went on. "Shaved. Ironed his shirt. For once, he didn't smell like beer."

RJ had made all that effort? That was…interesting.

"Who knew, under all that scruff and obnoxiousness, there was a remotely handsome man." Dorris turned to give Kitty a head-to-toe inspection. "What's that saying? A good woman can change a man?"

"No no no. I… I don't think…" Kitty's words tapered off.

"I'm in shock." Twyla pointed at her. "I'd say you are, too."

"No… He… I…" Kitty shook her head vigorously. "You know how RJ is. It's probably a trick…or something?"

RJ had been known to let the air out of someone's tires, trade out road signs, fill someone's air vents full of fish bait, or, if drunk enough, try to steal a stock trailer or horse tack. He might have a long history of minor vandalism but playing with a woman's heart hadn't been a part of that. If that's what this was about, it was more despicable than any prior offense. Besides, Kitty wasn't the sort of women to be toyed with.

"Why would you automatically assume that?" Twyla sighed. "Honestly, Kitty, you're not some mean old crone with warts and a giant crooked nose. You're a young woman—pretty and sweet. Why wouldn't a man ask you out?"

Tyson studied the woman in question. Twyla was right. But she forgot to add that Kitty could do a whole lot better than RJ.

"Do you think he's ham-some, Aunt Kitty?" Samantha was tugging on Kitty's arm.

"I do—" A sudden sneeze erupted. Then another. She pressed the handkerchief to her nose and squeezed the bridge of her nose.

"You do?" Twyla's gasp was pure shock.

Honestly, he was a little surprised as well.

"No." Kitty held up her hand. "I sneezed." She waved her sister away. "Can we stop talking about this now?"

"If he was serious, he'll be back." Twyla faced her sister, her brows high. "Might want to think about what you'll say when he shows up next time."

"If," Kitty murmured.

"He wants your help finding his momma a present." Samantha was bouncing around Kitty. "That's nice."

"It is nice." Kitty smiled at her niece.

"And he gave you his hanky for your sore Rudolph nose." Samantha pointed at the red plaid square of fabric. "That's nice, too."

He eyed the handkerchief in Kitty's hand. Any man who'd been brought up right would have offered up his handkerchief. But RJ had never been the sort to worry about things like that... Before.

On the surface, it did appear that RJ was being nice. Maybe that's why he was worrying. None of this was typical RJ behavior and, whatever this was, he didn't want Kitty drawn into it.

"He was on his best behavior. As surprising as it is, I'd say RJ is trying to get your attention, sister-of-mine." Twyla took Samantha's hand and led her to the counter. "Now, how about we get Mr. Ellis's order for him?"

"Okee-dokee." Samantha skipped along.

"Sorry you walked into this." Kitty shoved the hanky into her pocket. "It's not a big deal. I don't know why Twyla's carrying on like this."

"Because it's not every day my little sister gets hit on," Twyla called out.

Tyson frowned as Kitty's cheeks went red again. What was RJ up to?

"Where are the Ellis Feedstore shirts, Kitty?"

Kitty hurried to the counter. "Here." She pulled out a stack of folded shirts she'd embroidered the Ellis Family Feed and Ranch Supplies logo onto. "I think they turned out well. Take a look and make sure you're happy with them, though." She slid the shirts across the counter to him.

He flipped through the shirts and nodded. "Looks good."

Kitty slid them into a Calico Pig paper bag. "Everything ready for the girls' arrival tomorrow?"

"That's right." Dorris Kaye's hearing was unparalleled. If there was something worth knowing, she'd pick up on it from another room. Now she stood at the counter, wide-eyed with interest. "You and your daddy are taking in your cousin's kids?"

He nodded.

"That's a big ask for you two bachelors, isn't it?" Dorris sighed. "Is everything okay with your cousin? Why is the poor dear having to bring the girls to you?"

"Oh for goodness sake, Dorris." Barbara Eldridge's voice surprised him. When he turned, he found her sitting in the back corner of the shop, knitting needles clacking away. "Leave the poor man alone and come finish your scarf. With RJ dropping by, you've already got plenty to talk about."

Dorris huffed, her outraged expression giving way to a giggle. "I suppose I do. I never." She was shaking her head as she joined Barbara.

Kitty's sigh caught his attention. Sure enough, her eyes were closed and her cheeks were aflame. She'd always been shy, so knowing she'd be talked about and linked to RJ Malloy likely had her unhappy. Still, she saw him watching her and forced a smile onto her face.

That was Kitty—always smiling and trying to make others happy.

"I'm sure she'll find something else to talk about before too long." He kept his voice low, for Kitty's ears alone.

"It's fine." She wrinkled up her nose, pressed the hanky to it, and sneezed once—then again.

"Aunt Kitty's got them allergens." Samantha nodded gravely. "She's sneezed a trillion-million times. Daddy says her nose might 'splode."

"Let's hope not." Tyson chuckled.

Samantha nodded. "Yep." She bounced on the balls of her feet. "Aunt Kitty says I can come to your house to meet June and July and play with them, too?"

"Yes, ma'am. I'm betting the three of you will be friends." At least, he hoped so.

"I am nice." Samantha pointed at herself. "I'll be extra nice to them."

He chuckled. "I'm counting on you, Samantha."

"Sorry." Kitty sneezed again, her eyes meeting his as she held the bag of shirts out to him.

"No need. I get allergies myself every once in a while." His gaze bounced between her and the hanky. Whatever this was, knowing RJ, it wouldn't end well. He hesitated, then heard himself say, "I guess you don't need me tellin' you to be careful. Around RJ, I mean?"

Kitty's eyes widened. "There's nothing… That was just…" She shook her head and murmured, "It's fine."

Tyson sighed. That she was so flustered only increased his concern. Since when did RJ Malloy have this sort of effect on her? Or was it simply that she was embarrassed? As much as he wanted to believe it was the latter, he couldn't shake his discomfort. All of this was worrying. He didn't like it.

"Kitty's a big girl." Twyla propped one elbow

on the counter, her brown eyes pinned on him. "Plus, she's already got a big brother to protect her."

Twyla was right. "I'll hold my peace and mind my own business." He paid for the shirts, said his goodbyes, and left the Calico Pig.

But he hadn't made it a block before he was reaching for his phone and dialing Jensen.

"Hey, Jensen." Tyson kept walking. "You got a second?"

"Shoot."

"RJ Malloy showed up at your sisters' shop just now. He asked Kitty out." What was he doing? Had he really needed to call? Chances were, Twyla or Kitty would have told him everything—they were close like that. So why was he getting involved?

"What did you say?" The gruff edge to Jensen's words made Tyson feel better.

"You heard me. Cleaned himself up, even. Dorris Kaye will likely have the whole town buzzing over it before nightfall." It was his duty to alert his friend that RJ was up to something with his sister. If Tyson had a sister, he knew Jensen would do the same. Especially if his sister was as naive and sweet as Kitty. "I figured you'd want to know."

"Yeah, well… I don't like it." Jensen sounded

a whole lot like his father when he was angry—and he was angry.

Good. "Me neither." And he didn't like the way Kitty was blushing and flustered and having a hard time meeting his gaze, either. But he kept that to himself.

There was a long pause. "I appreciate it, Tyson, but I guess, if Kitty's interested, there's not much I can do about it."

Tyson came to a stop in the middle of the sidewalk.

"RJ's not my first pick, but if he gets his act together and treats my sister well, I guess I'll have no reason to complain. As long as she's happy, I mean."

Wait, what? Tyson swallowed. What sort of response was that? Jensen knew RJ. He loved his sister. He should want the best for her. That wasn't RJ Malloy—anyone with half a brain would know as much.

"You've got enough going on right now, so let me worry about it," Jensen said. "We'll see you tomorrow night?"

"Yeah." He frowned. "Sounds good." He hung up the phone, still reeling. Was Jensen serious or was he messing with him? Tyson wasn't amused. There was nothing funny about any of this. Not RJ showing up dressed to impress or Kitty's rattled state thanks to RJ or Jensen's suggestion that RJ and his sister weren't the worst suited couple...ever.

He took a deep breath.

Jensen was right about one thing. Tyson was busy and, with the girls arriving tomorrow and the Sweethearts Rodeo next month, he was only going to get busier. He didn't have time to take on something that had nothing to do with him.

"Fine." He climbed into his truck and slammed the door shut. He'd mind his own business. But if RJ stepped out of line or if Tyson's gut told him something was wrong, he wasn't going to stand around doing nothing. He knew what it was like to be humiliated and have his heart stomped on. There was no way he'd let that happen to Kitty.

CHAPTER FOUR

KITTY UNLOCKED THE front door of the Calico Pig and held the door open. She balanced the to-go cup carrier with their coffees and the brown paper bag holding their breakfast. "Why does everything from Old Towne Books and Coffee smell so good?" She held the door wide for her sister. "After you."

"I don't know, but don't squish my pastry because I'm starving," Twyla murmured over the box of sewing bits and bobs she carried.

"I wouldn't dream of it." She followed her sister inside.

It was going to be a good day. Saturdays brought tourists from all over—which Kitty loved. Someday, she wanted to travel. She liked the idea of expanding her world beyond the Texas Hill Country. Not for long, of course. Garrison was her home. But the idea of a far-flung adventure held all sorts of appeal. Since that wasn't in her immediate future, she enjoyed chatting with those who visited the Calico Pig.

"Did you get the mail?" Twyla slid the box she'd carried inside onto the counter. "I'll get it," she said, after Kitty shook her head.

Kitty unpacked their breakfast. "Yummy." Hazel and Ryan Diertz, the newlyweds who owned Old Towne Books and Coffee, had to be almost as smitten with coffee and baking as they were with one another. It came across in every bite or sip—carefully crafted flavors that delighted the nose and tickled the taste buds.

"Goodness, I can smell that all the way up here. And my stomach is growling." Twyla returned with a handful of envelopes. "What's this?" She opened one and froze.

"What's wrong?" Kitty knew what that look meant—her sister wasn't happy.

"What's wrong? It seems we've got our decree from the Garrison Ladies Guild. I can't believe this. Seventy cowboy hatbands adorned with sequins and hearts, forty tulle heart tutus, and seventy red-and-pink-fringed vests." Twyla waved the paper in front of Kitty's face. "And that's on top of running the shop and, you know, eating and sleeping and living."

All of that? "It's manageable." Attitude was everything. Yes, it was a lot to do and not a lot of time to do it in but…

"Kitty." Her sister shook her head, her irritation obvious. "Remember, I don't want to take on big jobs with a short turnaround like this anymore. It would be one thing if we had time to prepare, but we don't. And you know Martha—she's not exactly easy to please. If you agree to this, you're signing up for a month of no sleep, constant criticism, and headaches."

"Gretta said she'd help."

Twyla just stared at her.

"What?" Kitty pushed the braid from her shoulder, determined. Twyla was a glass-half-empty kind of person—she always had been. So it would be up to her to keep their spirits from waning.

"What do you mean, *what*? Gretta can't sew." Twyla's voice continued to rise.

Which is true. She tried again. "I'm sure she can do something else to help." She eyed the cinnamon streusel muffin in her hand, not nearly as hungry as she'd been minutes before. She'd never admit it to her sister, but the order was daunting. "But Mabel and Brooke do—so I'll reach out to them. If we can divide and conquer, the work won't be too bad."

"Mabel's got a wedding to plan. Brooke has a brand-new baby and a hair salon to run." Twyla's valid arguments were rapidly deflating her hope-filled bubble. "I feel like this is personal—like Martha is mad at Dad, and she's taking it out on us."

Martha Zeigler was loud and opinionated but

Kitty had never considered her vindictive or petty. "I doubt that."

"Because you always choose to see the best in everyone." The way her sister said it, it wasn't a compliment. "Someone could scream insults at you and you'd make some excuse—like they had a bad day or were going through a hard time or something."

"Getting angry is better?" Anger had played a far too substantial role in her upbringing. Her father had been brought up clinging to the Briscoe-Crawley family feud. When her mother died, his anger had compounded. Years of pointless squabbles with her brother, Jensen, had everyone walking on eggshells—and kept the air in the house charged with tension. The last couple of years had been easier between them, thanks to their mutual love for Samantha. That little girl was the glue that kept them together.

Needless to say, Kitty refused to let anger into her heart. She didn't want to waste her energy or time cultivating something so destructive. Life was hard enough without having a bitter mind-set. "I'll make some calls, Twyla. I'm sure I can find some people to pitch in."

Twyla snorted. It was such a familiar sound—so like their father—that Kitty giggled. Not that she'd dare say as much to her sister. There was no faster way to get her sister upset than to compare her to their father.

"What's so funny?" Twyla asked, her brows rising.

"Oh, nothing." But she headed to the front of the shop and flipped the sign to Open with a smile on her face. She was still smiling when Audy Briscoe's loud pickup truck parked in front of the shop and RJ Malloy stepped out of the passenger door. He said something, then hopped up onto the sidewalk and made a beeline to the glass-front shop door. There was a bunch of flowers in his hand.

"Morning," he said, stepping just inside the door. It was weird to see RJ like this. Normally, he looked like he'd just rolled out of bed and was suffering from a hangover. This RJ was bright-eyed, chipper, and neat from head to toe. "How's your day starting off?"

"Oh well, fine." Kitty mumbled. "You?"

"Looking brighter by the minute." He held out the flowers to her.

She blinked. "For me?"

"Yes, ma'am." He smiled.

"Why, RJ Malloy, look at you being all charming. You shine up like a new penny." Twyla came to stand by her side. "I hear you're working out on the Briscoe place?" She waved out the window at the waiting truck.

"I am. But we had to pick something up first, so I figured I'd drop these by." He nodded at the flowers.

"I never thought of you as a morning person." Twyla didn't bother hiding her full-body inspection of the man—or keep the skepticism from her voice. "Can't help but wonder what, exactly, you are up to?"

RJ shrugged. "The early bird gets the worm, don't it? Or I've heard tell that's the case." He cleared his throat, looking uncomfortable. "Anyway." He waited for Kitty to take the flowers. "I thought... These are for you."

"Thank you." Kitty stared down at the carnations and daisies. It was so unexpected she wasn't sure what else she was supposed to say.

"You know, Kitty loves flowers, but—" her sister pretended to whisper "—the real way to her heart is a man's ability with a needle. Can you sew?"

"Sew?" RJ tipped his straw cowboy hat back. "'Course I can. My maw made sure I knew how to patch my jeans or sew back on a button."

"Sounds like you were raised right." Twyla glanced at her. "Sewing on buttons wouldn't be all that different from sewing hearts onto hatbands, I wouldn't think?"

Kitty shot her sister a look. Yes, they needed help, but asking RJ for help was wrong. If—and it was a big *if*—he was sincerely interested in her, then she wasn't going to use that to her benefit. "Stop teasing, Twyla."

"Who said I was teasing?" Twyla smiled brightly. "I didn't."

"Well, lemme know. I can bring my own thimble." RJ smiled, nodded, then touched his hat. "I'll see you later, then." With a wink, he turned and headed out of the shop.

Twyla waited for the door to close before saying, "A wink and flowers. All before nine in the morning."

Kitty peered out the front window at the truck backing away from the curb, more confused than ever.

"I can tell what you're thinking and, if this is a joke, he's going to an awful lot of effort." Twyla crossed her arms over her chest. "I'm going to call Brooke and see what she has to say about it."

"No, no." She sighed as she carried the bouquet back to the counter. "This is my…conundrum. I'll handle it."

"Conundrum?" Twyla laughed. "That's one way to put it. And what about the other conundrum? Courtesy of the Garrison Ladies Guild?"

"I'll make some phone calls about that." Kitty pulled a vase from beneath the counter. "It's all going to work out, Twyla. You'll see. That's one of the best parts of Garrison—the way everyone rallies to help one another."

"Let's hope that's the case or we will be calling RJ and his thimble for help." She glanced at Kitty. "Though I'm sure you'd prefer it was Tyson offering and not RJ."

"Let's not start that again." She arranged the flowers in the vase.

"Nothing has started. That's the problem." Twyla grabbed one of her hands. "What's stopping you from going after the man you've been pining for as long as I can remember? If Jensen can fall in love with a Briscoe, why are you so resistant to even try with a man who's your friend? And a friend of the family?"

She had plenty of reasons… Because he *was* her friend. Because he was too good-looking for a homebody like her. Because loving him from afar kept her from experiencing actual heartbreak. "Finding a man handsome doesn't mean I'm pining for him."

Twyla stared at her for a minute before she said, "Well, okay then. Might as well give RJ a chance. He's obviously interested so, with him, there's no fear of rejection."

"You want me to date RJ Malloy?" All she could so was stare at her sister in disbelief.

"Why not? Have some fun. We all know RJ is good at having fun."

"If by *fun* you mean breaking the law?" She picked up her coffee. "I haven't had enough coffee to keep up with this conversation."

"So you're saying we'll pick this up later on?" Twyla giggled. "Oh, the look on your face. I didn't think so."

Kitty laughed, too. For all her sister's nagging, she meant well. Why Twyla was so determined to pair her up with someone was a mystery, though. Twyla was only eighteen months older than her and far prettier than Kitty. Where Kitty was shy and a people pleaser, Twyla was all fire and sass. Kitty's outside matched her insides: mousy brown eyes and hair and a completely forgettable figure. Unlike Twyla—with her flashing brown eyes, auburn hair, and a voluptuous figure that men noticed. Kitty knew they noticed, she'd seen it happen more than once. But her sister said men were too much work for too little reward.

It didn't help that they were their father's caretaker. He wasn't exactly a role model for his sex. In fact, after one extra-fiery argument, Twyla had asked, "I already have one man-baby to take care of, why would I choose to take on another one?" And, really, Twyla had a point.

There were times when the idea of having a special someone all to herself sounded enchanting, but that was just an idea. She'd tried, she had. But the numerous first dates she'd gone on had left her cold and lonelier than ever. Better to keep things as they were, known and comfortable and easy, than risk turning her life upside down for the unknown. She was pretty sure her sister felt the same way.

"I'll make you a deal." All of a sudden, she had an idea. The perfect idea for ending this conversation now—and for the foreseeable future. "I'll date if you date."

Twyla almost choked on her coffee. "Excuse me."

"You heard me." Kitty couldn't stop smiling. "It seems fair. Think about it. I'll go start making phone calls." She sauntered to the stockroom in the back, phone in hand. Now that she'd eliminated one problem, she could move on to the next. Hopefully finding folk willing to lend some time and talent would be as easy as shutting down her sister. Otherwise she might be forced to call RJ—maybe even Tyson and his nieces, too.

JUNE AND JULY wore matching dresses and expressions. Wide-eyed and uncertain. Tyson was doing his best to act like having two little girls standing in the middle of his living room wasn't one of the strangest things to happen in the last couple of years. It was likely the girls were doing the same—acting. He was pretty sure they were doing a better job of it than he was.

"We've got your own room set up for you."
Tyson held a hearts-and-flowers-printed duffel
bag in each hand. "I hope you like pink."

"We both like pink." July, the oldest at six
years old, nodded her head.

"Yep." June agreed, clinging to her sister's
hand.

"That's good, then." His father smiled down
at them. "Want me to show you?"

"Yes, please." July straightened her shoulders
and swallowed. "And thank you."

"Yep." June agreed, swinging her sister's arm
back and forth.

June had yet to say anything other than "Yep,"
since they'd picked up the girls from the airport.
To be fair, neither of them had said much since
they'd hugged their mother goodbye and watched
her board her connecting flight. Margaret had
assured him the girls would be okay—and there
wouldn't be a whole lot of tears and carrying on.
It had been reassuring.

But then he'd watched the two little girls,
tightly clinging to each other's hands, and their
little chins wobbling as they fought to hold their
tears at bay. It had been a kick in the chest. Not
knowing what to do about it made it ten times
more painful.

His father had shot him a look that said he'd
felt the same—which is why they'd wound up

stopping for ice cream on the way home. Ice cream, in Tyson's experience, was his father's way of trying to fix things without having to do the whole talking about your feelings thing… In their household, talking feelings was akin to standing naked in the middle of a rodeo arena, with stands packed with spectators while a few angry bulls circled—something to be avoided at all costs.

"Your house is big." July was staring around the living room. "Is that a real dead animal?" She stared solemnly up at the deer head mounted over the fireplace.

June's eyes got even bigger—something Tyson hadn't thought physically possible—as she, too, regarded the deer with the massive antlers.

The trophy mount had hung over the fireplace for as long as he could remember and, until now, he hadn't given it much thought. Tyson cleared his throat. "Well…yes."

"My grandfather shot that." His father crouched between the girls.

"Why?" July asked.

Tyson tucked his thumbs into his belt loops—content to let his father take this one.

"Well, now, back then you couldn't just go to the store for food. You had to go out and hunt to feed your family." His father stared up at the deer. "Grandpa said it was so big, it fed them for near a month. I guess that's why he did that? To honor and remember the animal that took care of his wife and kids."

"Oh." July nodded. "Okay."

June blinked but didn't say a word.

"Your room is down this way." His father waved the girls to follow him. "You're right across from Tyson here."

Was this supposed to comfort the girls? The way they were looking at him, he wasn't so sure. They'd video called once a month since June was born but that wasn't the same thing as being here, without their mom or dad, in a strange place. If he was feeling uncertain about this arrangement, he could only imagine how these little girls were feeling. They were probably all kinds of scared. He tended to keep a poker face—something that wouldn't help June and July feel safe—so he'd have to do better and smile more.

"This way." His father led them down the hall-way and opened the doorway at the end of the hall—opposite Tyson's door. "Some friends of ours have a little girl and gave us stuff to get the room ready for you."

"Pwetty!" June let go of July's hand and ran into the room, staring around her. "Ballinas. Look, July, ballinas." She spun in a circle, her hands up over her head in a circle like the bal-lerina in the picture.

It was impossible not the smile at the little girl's excitement.

"Juney and I do ballet." July wasn't spinning, but she was smiling. It was a start.

"You do?" *Ballet*. He was officially in uncharted territory. "My friend's little girl, Samantha, is in dance. Most of this stuff was hers."

"Really?" July sat on the edge of the bed, still inspecting the room.

"You'll get to meet her tomorrow." At the moment, he wished his father had planned the get-together for today. It was only four and he had no idea how to occupy the girls for the next however many hours… He'd have to read over the email Margaret had sent with their daily routine. Since they'd left the airport, his mind had gone blank.

"New fwiends, July." June hopped on her toes. "Yay. Does she like buttaflies? Or catapillas? Or lizzawds? I like all those."

He and his father exchanged a look.

"I'm not sure." His father scratched the back of his head.

"I bet so." June nodded, running to the bookshelf in the corner. "Look, July, books."

July slipped off the bed and joined her sister. "Wanna read?" She sat on the fluffy pink carpet in front of the bookcase and smoothed her blue skirt over her lap.

"Yep." June pulled a book from the bookshelf.

"Kitty and Mabel were right about the books." His father leaned closer to him. "Isn't there some story-something at the library?"

"Like I'd know this, Dad." Tyson pulled his phone from his pocket. "I'll find out." He texted Jensen.

Is there something for kids at the library?

What time does Samantha go to bed?

What does she like to do all day?

He waited, the little dots rolling across the screen until Jensen's answer popped up.

Storytime at the library was this morning. Nine am.

Eight p.m.

Play, read, watch princess movies, play with the animals, tell stories… Give me a sec.

Tyson read over Jensen's answers with mounting concern. Reading he could do, easy. But his father favored war movies, so the chances of finding something suitable for the girls were slim. Other than his horses, the only animal they had was Toby—just about the meanest cat he'd ever met. But since Toby had shown up, there'd been no mice or other pests of any sort in the barn or around the house, so he and his father tolerated the foul-tempered animal. There was no way he was going to introduce the girls to that feline.

Jensen's text rolled in.

Kitty wants to know if you want her and Samantha to come over?

He breathed a sigh of relief and held the phone out for his father to read. The relief on his father's face was answer enough.

That'd be great. Tyson responded. Then added, They like ballet. He hit Send.

Jensen's reply was a string of laughing emojis.

Yeah, real funny. He stuck his phone back into his pocket and put the duffel bags on top of the chest of drawers. While he started unpacking a whole lot of ruffly and girlie clothes into the chest of drawers, his father lowered himself onto the rug with the girls by the bookcase.

"This one, this one." June held the book out to his father. "My favowit." She smiled, revealing a missing tooth. "'Bout caws."

"Juney likes cars." July's delivery was all matter-of-fact.

"What about you, July? What do you like?" he asked, tucking some beribboned purple socks into a drawer. Why would socks need ribbons? Talk about impractical. Just like the pastel-colored ruffled front nightgowns. He shook his head and tucked the clothes away.

July sighed, her whole face scrunching up as she considered his question. "Books. Dance. Music. Singing." She shrugged. "An' takin' care of Juney."

"You call your sister Juney?" his father asked.

July nodded. "Daddy does, too."

"I'm Daddy's Juney-bug." June pointed at herself then at her sister. "July-bean. Like a jelly-bean." She grinned at her sister and, just like that, both the girls were giggling.

It was one of the most infectious sounds he'd ever heard. Free and easy and honest. As if their happiness had bubbled up straight from their hearts until it came pouring out. He had no choice but to chuckle along with them.

"I guess that means I need to give Tyson a nickname?" His father cocked his head to one side. "Any ideas, girls?"

Tyson shook his head. "Pretty sure I'm too old for a nickname now, Dad."

"Come on, now, what rhymes with Tyson?" His father grinned. "Bison. Or Syphon." He shook his head, chuckling.

"Bluebewwy?" June asked. "Poptawt?"

His father was laughing now. "Alrighty then. I don't see why not."

July giggled. "Those don't rhyme, Juney."

"Oh." June didn't seem the least bit discouraged by this information. "Fwog. I like fwogs."

His father managed to ask, "Frog, huh?" before laughing all over again.

Kitty and Samantha arrived twenty minutes later. He'd finished unpacking, read Margaret's email again, and the girls and his father had narrowed the choices for his nicknames to Mice-on and Cupcake.

"Hi, Mr. Tyson. I'm here." Samantha came running in the front door. "Where are they?"

"Down the hall." He pointed—and she took off running.

"It's probably obvious she didn't want to come." Kitty shifted the foil-covered plate from one hand to the next and tucked a strand of her long brown hair behind her ear. "She was bouncing in her booster seat the whole way here. How is it going? You don't look too shell-shocked."

"No?" He grinned. "Not on the outside, maybe. I appreciate y'all coming over. So far, so good but…"

A peal of laughter echoed down the hallway.

"That's a good sound." Kitty held out the plate. "Snacks."

He took the plate. "Thank you. For all of this." He gestured to the hallway.

"What are friends for?" She smiled at him. "If

you have something you need to do, I can keep an eye on them?"

"I didn't expect you to come over and babysit, Kitty." He held her gaze, hoping to emphasize his point. He *was* glad she was here. She radiated a sort of gentle calmness that was uniquely Kitty. He could take all the calm he could get right now.

"I don't mind." She shrugged, her hands fluttering.

He shook his head. He wasn't going to take advantage of her giving nature. "I do."

Once again, it was nice to see her without outrageous makeup or a red puffy eye. Just long lashes and a warm, tawny gaze. She looked good. When she smiled, like she was now, the corners of her eyes tilted up—like her whole face was smiling. But that was Kitty: whatever she did, she was all in. "Your eye all better?"

"Oh... Yes." She nodded, her cheeks going pink as she smoothed her fingers over her eyebrow.

Kitty was a pretty woman, he'd told Jensen as much. It wasn't a revelation. She'd always been pretty. And a woman. Though he'd never thought of her that way. Not really. She was just... Kitty. Jensen's sister. A childhood friend. The nicest person he knew. But not someone he'd pondered overmuch beyond that.

For some reason, she seemed different. He wasn't sure why, but it felt like he was seeing her for the very first time. *Really* seeing her. It was Kitty, but not, standing right here in front of him like she had dozens of times before. But she wasn't just Kitty anymore. She was a woman. A beautiful woman. And he was struggling to make sense of this new information...

Was this how RJ saw her? He swallowed hard, his hands tightening on the plate.

She sucked in a deep breath and her gaze fell from his. "I'll go see what the girls are up to." She hurried across the living room and disappeared down the hall.

What was that about? Tyson went into the kitchen and put the plate on the counter. He frowned out the window over the sink and shook his head. Why was this mess with RJ and Kitty getting to him? Why was he borrowing trouble? He didn't need it—didn't want it.

He ran his fingers through his hair and pushed off the counter. June and July were here—that was what he needed to focus on. That and work. He was too busy to worry over much else. That included Kitty being all pretty and womanly and RJ not being good enough for her. Not in a million years.

CHAPTER FIVE

"THAT WAS A perfect plié." Kitty clapped her hands at the three little girls lined up in front of the mantel. Their impromptu "ballet show" had put smiles on everyone's faces. Poor Tyson had yet to fully relax, but his posture wasn't ramrod stiff anymore.

"I know." Juney was beaming. "I pwactice lots."

"She does." July patted her little sister on the shoulder.

"Gotta practice *all* the time." Samantha dragged out the *L*'s for a solid ten seconds. "I practice my clogging, too. It is *so* noisy. Grampa sticks cotton in his ears." She pretended to put something in her ears.

"One time, I thought her grampa was upset because he wasn't answering me. It turns out, he'd put cotton in his ears because Samantha was clogging all through the house." It was a miracle her father put up with all "the racket"—but, then, it was for Samantha, and he'd do just about anything for his only grandchild.

Earl chuckled. "You don't say?"

Tyson was smiling, too. Not that she let herself linger too long over that fact.

"What's that?" Juney spun around again. "Clogging?"

"It's a kind of dance." Samantha shrugged. "You wear big shoes and stomp and dance."

Kitty wondered what Samantha's dance teacher, Gretta Williams, would think of that description? Definitely not the sort of thing to put in a marketing brochure.

"Big shoes?" Juney tiptoed to one side of the room, then tiptoed the other way—her arms outstretched. "See that? It's called *chassé*."

"Chassey?" Earl asked.

"Yep." June tiptoe-danced back across the room.

"You dance in your big shoes?" July paused. "How big are they?"

"It's a clog-dance-thingy." Samantha shrugged. "And they're…big." She held her hands out to show the other girl.

July sank onto the floor, smoothing the tulle skirt around her. "This is pretty."

"My aunt Kitty made them." Samantha sat beside July. "She makes me all sorts of dress-up clothes. My aunt Twyla, too. They sew and knit. Princess dresses and ballerinas and dragons and fairies—"

"Dwagons?" June stopped dancing and clapped

her hands. "I wanna be a dwagon." She held her arms wide and started running. "I wanna fly up and up."

Kitty watched as the little girl "flew" around the room. Somehow, her gaze snagged on Tyson again. He sat on the couch, but there was a tension about him that said he was anything but relaxed. *Poor Tyson*.

"I'm pretty sure Kitty can make just about anything." Earl Ellis spoke up, leaning forward in his recliner. "She even made a pet costume once. Remember that, Kitty? Wasn't it for Barbara Eldridge's goat, Nana?"

Kitty nodded. "A banana. A banana goat, get it? Banana boat. Goat?"

For the first time, Tyson laughed out loud. "Oh, that's bad." His laugh warmed her insides.

"I don't get it." Samantha turned to the girls and asked, "You going to school on Monday?"

July's big eyes turned to Tyson, then Earl. "I think so. Momma said so."

"Yes, ma'am. Tyson and I got the both of you registered last week. July, you're in Mrs. Webber's class. And June, you're in Miss Pena's prekindergarten class." Earl paused. "We got to meet both ladies and they're real nice."

"Miss Pena was my teacher. She's funny and likes turtles lots." Samantha held up her fingers as she went through the list of the teacher's likes.

"Coffee. Chocolate. And nail polish. Her nails are bright and sparkly."

"I like towtles." June stopped dancing. "And pwetty, spawkly nails." She stared down at her fingertips.

"I can bring some nail polish tomorrow, if you like?" Kitty offered. "If you want sparkly nails for your first day of school?"

"Yes, please, Miss Kitty." June's nod was all excitement.

"Mrs. Webber is my teacher. We can be class buddies and do class chores together and eat lunch, too." Samantha reached over and took July's hand. "And we have a class guinea pig named Pig." She paused. "I have a friend, Kirby, who's funny. And I have another friend, Abigail. Sometimes she cries a lot."

"Me, too." June was back up, dancing and spinning around the room.

"Abigail cries because of Levi." Samantha screwed up her face and stuck her tongue out the side of her mouth. "Levi gets in trouble a lot."

Tyson chuckled.

"He chases us on the playground and makes lots of stuff up." Samantha kept making the face. "Daddy says he's a...new-somes."

"Nuisance," Kitty corrected her niece. "But that's not really a nice thing to say. Levi's just got a lot of energy is all." His mother, Gretta, was a single mother and owner of the Hill Country Dance Studio. Kitty had spent plenty of time with Levi when she'd done costume work for various performances and festivals. As long as he had a job or some way to direct his energy, he was fine.

"That's just boys in general, I think." Earl turned to Tyson. "Tyson, here, would get himself into all sorts of trouble if he wasn't busy. You remember?"

"I don't know what you're talking about." But Tyson's crooked grin said otherwise.

"*I* do." Kitty shook her head. "You and Jensen—sometimes, Mikey and Rusty, too. Starting in grade school. Jensen has so many stories." She tapped her chin. "Lemme see, now…"

Tyson's dark brown eyes landed on her, one eyebrow rising high. "Without proof, nothing happened. It's that easy."

"Proof?" She tapped her temple. "I was there for some of it. I remember."

"What did they do?" Samantha was all wide-eyed curiosity. "Daddy would get into trouble?"

"Not big trouble." Kitty was quick to backtrack. "Talking too much, mostly. Oh, wait, didn't you put a whoopie cushion on the teacher's chair?" As soon as the words were out, she realized her mistake. This wasn't the sort of thing she should be sharing in front of three impressionable little girls. If Samantha reported this back to Jensen, her brother would not be pleased with her.

"Tyson Matthew Ellis." Earl turned to his son. "You told me Jensen did that. You little scamp."

"Dad. It was a substitute teacher." Tyson shot her a look of disbelief. "You're gonna rat me out now, Kitty?"

"What's a whoopie cushion?" July asked, her gaze bouncing between the adults in the room.

"Oh…" Kitty had to fight to hold back her laughter.

"A cushion." Tyson stopped, cleared his throat, then said, "That makes a…extra…cushion."

That did it, Kitty couldn't stop herself from laughing. She hadn't meant to get Tyson in trouble, but how was she to know Earl would get upset after all this time? And Tyson, looking every bit like the chastised little boy she'd once known, was too much for her. She covered her mouth but it didn't do much to muffle the sound.

Samantha started giggling. "You're funny, Aunt Kitty."

"Real funny." Tyson's deep laughter filled the room—rich and warm enough to make her insides go soft.

"I'm hungwy." June hopped up and down.

"I got this." Earl stood, glancing at the clock on the wall. "It's about that time, isn't it? Your

Mom said you like macaroni and cheese? I got stuff to make it."

"Yep." June kept hopping. "Yummy."

"It's her favorite." July patted the floor beside her. "Too bouncy, Juney. Remember what Mommy said."

"Small bounces only." With a big sigh and a flounce of tulle, June sat. "Sawwy."

"It's all right, Juney." Earl smiled. "I don't mind big bounces. As long as you're happy and nobody gets hurt, you bounce all you want."

June's grin was huge. "Okay."

"Let's go play." Samantha hopped up. "I brought toys. Some horsies and dollies." She helped June and July up. "A dragon, too."

"We'll have to go in ten minutes." Kitty pointed at the clock.

"But we're still coming back tomorrow, right?" Samantha waited for her nod. "Okay. Let's go." The three of them went running back to the bedroom.

"Shame they're not getting on better." Earl chuckled.

"Kids are amazing. Samantha's just so…guileless. She can always find a reason to be happy—which we should all do. When she loves, it's with her whole heart. And she makes friends wherever she goes. Basically, I want to be Samantha when I grow up." She returned the cushions to the couch and picked up the extra tutus the girls had carried into the living room. "I don't know why we adults go and make things so complicated."

"Ain't that the truth?" Earl scratched the back of his head. "Might learn a thing from June and July while they're here, hmm, Tyson?"

"Pretty sure that's a given, Dad." Tyson's crooked grin had Kitty's heart tripping over itself. When his gaze met hers, it happened again. "You sure you can't stay for dinner?"

"We can't. Samantha has a daddy-daughter date. Once a month, Jensen likes to do something, just the two of them." She loved the love her brother had for his daughter. And that his soon-to-be wife, Mabel, was equally supportive of that bond.

"And what about you?" Earl grinned. "It's a Saturday night. You got plans to go kick up your heels or paint the town red this evening?"

Kitty laughed harder than she should have. "You know me, Earl. Big, big plans for the evening." Big plans as in putting on her pajamas and working on the costumes for the Valentine's Festival. Those would be her big plans for the foreseeable future. "Wining and dining. Maybe even some dancing, too." She laughed—so did Earl.

Tyson, however, did not.

HAD KITTY BEEN TEASING? He scrubbed the plate with the bristle brush, then stuck it in the dishwasher. She had to be, didn't she? He scrubbed the next plate extra hard. Why did he care? That was the part he should be concerned about. He reached for the pot and knocked it onto the floor—sending soapy water and noodles all over the kitchen floor. He sighed, stared down at the mess he'd made, and shook his head.

"You throwing pots in here?" His father stood in the kitchen doorway.

"It was an accident." He grabbed some paper towels and wiped up the mess.

"I figured as much." His father patted him on the shoulder. "The girls are in bed and wanted to say good-night to you. I can finish up in here."

"You sure?" But he didn't resist when his father took the kitchen towel from him. "I'll clean up the floor when I'm done. It's my mess."

His father gave him a gentle shove toward the door. "Go on, now. Little Juney can hardly keep her eyes open."

He glanced at the clock. So far the girls had followed the schedule Margaret had sent to him—dinner at six and bed by eight. He smiled at his father and headed to their bedroom. He rolled his neck and took a few deep breaths, shoving aside his frustration. The girls were spending their first night in a strange place—

they didn't need him coming in moody and up-setting them. They didn't do anything wrong. Neither had Kitty. If she was out with RJ, that was her choice. And, like Jensen said, if she was happy, he should be happy for her. He should.

He'd almost reached the bedroom when he heard the girls talking.

"I miss Daddy." June sounded close to tears. "I want Mommy."

"I'm here, Juney. Grandpa Earl and Uncle Tyson are here, too." He'd already picked up on how seriously July took her big-sister duties.

"But I want Daddy." June sniffed. "And Mommy. Who's gonna check for monstahs?"

"I will. I'll check under the bed." The springs of the bed shifted. "And the closet."

"You can't, July. You awe too little to scawah a monstah away. It could eat you." June's little voice sounded panicked. "Stay hewah and hold my hand."

"Okay." July's sigh reached him.

Monsters, huh? Tyson shook his head and entered the bedroom. "You two comfy?" Both girls were in the single bed together, the pink and purple comforter pulled up to their chins. "You don't want me to set up the other bed for you? Then you'll each have your own bed."

They shook their heads in unison.

"Okay." He smiled and sat on the edge of the bed. "You need anything? Glass of water?"

"No, thank you," July said.

June shook her head.

"Another blanket?"

More headshaking.

"It's here if you need it." He patted the extra quilt folded up at the foot of their bed. "How about a monster check?"

Both girls stared at him.

"Dad and I did it before we picked you up, and we were monster-free but, if you want, I can check again before you go to bed?"

"Yep." June nodded. "Under the bed and—"

"And the closet, too?" He stood and headed for the closet. This was familiar. A long time ago, his father had done this very thing for him. When he'd been about their age, come to think of it. "Let's see." He moved the clothes to one side, then the other. Stood on his tiptoes and ran his hand along the shelf at the top of the closet, then stooped to finish his inspection. He stood and nodded.

"All cwear?" June was on her knees, perched on the edge of the bed.

He gave her a thumbs-up.

June scooched back and got under the covers again. "Whew."

He dropped to his knees by the bed and lifted

the bed skirt. "You know, there's probably not enough room for anything under here with the extra mattress."

"Could be a skinny monstah."

He grinned. There was no arguing that logic. "Let's check." He made a big production of it. Crawling around the bed, lifting the bed skirt, while using his phone's light. "Nothing." He sat back. "Good?"

They both nodded.

"I wasn't scared." July yawned. "It was Juney."

"'Cuz July is the bwavest sistah evah." June flopped back onto the pillow and rolled onto her side to face her sister. "I'm so lucky she can pwotect me."

"You are." Tyson smoothed the blanket tight. "You are lucky to have each other."

"That's what Mommy says." July's eyelids were drooping. "Sometimes, taking care of Juney is lots of work."

"You're a good big sister." From the way June draped an arm over her big sister and cuddled close, June agreed. He stood, flipped off the light, and paused to say, "I'll be up for a bit, yet, but I'm just down the hall if you need me."

"Night-light?" June asked.

"I'll leave the light on in the hall, okay?" Tyson mentally added night-light to his shopping list. "We can pick one up when we go into town."

"A ballina night-light?"

Tyson chuckled. "We'll see what we can find." He wasn't sure Old Towne Hardware and Appliances would carry a ballerina night-light but, knowing Nolan Woodard, the man would order one if Tyson asked him to. "Y'all get some sleep now. And have good dreams."

"'Night, Uncle Tyson." July murmured.

"'Night, Unca Tyson." June echoed. "Sweet dweams."

He left the door cracked and went back to the living room to find his father on the phone.

"You don't say." His father had his phone to his ear, his brows rising high. "When did this happen?" He shook his head. "Last I'd seen of Dwight, he'd been all puffed up and proud of having Martha on his arm." He nodded, murmuring the occasional, "Uh-huh," and "Mmm-hmm," in response to whoever he was talking to—likely, Dorris Kaye. "Seems a shame. I can't imagine either one of them finding someone willing to put up with them."

Tyson headed into the kitchen to finish cleaning up, but his father had beat him to it. Instead, he took two glasses from the cabinet, filled them with milk, and grabbed the box of chocolate sandwich cookies from the pantry. He didn't know when this had become their nightly routine, but it was. Milk. Cookies. His father's evening telephone conversation with Dorris Kaye catching him up on all the latest gossip and news. While Tyson wasn't a fan of gossiping, he couldn't deny hearing Dorris Kaye's spin on things was entertaining. A time or two, he'd been present for the *event* she went on and on about, and his take on what had happened versus that of the older woman were a night-and-day difference.

"No, really? You don't say?" His father was smiling. "Hattie's gonna have a baby? She and Forrest didn't waste any time now, did they?"

Tyson sat, stunned by this news. Hattie and Forrest hadn't been married six months and they already had a baby on the way?

"You're right. No sense waiting." His father took the milk Tyson offered him. "That's all?" He stared into his glass of milk, a furrow forming between his brows. "I don't trust that boy. I know, I know, but he's got to act like a man before I'll call him a man, Dorris."

Tyson sat back in his chair, dunking a cookie into his milk. From the sounds of it, there'd be plenty for the two of them to talk about once his father got off the phone. He ate one cookie and dunked another.

He didn't know what was sadder: being thirty-four years old and spending his Saturday night with his dad, eating milk and cookies, or that he was perfectly content to be sitting here, with his father, eating milk and cookies?

"Well, that was something. 'Night. Yes, ma'am." His father hung up the phone.

"Hattie's pregnant?"

"Another baby Briscoe is on the way." His father chuckled. "Happy times for that family, to be sure."

Tyson nodded. "And for Hattie's folks, too." The Carmichael family were good, salt-of-the-earth folk.

"Don't you know it." But his smile dimmed. "What's this nonsense I hear about RJ? Him bringing Kitty flowers? Asking her to dinner? He's really courting her?" He reached for a cookie, all the while shaking his head. "Why isn't Jensen putting a stop to it? Or Dwight? I have a hard time believing her daddy'd be okay with this." He paused, then went back to shaking his head. "Dorris said he looked all handsome and neat when he came to see her. I don't care how spruced up he's getting, that's just putting lipstick on a pig."

Tyson ate another cookie and kept quiet. His father wasn't saying anything he hadn't already thought. But, since he was going to try to stay out of this from now on, there was no point talking about it and getting himself worked up.

"RJ Malloy?" His father went on. "And Kitty

Crawley? I don't like that. Not one bit. You can't be happy about that?"

No. No way. He shoved another cookie in his mouth.

"Might just have to talk to her tomorrow." His father sighed. "I know it's not my place, but if her own family isn't going to stand up for her, I'm going to."

"She might not thank you for meddling, Dad. What if she wants to date him?" Tyson set his glass on the coffee table, his appetite gone.

The disbelief on his father's face gave way to a smile—then a laugh. A big, deep belly laugh at that. He laughed along with his father all the while wishing he could be as certain that Kitty had no interest in RJ. But he couldn't shake the unease in his stomach. Something wasn't right. Whether that was Kitty or RJ or himself, he wasn't sure. Hopefully, he'd figure it out soon.

CHAPTER SIX

KITTY FLEXED HER HAND, then picked up the needle again. Sewing tulle wasn't easy. From past experience, using a machine led to her stitches pulling free and needing to be done all over again by hand. Since there was no time to waste, she decided she'd skip the machine altogether. But maintaining a tiny rolled hem was painstaking work. And sewing tulle onto the elastic waistband wasn't exactly a cakewalk.

"Turn on your work light or you'll strain your eyes." Twyla was cutting out the vest pieces from yards and yards of pink and red fabric.

Kitty reached up and turned on her light, then went back to stitching.

"I figured I'd find you both in here." Mabel came into the sewing room carrying a tray. "I brought you some tea and a snack." She set the tray with mugs and a plate of cookies on the table.

"Thank you." Kitty smiled.

"I was needing a little pick-me-up." Twyla set

aside her scissors and perched on a stool by the table, cradling her teacup in both hands. "Thank you, Mabel."

"It's the least I can do. Jensen says you've been at it since this morning?" Mabel leaned against the worktable.

She nodded. "Lots to do."

"Lots." Twyla was still irritated by the workload—the word dripped with annoyance.

"So I see." Mabel eyed the bolts of pink and red stacked on the far end of the worktable. Beside that were rolls of red and pink elastic and ribbon. "Jensen said something about a sewing party?"

"Next weekend." Twyla nodded.

"I reserved a room at the Community Center. So far, I've got four people showing up." Which was half of what Kitty had been hoping for. "It will be a huge help."

"I'm guessing not enough?" Mabel sipped her tea. "I'm sorry I'm useless with a sewing machine… I'm happy to help with the sequins and stuff if it doesn't require too much accuracy. If you ever need me to settle a horse or, you know, something animal-related, I'll be there."

Kitty smiled, doing her best to keep her stitches tiny and regular. "I wouldn't call anyone else." Mabel had a certain knack with animals, especially horses. It wasn't that she talked

to animals so much as understood them. Her
official job was animal behavioralist. Samantha, however, liked to say that, since Mabel was
pretty and could talk to animals, she was a princess. If anyone dared say otherwise, Samantha
was quick to put them in their place.

"I know you're busy but I was hoping we could
talk for a minute?" The hint of concern in Mabel's voice was just enough to make Kitty pause
and look up.

"Is everything okay?" Twyla reached for a
cookie.

"Yes." Mabel shook her head. "I don't think
it's a big deal but…" She shrugged. "It had to do
with you, Kitty. But I know you two share everything so…"

Kitty stuck the needle through the tulle and
elastic and put the in-progress tutu on the table.
She reached for the cup. "I'm all ears."

Twyla sat, wide-eyed as she nibbled her
cookie.

"I want to apologize for my brother, Audy."
Mabel sighed. "Since he married Brooke, he's
gotten so much better about acting like an adult.
He's a father, after all. Two times over now. You'd
think he'd realize he should think before he says
things that could cause problems."

Other than being an all-around rodeo champion, one of four Briscoe brothers, and Brooke

then-Young now-Briscoe's husband, Kitty didn't know much about Audy Briscoe. But then she remembered what RJ had said. She swallowed. "Is this about RJ?"

"This should be good," Twyla murmured.

"You know the two of them are friends?" Mabel waited for her to nod, then continued. "And Audy's been trying to help him out. RJ's always been… A mess."

Kitty nodded again.

"When they were younger, Audy and RJ lived for causing mischief. I admit, Audy was as much an instigator as RJ was back then, too. But now everyone else is growing up and moving on and RJ really hasn't. When he said he wanted to try to do better, Audy offered to help."

"Well, that's good." Kitty meant it, too.

Even Twyla nodded.

"Yes. And no." Mabel sighed. "Audy got him a job on the ranch and he's doing really well, I've been impressed. At this rate, he'll be taking on the foreman position before too long." Which, Kitty knew, took a lot of hard work. "But then Audy stuck his foot in it. He said it was really all because of Brooke and the kids that he'd become a better man."

"I bet Brooke was all smiles when she heard that. I know I would have been."

"Well, yes, but that seems to have led to what's happening with you." Mabel gave her a long look.

Kitty frowned. "How do you mean?"

"RJ's decided to find a woman that will make him a better man." She pointed at Kitty. "And, from what I've seen, he's very determined."

"Who knew RJ had such good taste." Twyla winked at her sister.

"Me? But… So, it's not a joke?" She'd been certain it was.

Mabel shook her head, her long dark hair swaying about her. "I think, maybe, Audy meant it that way, sort of. But it appears RJ takes things literally."

She didn't know what to say.

"I never thought I'd say this but he is actually trying to better himself." Mabel shrugged. "I don't know how you feel about him. Not that I'm trying to talk him up or advocate on his behalf or anything."

Kitty blinked. How did she feel about RJ? Up until five days ago, she rarely thought about him—let alone felt anything for him.

"He did say that you were the only woman in Garrison who was likely to make a real man out of him." Mabel smiled. "Which I thought you might want to hear."

It was surprisingly sweet.

"I know Dorris Kaye is involved and there's

already talk, so I wanted to tell you his intentions and put your mind at ease." Mabel took a deep breath. "Now you know and I'll stop talking about it. Unless you want to talk about it?"

"I think we should talk about it." Twyla scooched her stool closer.

"I… I don't know what to say." Kitty set the cup down on the table and forced a smile.

But she was saved from having to say a thing by Samantha's arrival. "I rode Firefly around and around and around the pen." Her words came out in a rush.

"You did?" Mabel hugged her. "I'm so proud of you."

"Firefly is the bestest horsie." Samantha was breathing hard. "I ran all the way here to tell you."

"I'm glad you did." Twyla offered her a cookie.

"Firefly is a good horse. And the only horse I know that gives hugs." Kitty loved seeing such happiness on Samantha's face. Not too long ago, she was terrified of anything on four legs—no matter the size or species. Things like petting a dog or riding a horse were panic-inducing ideas. Now they were part of Samantha's everyday life.

"And Daddy says we all need to get ready to go see July and Juney." Samantha looked down at her jeans. "I need to wash up 'cuz I smell like horsie. Pee yew." She pinched her nose, smiled, and ran out of the sewing room.

"She's been talking about Juney and July all morning." Mabel put Kitty and Twyla's now empty cups back on the tray and stood. "I can't wait to meet them."

"You know Samantha—they were friends within the first five minutes." Kitty didn't know who'd been happier about that, the girls or Tyson and his father? Probably Tyson and his father.

"I might be gifted with animals but I don't have her gift with people." Mabel headed for the door. "I'll go help Samantha get ready. Either of you need anything?"

"I'm good," Twyla said.

"Me, too." Kitty smiled her thanks and reached for the tulle she'd been working on. As soon as Mabel left, she propped an elbow on the table and rested her head.

Her sister's hand rested on her shoulder. "Is it that bad?" She moved to sit in front of Kitty.

"Being talked about?" She wrinkled her nose. "It's not good." About the only thing in the world Kitty hated was being the center of attention.

"Forget about that part. You can't control it anyway." Twyla gave her shoulder a squeeze. "It's kinda nice to know you've caught some-one's eye, isn't it?"

Was it? She shrugged.

"Don't worry over it, Kitty. Be flattered. Smile. Go on about your business and let things take their course. You do what you want—and only what you want." She stood. "I guess I'll go freshen up, too. I can't believe Dad said he'd go with us. I hope he doesn't scare those two little girls."

"It's good to get him out of the house." She contemplated taking some sewing with her but decided against it. "Maybe we should take two cars?"

"Might not be a bad idea. Dad won't want to stay too long anyway."

They tidied up the room, turned off the lights, and went to get ready.

Kitty changed her dress three times before she gave up, tugged on an old favorite, and ran a brush through her hair. She wasn't out to impress anyone. There was no need to make a fuss or get dolled up. Still, she ran a natural gloss over her lips and brushed on enough mascara to make her lashes thick and long.

"You look nice." His father scowled at her as soon as she stepped into the great room. "Why're you getting all dressed up?"

"I'm not." She peered down at her dress. "It's an old dress."

"Hmph." Her father kept on scowling the entire ride to the Ellis place.

Next to the Crawley Cattle Ranch, the Ellis place was modest in size—something her father remarked upon the minute they pulled through the gate. He went on to grumble over the state of the gravel road and the length of the walk to get from where they parked to the front door of the house. Even though Kitty found it exhausting, her father seemed to enjoy complaining and criticizing.

"Come in, come in." Earl Ellis opened the door, his smile welcoming.

"Thanks for having us, Earl." Jensen shook the man's hand. "There's a lot of us."

Earl chuckled. "Nice to have the company. It gets mighty quiet out here, just me and Tyson."

"Quiet sounds nice to me." Her father nodded at Earl. "Not enough of it on my place."

"You wouldn't have it any other way, Dad." Kitty patted his arm. She'd never forget how worked up he'd been when Jensen said he and Mabel might build a place of their own.

"Samantha!" Juney came barreling across the living room. "You awe hewah."

"Juney." Samantha hugged the little girl. "Hi."

"Come on." Juney grabbed her hand and tugged her along.

"That'll be the last we see of them for a while." Tyson stepped forward. "Juney and July have been up since the crack of dawn, asking if it was time for Samantha to come over yet."

The first thing Kitty noticed was how tired he looked. The second? The warmth in his eyes when he turned her way and smiled. She felt it, from the tips of her toes to the top of her head. But instead of going all moony-eyed and locking up like she'd always done, she took a deep breath, counted to ten, and pinned her smile in place. She'd promised herself today would go off without her knees going to Jell-O even once. She could do it. She would do it. All she had to do was convince her heart to stop thundering so loudly and it would work out just fine.

TYSON HAD NEVER slept on a twin bed with someone else. He'd certainly never slept on a twin mattress with two tiny ninjas before. But that's exactly what had happened last night. Juney had woken up about ten, crying and distraught, and there was nothing he or July could say or do to fix it. Except lying down on the bed with them. He'd suggested they all move into his room—at least he had a queen-size bed—but that had triggered a whole new round of "monstah" fears and anxiety so he'd dropped it.

Once Juney had nodded off, he'd tried to go back to his room. Tried. She was out cold so he'd carefully begun to disentangle himself from the girls' limbs—but then Juney's eyes had popped open and they were back to square one. Eventually, he'd given up and tried to doze.

He'd downed almost an entire pot of coffee by himself this morning and he was still dragging. The only saving grace was knowing the girls would be happily occupied with Samantha for the better part of the afternoon. With any luck, no one would notice him sitting in the corner in a stupor—likely drooling on himself.

But he hadn't counted on the sheer business that adding five extra people to the house caused. Once it was established that the brisket had another hour on the grill and there was nothing else to prep or worry over foodwise, they all settled in the living room. Dwight commandeered what was normally Tyson's recliner. He sat and stared, answering his father's questions with as few words as possible.

"You hear about Hattie and Forrest?" his father sat opposite Dwight.

"What about 'em?" Dwight's frown deepened. "They're all right, aren't they? They're good kids, the both of them."

Tyson was surprised to hear the man say something remotely complimentary of someone that wasn't his blood.

"Hattie's pregnant." Mabel sighed. "I am going to be an aunt again."

"I'll be. That is something." Dwight almost looked happy. Well, he didn't look angry, so that really was something.

"She is?" Kitty's whole face lit up with happiness. "Oh, that's wonderful. I bet they're ecstatic."

He'd always marveled at Kitty's ability to share in someone else's joys and sorrows—like it was her own. She wasn't putting on airs or attention seeking; it was sincere and heartfelt. There was no trace of jealousy or envy in her voice, just delight. Life, through her eyes, would likely be a happier place.

Once again, he had to fight against this sudden fascination for her. He didn't understand where it came from or what to make of it. When had it become a struggle to keep from staring at her? When had she started to look so…to be so… He tore his gaze from her and shook his head.

"Looks like you had a rough night," Jensen murmured.

He nodded.

"How's it going down at the stockyard?"

"Good. The renovations wrapped up last week." Tyson rubbed a hand over his face and sat up straighter. "It looks a whole lot safer now, let me tell you. A whole lot nicer to look at, too."

"Every once in a while the Garrison Ladies

Guild comes through in a big way." Jensen nodded. "You just have to bear with the rest of it."

"You mean the meddling? Opinions? And general invasion and judgment of every aspect of your personal life?" He grinned. "I guess it's a small price to pay for all the good they do." And now that it was done and the results were as impressive as they were, he would suffer through the daily badgering and pushiness the Ladies Guild served up all over again—no doubt about it.

"If you say so." Dwight Crawley sounded off.

"How else were the stands going to get replaced, Dad? It hadn't been put into the city's budget for the year, so it was either cordon off places too dangerous to sit and use or take the help the Ladies Guild offered." Jensen glanced at Tyson. "Seems like you made the right choice for the community."

Tyson nodded.

"If you think that gift will come without strings, you're in for a wake-up call." Dwight sniffed.

"Dad." Twyla sighed. "It's a little early in the visit to go all doom and gloom."

"I wasn't. I'm just saying it like it is." Dwight glanced his way. "I guess it's better than getting sued over some accident."

Tyson nodded. They'd been lucky. "I was worried we were going to have to sit out this rodeo season. A whole section of the wooden bleachers was so rotted, someone could have easily broken through and fallen to the ground beneath."

"Then the Ladies Guild did a good thing." Mabel gave him an encouraging smile. "I, for one, can't wait to see the place."

"You're welcome to come over and take a look, anytime." Tyson smothered a yawn.

His father chuckled. "I found Tyson, here, buried under June and July this morning—in their little bed. He had an elbow in one ear and a foot smashed in his cheek."

That had everyone laughing—even Dwight.

"You don't have to entertain us, Tyson. Go take a nap." Kitty stood. "I'm off to paint three little girls' fingernails and toenails."

"I'm coming." Mabel stood and held her hands out in front of her. "Hmm, I might even ask you to paint mine, too."

"I'll do it." Twyla was up, too, trailing after them. "I have steadier hands than Kitty, anyway."

Their voices faded as they made their way down the hall to the girls' room. Just about the time the door closed, his father turned to Dwight and asked, "I was talking to Dorris and she said something that surprised me. What in the Sam hill is going on with you and Martha?"

"Why are you talking to Dorris Kaye?" Dwight

shook his head. "That woman's got something to say about everyone—and most of it ain't true."

"So you and Martha didn't have a fight?" His father crossed his arms over his chest and waited.

"What business is it of yours?" Dwight mirrored the other man's actions. "You're getting as bad as they are, Earl. Nosing around."

"I'm talking to you, aren't I? I'm not going to tell them what you say." Earl sighed. "But I am going to listen and see what I need to know and get it taken care of. You're a mean ol' cuss, but you're my friend. Martha is just as mean but that seemed to suit you all right. So what happened?"

Tyson wasn't sure whether to leave the room or remain perfectly still.

"Nothing worth talking about." Dwight grumbled.

"Being stubborn this way is only going to cost you." His father grumbled right back. "Sometimes you've got no more sense than a box of rocks, Dwight Crawley."

Jensen's choked-off laughter had both men turning on him. "Sorry." He cleared his throat. "Not many people talk to Dad that way."

"When you've been friends as long as we have, you tell it like it is." His father pointed between the two of them. "You two will get there. Keep having each other's back, and you'll see."

He and Jensen exchanged a look.

"Which reminds me..." His father leaned forward, his eyes narrowing. "Dorris said something else that got me worried." He rested his elbows on his knees. "What are you thinking? Letting your sister get involved with RJ Malloy?"

Tyson ran a hand over his face. "Dad."

"What now?" Dwight sat up, his head swiveling round to level a hard-eyed look Jensen's way. "Your sister? Which one?"

"Hold on." Jensen held up his hand. "I never said I was okay with it. I was trying to get—"

"Unca Tyson." June came skipping into the room. "Unca Tyson, come on." She grabbed his hand. "You have to show Miss Kitty and Miss Mabel and Miss Twyla how to look for monstahs."

"I do?" He grinned.

"They don't know how." Juney shrugged. "I dunno how come? You gotta show 'em."

"Look for monsters?" Jensen frowned. "If this turns into something I have to deal with from now on with Samantha, you're gonna pay."

Tyson laughed. "I don't know what you're talking about." He let Juney lead the way.

"He's hewah." June announced once they'd reached the room. "Show 'em, Unca Tyson."

"Will I get my nails done if I do?" Tyson had meant it as a joke.

"Yes!" Three little girls and three women answered in unison.

"You asked for it." Twyla held up a bottle of green-sparkly polish. "I bet this shiny one will help chase off all the monsters."

Kitty giggled. "Twyla, behave." She glanced from the nail polish to Tyson, then giggled again.

How had he never noticed how cute she looked when she laughed? Why was he noticing now? He swallowed.

Mabel stopped painting Samantha's nails and looked up at him. "We're all eagerly awaiting to see you in action. Juney said you saved their lives."

"I did?" Tyson turned to the four-year-old, who nodded so sagely he had to grin. "Does that make me a hero?"

"Yep." June nodded. "You awe a weal hewo, Unca Tyson."

"But you snore." July blew on her fingers. "So loud."

"Sorry about that." He shrugged.

"It's okay. Daddy snowahs, too." June bounced up and down. "Show 'em. Show 'em so the monstahs don't get 'em."

All eyes were on him.

"Okay." He rolled up his sleeves and stretched. "You can't cut corners." He was fully aware of Kitty's eyes on him. Maybe that's why the whole thing went from two minutes to five. He liked knowing that he was the one that put that smile on her face. And him crawling around on the floor like an idiot is what made her laugh so hard. When he was done, he sat on the floor and leaned against the bed. "And that's that."

"That was something, all right." Mabel shook her head, smiling.

"Who knew you were such an entertainer?" Twyla went back to painting July's nails.

"I'm impressed. You did a very thorough job." Kitty was still smiling—it was infectious.

"You can't be too careful," he said. Why was he feeling proud when he'd just gone and made a complete fool of himself?

"You can paint Unca Tyson's nails now." June sat on the floor beside him. "Miss Kitty did mine. See?" She wiggled her bright pink-tipped fingers.

"I do." Tyson nodded. "But it's okay. Miss Kitty doesn't have to paint my nails."

"After that, yes, she does." Twyla glanced at the nail polish Kitty was holding. "It's either pink with Kitty or green sparkles from me."

"You don't want pwetty nails?" June peered up at him and grinned. "We will match. Matching is fun."

There was no getting out of it now. "Okay." He sighed and held his hands out. "Do you mind, Kitty? Pink is more my color."

Mabel and Twyla found this hysterical.

"I don't mind at all." She scooched across the floor and faced him. "Juney is right. You're very brave." She winked at him and took his hand in hers.

That wink cut off Tyson mid chuckle. He wasn't sure if it was the wink or the smile or the fact that she was holding his hand that put the lump in his throat. When she leaned forward to paint his nails, her long hair spilled down over her shoulder like a silky wave. A silky wave he wanted to touch. He swallowed hard, but the lump didn't move. His head was spinning, and he was having a hard time steadying his breath, but there was one thing he knew. Kitty was making him feel all…this. Now all he had to do was figure out how to stop it.

CHAPTER SEVEN

KITTY CARRIED THE pot of coffee around the table, refilling cups as she went.

"It doesn't feel right with you playing hostess, Kitty. You're our guest." Earl made to stand, but she put a hand on his shoulder.

"I was up and the coffee was ready." She smiled down at the man. "It's no bother." She refilled her brother's cup next.

"That's my Kitty. Always taking care of folk. Someday, she's going to make some fellow a good little wife." Her father's tone was surprisingly affectionate. "And the best mother."

"You wanna be a mommy, Miss Kitty?" July cocked her head to one side.

"I've always wanted to be a mom." Even though she was the youngest, her nature had turned her into the family nurturer. She hoped, someday, she'd do the same for a family of her own.

"You be a good mom." There was some left-over whipped cream on June's cheek. "Wight, July?"

July nodded.

"Aunt Kitty does like someone." Samantha's gleeful declaration put Kitty's stomach in knots and snagged everyone's attention. "She says he is ham-some."

"Wait." She shook her head, her face going hot. "I don't—"

"Samantha." Jensen shook his head. "That's Aunt Kitty's personal business. Who she does or doesn't like, that's the sort of thing only she can share that. Not you or me or Grampa or anyone but Aunt Kitty. It's private and wrong to talk about it."

"Okay." Samantha was crestfallen. "I'm sorry, Aunt Kitty."

"Oh, now, sugar, it's okay." Her father reached over to pat Samantha on the head. "You didn't know. And your daddy didn't need to be so hard on you. We're all friends here, anyway."

"Dad." Jensen shook his head. "Friends or not, I don't want Samantha growing up a gossip."

"It's fine." Kitty cut in, more than ready for the conversation to be over. "No harm was done." She smiled at her niece.

"So, it's a secret?" Samantha asked. "No one should know?"

Once again, everyone was looking and waiting for Kitty's response.

"If Aunt Kitty did like someone, it would be

a secret." It was Twyla that came to the rescue. "Grown-up stuff is hard that way sometimes."

"You could make a Valentine's card." Samantha perked up. "Mrs. Webber says Valentine's cards are for your sweetie. We're going to have a Valentine's party and we have to make cards for all of our friends in class and our sweetie, if we have one." She paused. "I don't have one."

"Me neither. Dad says boys are stinky." July shook her head. "I don't want a boyfriend."

"Nope." June stuck her tongue. "No boys."

"I'm glad to hear it." Earl was laughing. "You stay away from those stinky boys for a few more years, at least."

"I'd say a good ten to twelve more years?" But her father was smiling. "And only if your daddy or grandpa say it's okay."

Kitty returned the coffeepot to the sideboard and sat at the table, between June and Mabel.

"Is that why Aunt Kitty and Aunt Twyla don't have boyfriends, Grampa? You won't let them?" Samantha sat back in her chair.

"Let us?" Twyla laughed. "No, honey, that's not why. My standards are too high. I have yet to meet a single man in Garrison that measures up. It would take a lot for me to fall in love with a man."

"Unca Tyson is good." June pointed at Tyson. "He's a hewo and stuff."

"That's true." Twyla regarded Tyson. "He is a good monster hunter. And he can pull off pink nail polish. Both rarities, for sure. But, sadly, he doesn't give me the tingles."

Tyson shrugged. "Your loss."

"Tingles?" July frowned. "Do they hurt?"

"I don't like owies." June shook her head. "Nope."

"It's more like butterflies in your tummy. If you like someone you can't wait to see them. You get all warm when they're close and smile when they're around. That person makes you happier than all the other people—" Kitty broke off, realizing she was the last person at the table that should answer this question. "I'd assume."

While the three little girls seemed content with her answer, the adults around the table were regarding her with a wide variety of expressions. Earl's gentle smile was a stark contrast to her father's narrow-eyed glower.

Mabel reached over to pat her hand and whispered, "I think that sums it up perfectly."

While her sister-in-law to-be meant to be supportive, it only added to Kitty's discomfort. Really, what had she been thinking? The handful of dates she'd had in high school and college had all ended up in friendships. In fact, she and Twyla were the only ones at the table who'd never, actually, experienced love or the loss of it.

Tyson's divorce hadn't been all that long ago. She'd been a firsthand witness to the pain and rage he'd suffered. It was one of the few times Kitty'd felt really, truly angry at someone. How could Iris have hurt the man she'd sworn to love so deeply? How could she break the vows they'd made in front of friends and family? How could the woman live with herself, knowing she'd broken the faith of an already wounded man? There was no answer that would make what Iris did okay. And, honestly, Kitty didn't like thinking about the woman.

But she did wonder about Tyson. Did he still miss Iris? Did her betrayal still eat at him? Had the nonsense she'd babbled made him think of his ex-wife? Or upset him?

She glanced his way. Except for the clenching of his jaw, Tyson's expression was unreadable. He was good at that, keeping his thoughts and feelings from others. It was a way to protect himself. After everything he'd been through, it was understandable—but sad.

That's why seeing him so animated with the girls had been such a thrill. Watching him poke around the closet and crawl around on the floor had made her smile. He was the most carefree he'd been in years. Not to mention he'd let her paint his nails.

His gaze shifted and their eyes locked. For

one minute, there was only Tyson Ellis in that room with her. Oh-so-handsome. That strong, angled jaw. The thick, arched brows. His deep brown eyes. And his mouth... Curling into that crooked grin that made her boneless and flustered. Thankfully, she was sitting down or she'd have wound up a puddle on the floor. Which meant she'd broken her promise to herself tonight. She sighed.

"I'm going to clear the table," Mabel whispered.

"I'll help." Better to wash dishes than continue cataloging all of Tyson's dreamy assets. She stacked up all the dessert plates within her reach and stood, carrying them into the kitchen.

"You're not doing the dishes." Tyson had followed her, carrying the rest of the plates.

"I don't mind." She wouldn't look at him, not yet. Instead, she stacked the dishes on the side of the sink and opened the dishwasher.

"Kitty." He stepped closer and rested his hand on the kitchen counter.

She faced him but, to avoid any potential knee-weakening outcomes, she focused on the button in the center of his chest. "Let me, Tyson. You and your dad have your hands full with the girls. *And* you made us all dinner."

"Is there something on my shirt?" He ran a hand over his shirtfront.

"No."

"Then why are you staring at it?"

Because you're standing too close. Because you make it hard for me to breathe, let alone think. She took a deep breath. "What?" Her laughter was forced but it was the best she could do. "I am not staring at your shirt." She turned away from him and reached for the faucet. "You're silly." *Stop talking.*

"You okay?" His voice was soft enough to send a thrill down her spine.

"Fine." She wasn't fine, not at all. If she was, she wouldn't care that he was standing behind her. "I was thinking about what my sister said... About having high standards. I don't think she does." She had no idea where she was going with this but she kept talking. "Is it too much to want respect and loyalty from your partner? Someone that would work hard and support you in all things? I don't think that's unreasonable, do you?"

"No."

"Sometimes I think it's an excuse. It's easier not to try than to try and fail or get hurt." Was she talking about Twyla? Or herself? Both of them, maybe.

"You don't have to hand-wash the dishes." He reached over and took the plate from her. "You rinse, I'll load?"

"Sure." The pink nail polish made her grin. "What?"

"Your nails." She went back to rinsing.

"They look good." There was a smile in his voice. "Don't be offended if I wind up taking it off before work."

She made the mistake of looking up at him, her feigned horror giving way to actual horror as she realized just how close he was. "I…" She took a step back. "I'm offended."

A deep V settled between his brows. "I'll leave it, then."

"Joking." She smacked him with the kitchen towel, beyond flustered. "I was teasing." And now she'd hit him with the kitchen towel. "Sorry." Maybe she should just run and hide and pretend none of this had happened?

"You're sure you're okay?" He put a hand on her shoulder, so she had no choice but to look at him. "You're acting strange."

That was an understatement. "Am I?" She took a deep breath. "I'm stressed. I've got so much to do for the Valentine's Festival." That was true. "Costumes. Lots and lots of them. It's great because, someday, I want to open a custom online costume shop—so this is something I can add to my portfolio. It's just a lot in a quick amount of time, and I'm a bit of a perfectionist when it comes to my work. Twyla's not happy with the workload, though, and insists we needed help. I rented out the Community Center next weekend and have recruited some extra hands to help with the sewing but, you know, that means I have to let go of being a perfectionist. So I will. And I'll be grateful...for the help." She stopped, wondering where all that had come from, if anything she'd said made sense, and why, exactly, she'd spewed it all on Tyson.

"Sounds like a lot." His gaze was a little too intent. "And you had to take time from that to come here."

"Oh, no, this was great." She closed her eyes long enough to catch her breath. "I... You know, maybe I should go. I'm sure Dad is getting tired. I brought two cars just in case he wanted to leave early. And I didn't want to cut into the girls' playtime."

The V between Tyson's brows deepened. "You're leaving?"

"No, I'll help finish up in here first—"

"I can handle the dishes, Kitty." He grabbed her wrist before she could reach for another plate. "If you need to go, go. I was just, I dunno. I guess I'm not used to seeing you this way." He swallowed.

"Oh." She gently tugged free of his hold. "I'm sorry." The skin where he'd touched her tingled.

"You don't need to apologize. I… I'm just worried." He hesitated, then said, "About you."

This was what a friend would say. There was no reason for her to feel any flutters or giddiness because of it. How had she worked herself into such a state? "I shouldn't have dumped all of that on you. Really. I'm fine." She took another step back, then another. "Next time I see you, I'll be back to normal." She reached for the kitchen doorknob—right as the door swung open and whacked her in the head.

THAT CRACK, the sound of impact, was still echoing in the kitchen when he caught Kitty. It'd played out in slow motion. Her backing away from him. The door slamming into her head and knocking her forward—and her falling. Instinct must have kicked in because he didn't remember making the conscious choice to move. He must have, because he was cradling her close as he knelt on the floor. "Kitty?"

She was dazed, but her eyes were open. "Hmm?"

"What happened?" Jensen peered around the door, then hurried inside. "Kitty."

"Yes?" Kitty blinked rapidly. "What?"

"Ice." Tyson smoothed her hair aside to discover a gash and an angry red knot rising. "She needs ice. And some pain reliever." He winced at the cut bleeding freely. "And a towel."

"Ow." She reached up to touch her head, then leaned away from her hand. "Ouch, oh, ow."

"I'm sorry, Kitty-cat." Jensen was hovering.

"You use a battering ram to come through the door or what?" Tyson glared up at his friend.

"How was I supposed to know she was standing there?" Jensen snapped back. "You think I meant to hurt my own sister?"

"No. Of course not." But it had scared him. "I need a towel. She's bleeding."

"Where…" She shook her head, then froze, a hiss slipping from between her lips. "This… hurts."

He took the towel Jensen offered him and gently pressed it against the gash. "I bet." She looked so pale. Seeing Kitty frail this way scared him even more. "We need to take her to the hospital. She needs stitches—and she might have a concussion."

"I'll drive." Jensen nodded. "Lemme pick her up—"

"I got her." Tyson scooped her into his arms. "Let's go."

The second they stepped out of the kitchen, minor chaos erupted. Understandably, everyone wanted to know what had happened but Tyson was having none of it. Kitty was bleeding and hurt—they could get their answers later. "We need to get her to the hospital." He headed for the front door. "Dad, get me an ice pack."

"I'm fine." Kitty's mumble was too weak to reassure any of them.

His father ran into the kitchen.

"You will be. Good thing you've got that Crawley hard head." Tyson smiled down at her. "You just keep those pretty eyes of yours open, okay?"

"Okay." She smiled back.

"Here." His father handed him an ice pack. "You take good care of her."

"Let's go, Jensen." He waited for Mabel to open the front door, hurried down the steps, and headed for Jensen's truck. "Lean on me?" He put her on her feet but kept his arm anchored around her waist as he pulled the back door of the truck crew cab open. "We're going inside now, ready?"

"Okay." She was holding her head now, pain bracketing her every feature.

"Hold on, Kitty." He lifted her into the back seat and slid in beside her. "Try and keep that towel and ice there." He buckled her seat belt. "You okay?"

"Not really," she whispered.

"Mabel, call Doc Johnson." Jensen climbed into the driver's seat and started the truck. "Tell him we're coming in." He rolled down the window to add, "Concussion, likely."

"I'm coming." Dwight Crawley was making his way to the porch steps.

"Mabel will bring you, Dad." And Jensen peeled out of the drive.

"Ooh, you're going to be in trouble." Kitty's voice wavered. "He's going to be so mad…"

"You let me worry about Dad." Jensen flew down the driveway to the main road.

"Slow down, Jensen. Getting in a wreck won't get us there any faster." It killed Tyson to say it, though. He wanted Jensen to speed. He wanted to get to the hospital—now. But she was already hurt. The idea of something worse happening to her wasn't something he could handle. "It's okay," he murmured again, taking her hand in his.

"I'm fine." She slumped against him, her head on his shoulder.

He reached around her to hold the ice pack and towel in place.

"Hey, Kitty-cat." Jensen called. "You stay awake. Tell me a story."

"What story?" Kitty's voice was muffled against his shoulder.

"How about the time we lost Samantha." Jensen kept checking on her via the rearview mirror.

"You lost Samantha?" Tyson prodded, trying to keep her alert.

"We didn't. We only thought we did." The truck hit a bump, jostling them and making her cry out.

Tyson bit back a slew of colorful words and tried not to shoot Jensen a warning look. The man was upset, he got that. Likely, he was feeling guilty for hurting his sister. But if he didn't keep his eyes on the road and drive carefully, Tyson was going to have a whole lot to say to him in the ER waiting room.

"What happened? Where did this happen?" Tyson kept careful pressure on her head wound, aware that the fabric was sticky beneath his fingers. It didn't mean it was serious—head wounds bled a lot. But knowing that didn't do a thing for the panic crushing down on his chest.

"Shopping." Kitty sniffed, her voice halting. "Jensen let her out of the cart and she took off." A sob escaped her before she pressed her hand to her mouth.

"Hey, hey." Tyson rested his cheek atop her head. "If you need to cry, you cry."

"It hurts." She sniffed. "To cry."

"Aw, Kitty. I'm so sorry." Jensen sounded close to losing it himself. "I am the worst big brother. I am. I wasn't thinking—"

"It's okay, Jensen. Everything is fine." She

took a wavering breath. "Please don't worry over me."

Tyson grinned, he couldn't help himself. It was such a typical Kitty thing to say. "That's what you do when you care about someone, Kitty. You worry. Let him worry."

"Okay." Her hand tightened on his. "Are you worried?"

Yes. I am. Tyson pressed his eyes shut. Of course he was worried. He was going to worry until the doc said otherwise. He'd likely be worried long after that, too. He was scared to death—and it took a lot to scare him. "No. I'm not worrying because I know you're going to be fine."

"Not even a little bit?" she whispered.

"Maybe." He ran his thumb back and forth across her hand. "A little bit." If she listened, she'd be able to hear his heartbeat. There was no hiding from that—how it was pounding.

It was the longest drive of Tyson's life. He and Jensen did their best to keep her engaged but he could tell she was having a hard time staying awake. When the Colton County Emergency Center and Hospital sign was finally visible, it was easier to breathe. "Almost there."

"Mmm."

"Kitty." He gave her hand a squeeze. "Come

on, now. Tell me something. Something no one else knows."

"I can't." She sighed. "It's a secret."

"I'm good at keeping secrets." They were almost in the parking lot now. "Nothing you say can surprise me." He waited just long enough for Jensen to put the truck into Park before opening the door. He unbuckled her seat belt and slid, holding her close, until he had one foot on the ground.

"I can take her." Jensen reached for her. "She's my sister. I did this. Lemme get her inside."

He didn't argue. He shifted her from his arms to Jensen's and took the keys. "I'll park the truck."

But Jensen was already hurrying her inside.

The waiting room at the Colton County Emergency Center wasn't large because Colton County wasn't all that populated. By the time the Crawleys and a handful of friends had gathered, there were no chairs to spare. Tyson didn't bother to sit. He paced.

When Doc Johnson came out, Tyson had to stop himself from shoving through the throng of family to hear what he had to say.

"The good news is there's no skull fracture. She did get ten stitches to close up that gash and she has a doozy of a concussion. I'm thinking, to be on the safe side, we'll keep her tonight. Just to keep an eye on her."

Tyson crossed his arms over his chest, holding back the questions he had no right to ask.

"You think that's necessary?" Dwight Crawley looked to have aged ten years in the last half hour. "She wouldn't be more comfortable at home?"

"Dad, if he wants to keep an eye on her, she needs to stay here." Twyla slipped her arm through her father's. "I think we should listen to Doc Johnson."

"I don't anticipate a thing going wrong but there's always potential complications with a head trauma." Doc Johnson patted Dwight Crawley on the shoulder. "She's young and healthy, Dwight. I'm sure, by tomorrow, she can go home and, in a few days, you'll all forget this happened."

Tyson doubted that. He sure wasn't going to forget tonight. His heartrate still hadn't returned to normal. And poor Jensen was eaten up with guilt—it was written all over his face.

Doc Johnson said, "We'll get her into a room soon. Once you all say your good nights, you'll have to clear out. Hospital policy is one guest overnight, I'm afraid." With a nod, he went back through the ER doors.

"I'll stay with her." Twyla volunteered. "Jensen, you can take Dad home."

"No." Jensen shook his head. "I'll stay with her. This is all my fault."

"It was an accident." The words were out before Tyson realized it. "You've got Samantha waiting for you—probably worrying. She'll want you to tell her everything's all right."

"He's right." Dwight Crawley nodded. "I want to thank you, son, for your quick action." He held out his hand to Tyson. "You took care of my girl. I won't forget that."

Tyson shook his hand.

"You've got blood on your shirt." Twyla pointed.

"It's fine." He waved aside her offer. "Thank you, though."

The ER doors opened and Martha Zeigler came in. It was the first time he'd ever seen the woman looking vulnerable. When she approached Dwight, there looked to be tears in her eyes.

"Earl called. How is she?" Martha clasped Dwight's hand in hers. "What can I do?"

"She's fine. She is…" But Dwight sputtered to a stop and he shook his head.

Martha wrapped him in her arms and patted his back. "You stop acting tough. It's just me."

Surprisingly, Dwight Crawley clung to the woman and buried his face against her neck.

"Let's sit and catch your breath." She led the older man back to their seats and sat beside him.

Tyson watched, mystified.

"Huh." Jensen shook his head. "Go figure."

"You can take credit for that." Twyla nudged her brother. "Getting those two back together. Well, at least, talking to each other again."

"And this is a good thing?" Jensen didn't look convinced.

"Yes, it's a good thing. Dad's been an outright jerk since whatever happened to put them on the outs with one another." Twyla sighed. "I, for one, am grateful. And you need to call Mabel and let her know what's going on."

"I will. I'm gonna stay until she gets a room." Jensen pulled his phone from his pocket and walked out the ER doors.

"What's your excuse for sticking around?" Twyla smiled up at Tyson. "I mean, she's here, safe and sound and all. Thanks, again, for that. But no one expects you to stay."

"Oh." Tyson's nod was slow. "Right." He could leave. But…there was no way he could leave.

"I guess you have to get a ride home, though?"

"Right." Because he'd ridden with Jensen. And since his father and Mabel had stayed at the house with the girls he'd have to ask Jensen for a ride home, too. "It would be a long walk."

A nurse walked into the waiting room. "Miss

Crawley is on her way up to room 203. You can all go up and say a real quick goodbye."

He stood where he was. Twyla had made it perfectly clear he had no place here. He knew that, he did. He shouldn't get onto the elevator with Twyla, Dwight, and Martha. She was fine.

"Coming?" Jensen asked, tucking his phone into his pocket as he headed to the elevator.

No. I'm good. He swallowed. "Yeah." Tyson followed, ignoring the smile on Twyla Crawley's face when he stepped foot on the elevator. Or the side-eye from Martha Zeigler. They didn't matter. He needed to see her—for a minute. That would be enough to erase the last, lingering fear still clawing at his chest.

CHAPTER EIGHT

KITTY'S HEAD HAD a heartbeat. It wasn't painful, she'd been given meds for that. But the throb was something. So was the heaviness. The only upside was the slow clearing of the fog in her brain. Since she'd tumbled onto poor Tyson, things were murky. With the exception of the pain, that is. She was numb now, but she remembered it clearly.

"There's my sister, the unicorn." Twyla walked into her hospital room. "Hopefully they've given you enough pain meds for you to be feeling magical."

"What do you mean *unicorn*?" She reached for her forehead.

"Don't touch." Twyla grabbed her hand. "I was teasing you. Your lump is on the side, don't worry." She leaned forward to kiss her cheek. "I meant *unicorn* as in one-of-a-kind special."

"Oh." Kitty took a deep breath. "I can be that kind of unicorn."

"How are you, darlin'?" Her father took up the

space on the other side of the bed. "You gave this old man a fright."

"I'm good, Daddy." Her father only resorted to pet names when things were stressful. This, apparently, had stressed him out. "I inherited your hard head so don't worry."

He snorted. "Well, my heart about stopped when Tyson carried you out of the kitchen."

She had a vague recollection of Tyson carrying her. "Poor Tyson. I'm heavy." She reached for her father's hand.

Jensen stood at the foot of the bed, shaking his head. He opened his mouth, then shut it, his jaw clenching.

"Oh, stop it." Kitty tried to sit up, swayed, and fell back against the pillows. "I'm fine, everyone. Fine. I don't want to see long, pained faces or guilt-ridden expressions, you hear me?" She rested a hand against her head. "If you're going to do that, I'll get the nurses to kick you out. Got it?"

"Got it." Jensen squeezed her foot. "I love you, is all."

"I love you, too." She crossed her arms over her chest. "Now, smile or something. Just don't do that." She pointed at his face and his teary eyes.

"What can we bring you?" Martha Zeigler stood in the doorway. "Anything you want, it's yours."

Kitty blinked. Was she hallucinating? Doc Johnson said she needed to be very aware of abnormal things like slurred speech or numbness or decreased coordination. He'd said she might be confused—was a hallucination the same thing as confusion?

"Martha came as soon as she heard what happened." And, from the looks of it, her father was thrilled.

"Thank you for coming." Kitty smiled at the woman. "You didn't have to. All this fuss over—"

"You." Jensen squeezed her foot. "Like Tyson said, we have the right to worry about you. It means we care. Everyone in this room cares about you."

Tyson had said that? Yes, he had. When she'd had her head on his shoulder. Oh…she'd had her head on his shoulder. Unfortunately, the uptick of her heartbeat was instantly reported by the monitor she was connected to.

"You okay?" Twyla glanced from the rising numbers on the monitor to her sister's face.

She nodded, then winced. It didn't hurt but the pull against her stitches was uncomfortable.

"You hurting?" Jensen was staring at the monitor now.

Kitty took several long, slow breaths and concentrated on the emoji-style pain chart posted on the opposite wall until her heart rate returned to normal. "All good."

Twyla sighed. "Well, I'm staying here tonight, and if that happens again, I'm getting the nurse."

"You're staying here?" She looked around the sparse hospital room. "Twyla, that's just silly."

"Shush." Twyla pulled a chair to the side of the bed. "If you're going to suffer, I'm going to suffer with you. It's my sisterly duty."

"Except you'll be too tired to take care of me when I get home." She wrinkled up her nose. "You should go home and sleep in your own comfy bed."

"Look at you trying to manipulate me." Twyla's brows rose. "I didn't know you had it in you."

"Manipulate?" She relaxed into her pillow and closed her eyes. "Fine. Get a crick in your neck. But don't get mad at me over it."

"Deal." Twyla took her hand again.

"It's the closest thing to a bed I could come up with…" Was that Tyson's voice?

Kitty sat up and opened her eyes to see, yes, it was Tyson, carrying a large vinyl recliner into the room.

"The nurse said it'll fold way back." He placed it next to the bed. "Don't know how comfortable it'll be, Twyla, but I guess you'll find out."

Tyson was still here… He'd gone off to find Twyla a more suitable bed. She started taking preemptive deep breaths. After years of keeping her feelings hidden, she wasn't going to be outed by a heart rate monitor. She slid her hand under the sheet and slid the taped sensor from her fingertip.

"Maybe Juney is right. After all you've done today, I'd say you might be hero material." Twyla beamed up at him. "I guess I should give you a big ol' thank-you kiss but... I don't want to."

Kitty gasped in surprise. "Twyla." But then Tyson's brown eyes shifted her way and her mind went blank.

"Hey." He grinned.

Gracious. That grin. She was *so* glad she'd pulled off her pulse oximeter. "Hi." It was hard to peel her eyes from his handsome face, but she managed it. Only to discover an alarmingly large red spot on his shirtfront. "Is that... Did I do that to your shirt? Oh, Tyson."

"It's just a shirt, Kitty." He shoved his hands into his pockets, but his gaze stayed, warm and steady, upon her. "How are you doing?"

She nodded, then winced—her eyes closing. "Okay." She blinked. "I guess I need to remember not to move my head for a while." He seemed to be standing closer to the bed now. Maybe her eyes were playing tricks on her. "I'm not certain what happened, exactly. Things are a little fuzzy."

"Don't force it." Twyla cradled her hand in both of hers. "I imagine it'd just upset you, anyway."

But images were already clicking into place. Like the girls' faces when Tyson had carried her through the house. "Are the girls okay? I hope this didn't scare them."

"Katherine Ann. You are not going to chastise us for worrying over you, then turn around and start worrying about someone else. The girls will be fine. Jensen already called and filled Mabel in. Accidents happen. That's part of life." Her father rested his hand against her cheek. "Now, if you don't rest your pretty little head and take care of yourself, I'll ask Doc Johnson to keep you here another day or two—to make you get some rest."

She pretended to zip her lips shut.

"Good." He stooped and kissed her cheek. "We'll clear out and let you sleep. And you'd best sleep, hear me. No worrying over nothing." He shook his finger at Twyla. "I expect a full report in the morning."

Twyla saluted him. "Is that how you salute? No idea." She did it again, then shrugged.

Her sister's antics had her laughing—which hurt. She pulled her hands free and pressed against the bandages around her head. The pressure helped a little. Better to keep her eyes closed until the threat of tears wasn't obvious.

"Stop being funny, Twyla Marie." Her father's words and threatening tone had Kitty laughing all over again.

"Dad." Twyla sighed. "That's you."

"I love you all." As long as she held on to her head, it wasn't so bad. Her eyelids were definitely getting heavy. "But I'm really tired so you should all go home and get some rest."

"Come on, Dwight." Martha's voice was pitched low and encouraging. "Let your girl sleep and we'll come back in the morning."

"With breakfast." He gave her another kiss. "'Night, darlin'."

"'Night, Daddy." She smiled. "'Night, Miss Martha." She waved them off.

Tyson and Jensen were headed for the door when the nurse came in. "Did you lose your pulse oximeter? The alarms are going off at the nurses' station."

Lose, no. Take it off? Yes. She cleared her throat. "I guess so." She held up her hand so the nurse could reattach it. "I'll be more careful."

"Nurse, you should know she won't complain even if she's hurting." Jensen, and Tyson, were still standing in the door. "Other than that, she'll be an easy patient."

"I'll keep an eye on her." The nurse pulled

a keyboard from underneath the monitor and started typing. "Anything else I should know? Any allergies? How's your pain?"

Kitty gave the woman a thumbs-up.

"Oh, here." Twyla put Kitty's purse on the bed beside her. "Your phone has been pinging and ringing for a while." She fished the now-ringing phone from the bag, pressed the button, and handed it to her.

Kitty fumbled with the phone, frowning at her sister. "Hello?" She didn't want to talk on the phone. She wanted to sleep.

"Kitty? It's RJ. You okay? I heard you had an accident."

She glanced at her sister—who was grinning. "Hi, RJ. I'm okay."

"Well, I'm in the neighborhood. Want me to bring anything to you?"

"Oh, no. That's okay. Twyla is here and I'm only allowed one visitor now that it's so late."

"Well, that makes sense." He sighed. "You needin' your rest and all."

"Yes." She pleated the blanket covering her legs. "I do."

"I'll let you get some sleep, then." He cleared his throat. "I was real worried about you, Kitty. I'm mighty glad to hear your voice and know you're well."

She wasn't sure what the appropriate response was. "Thank you...for checking on me."

"Of course. I'll see you tomorrow. 'Night." And he hung up.

"That was sweet." Twyla's grin was full of mischief.

"You knew it was RJ when you answered the phone, didn't you?" She sighed. "I thought you were anxious for me to get some rest?"

"He's not coming up here, is he?" Jensen asked. "We're only leaving because Doc Johnson said no more visitors."

"That's right. Visiting hours are over." The nurse kept on typing. "Your boyfriend can come visit you at eight tomorrow morning, though. It sounded like he was worried about you."

Kitty held up her hands. "Oh, he's not—"

"He did sound worried, didn't he?" Twyla rested her elbows on the side of the bed. "I bet he brings you flowers when he comes to see you tomorrow."

"A good boyfriend would." The nurse finished typing, then folded up the keyboard and the monitor. "I guess we'll see in the morning."

"He's not her boyfriend." Tyson's scowl could rival one of her father's. His tone wasn't much better, either. Even as he said, "Get some rest, Kitty," he sounded angry. Without another word, he left.

"I guess we're leaving?" Jensen shook his head.

"Why are you two still here?" Twyla shooed them away. "Maybe go get Tyson a beer before he blows a gasket or something."

"Maybe." Jensen was chuckling when he left.

"I'll be back in a bit." The nurse followed Jensen out.

"Well, that was weird." Kitty sighed, her head beginning to ache.

"It was, right? Tyson seemed pretty upset." Twyla shrugged. "But you're not allowed to worry about him, Kitty. He's a grown man. More than capable of taking charge and fixing things."

She wasn't sure what *things* Twyla was referring to, but she was too tired to ask. "I hope he's okay," she murmured—and fell sound asleep seconds later.

TYSON SIPPED HIS BEER. He was out of sorts—too out of sorts. That's why he was sitting in a bar with Jensen. He needed to get his head straight before he went home. And he was nowhere close. His mind was all over the place, replaying parts of the night and tearing him up all over again. He never wanted to experience that sort of pure helplessness again. It had gnawed at him while he'd held Kitty close, her head bleeding, and the whole way to the hospital. And waiting for word on her condition for what felt like an eternity had just about driven him out of his mind. Now there was a sense of relief. After all that, Kitty was okay. That was good. That was important. He shouldn't have let Twyla's teasing irritate him. Or RJ's call and his…existence, either. The one thing he was struggling to understand was his anger. He had no reason to be angry—but he was.

"You want another round?" It was the first thing Jensen had said since they'd sat at the bar and ordered their beer.

He shook his head. "I'm good." At least, he was trying to be.

"You sure about that?" Jensen faced him. "You look ready to throw down with the next person that looks at you funny." His gaze was direct. "You want to talk about it? Or you wanna keep stewing in it?"

"The second one." What was he supposed to say? That seeing her hadn't given him the comfort he'd hoped and he'd rather be sitting at her bedside than sitting here, having a beer in the bar. That he didn't like RJ calling Kitty. That it rubbed him all the wrong way when Twyla teased that RJ was Kitty's boyfriend. He wasn't going to say any of that. He definitely wouldn't admit that every time Kitty came to mind, things got brighter and more vivid and real and it terrified him. *What is wrong with me?*

"Your call." Jensen finished his beer and sighed, a curse slipping before he asked, "You're not really in a fighting mood, are you?"

"You said it, not me." He rolled his neck.

"Good, because—" Jensen pointed at the bar entrance "—RJ is here. And he's coming this way."

His grip tightened on the glass. "Why would I care if RJ is here?" He downed the rest of his beer.

"Tyson. Jensen. How's Kitty doing?" RJ stopped and leaned against the bar.

Tyson turned and looked at the man—really looked. All he saw was sincere concern. Concern for Kitty… Tyson swallowed and stared at his empty glass.

"She's got a concussion. Cut her head and got a few stitches, too." From the sound of it, Jensen was still feeling guilty.

"How in tarnation did that happen?" RJ tipped his hat back on his head. "She fall off a horse or something?"

Tyson didn't want to relive the whole ordeal to appease RJ's curiosity so he asked, "How'd you find out she was in the hospital?"

"Oh, you know. Talk spreads faster than wildfire in these parts. I guess your daddy, Earl, called Martha and Martha called Dorris and Dorris called me—knowing I've got feelings for

Kitty and all." RJ waved down the bartender. "Another round, please."

Even though RJ's feelings for Kitty weren't a secret, RJ's easy confession was a slap to the face. There'd been no hemming and hawing, just a straightforward declaration. RJ wasn't afraid to say he had feelings for Kitty. Even to her brother. He wasn't struggling with his feelings—he owned them.

"Feelings." Jensen leveled RJ with an unflinching stare. "Honest-to-goodness feelings? With a plan for the future? Because if we're talking about anything less, I'll ask you to walk away from my sister. *Now.*"

About time you said something like that. If Tyson had any beer left, he'd have toasted Jensen.

"I'm hoping there's a future with her." RJ nodded his thanks as the bartender set three glasses of beer on the bar before them. "That's what I'm aiming for, anyway. The kids. The dog. All of it. You have my word on that."

Well, that's just great. The idea of Kitty and RJ living some kind of white-picket fence life had his stomach flipping over and beer rising back up his throat. Objectively, he respected RJ for being so aboveboard and clear about his intentions. But he neither liked nor approved of a single thing the man had said. He'd never be okay with RJ courting Kitty. But he'd have to be. This—Kitty and RJ—had nothing to do with him. It didn't matter that he had a whole lot of objections and even more feelings about the matter.

"But I could use a little help." RJ chuckled.

Tyson ran a hand over his face. How was he supposed to sit here and listen to this?

"How's that?" Jensen took a sip of beer.

"Twyla said something about some big sewing project. Now that Kitty's laid up, I figure she's going to need help with it." He smiled. "I can sew, my ma and gramma can, too. I figure the more hands, the better."

I'm the bad guy here. Tyson knew about the stress Kitty was under. It had all come pouring out of her minutes before she'd had her accident. Had he stopped to consider how this would set her back? No. He'd been too caught up in himself. And that needed to stop. "You're right. We should all pitch in and help."

"You sew?" RJ scratched his head. "Huh."

"If needed." He was pretty sure this qualified as a need situation. "Kitty said something about renting out the Community Center on Saturday." But he couldn't remember the specifics.

"I'll be there." RJ lifted his glass. "To Kitty. Wishing her a quick recovery."

"Amen to that." Jensen lifted his glass.

Tyson did the same. If toasting with RJ got

Kitty on her feet faster, he'd toast all night. He downed half his glass.

"How's it going working for Audy?" Jensen asked.

"Well, now, that's the thing. Rodeo Audy—the one I knew best—is a whole lot different than Running the Ranch Audy. I'm thinking his reformation has just as much to do with Brooke, Joy, and their little nugget, Clara, though. He's the first one to say his whole world revolves around them. But he doesn't seem to mind it too much." RJ grinned. "He's definitely had me lookin' at things differently. Like, maybe, being settled down could be a good thing."

Jensen chuckled. "Yessir, it can. I can vouch for that."

It seemed like just about everyone in Garrison was falling in love or getting hitched the last few years. If Tyson's own attempt at domestic bliss hadn't been such an epic failure, even he might have been tempted to try again. But, it had, so he wasn't. Not in the least.

They spent the next hour talking about anything other than Kitty. Every time things started to move back in that direction, he made an effort to redirect things. From Tyson's bronc riding days to living outside the rodeo circuit, ranching, farming, running a small family-owned business, family—they covered a whole lot of ground.

When it was all said and done, Tyson had no reason to dislike RJ. The man was working hard to change. He didn't shy away from his past or the foolish things he'd done. He'd made a promise to himself to do better and he was trying.

And yet, Tyson couldn't like him.

On the drive back to his place, he intentionally shifted his thoughts from RJ. Tomorrow was the girls' first day at school. He didn't know what to expect, but he and his father were both planning to be there.

"What are you going to do?" Jensen asked.

"About?"

Jensen sighed. "My sister."

"What do you mean? There's nothing for me to do." He needed to remember that.

"Oh?" Jensen sighed. "I'm not saying I'm rooting for RJ, but the man knows what he wants."

Even though the truck cab was dark, Tyson found himself glaring at Jensen. "I got that."

Jensen had the nerve to laugh.

"She's your sister." He ran his fingers through his hair, irritated all over again. "I…worry. This whole thing with RJ is weird. You're not worried?" Why wasn't he worried?

"You're worried about Kitty—as your friend?"

"She is my friend. Always." He shook his head.

"You don't think you're getting too worked up over this? Her and RJ?"

Maybe. Possibly. Probably. But he wasn't ready to admit it. "I don't think you're worked up enough." Tyson pushed back.

Jensen sighed. "You want her to be happy? You want her to find a man that will support her, protect her, and make her happy? As her friend?"

"She deserves nothing less." She deserved that and more.

"What if that's RJ? What if he's the one chance at the family she's always wanted? It's not like she's got men lined up around the block."

"'Cuz they're stupid," he ground out.

Jensen laughed again. "Sometimes it's hard to see what's right in front of you." He sighed and said, "If this is her choice, I'll support it."

Tyson swallowed against the knot in his throat. Didn't Jensen get that RJ didn't deserve her? This was Kitty. She was special. She was important.

"I think you need to take a step back and think about this, Tyson. Unless you know of someone better suited for her, someone willing to step up, you need to give RJ a chance." Jensen turned on his blinker and slowed down. "I'll drop it."

What infuriated Tyson all the more was Jensen was right. About all of it.

They parked and headed inside to find the

three girls and his father, sound asleep, piled up on the couch with the television on and some cartoon princess movie playing.

Mabel sat in the recliner, her phone in one hand and a tablet on her lap. As soon as she saw them, she motioned for silence and set everything aside, tiptoeing across the room and into Jensen's waiting arms. "She resting?"

Jensen nodded. "Hopefully. Twyla was full of mischief, so who knows."

Mabel frowned.

Tyson wholeheartedly agreed with that frown.

"We should go." Mabel nodded at the clock.

The next ten minutes were spent shifting sleeping bodies into car seats and beds. Tyson was astounded at how soundly the girls slept. How is it he could lift them from the couch, carry them down the hall, tuck them into their own bed, and leave without them stirring? But, last night, June got wide-eyed awake at the slightest sound he made trying to sneak out?

When the girls were in bed, he wandered back to the living room to find his father, two glasses of milk, and their evening plate of sandwich cookies waiting on the coffee table.

"You wanna fill me in on what happened tonight?" His father shook his head. "All I know was Kitty was white as a sheet and bleeding and you were beside yourself."

He had been. "Her head got smacked with the door. Hard." He could still hear the sound. "She went down and I caught her." He could still feel her, limp, in his arms. His heart twisted up until it was aching something fierce. He rubbed the heel of his hand against his chest, but it didn't help. "She's stitched up, got a concussion, and staying overnight at the hospital. Doc thinks she'll be fine tomorrow."

"Good. Good," his father murmured. "And you? How are you holding up, son?"

He leaned forward to rest his elbows on his knees and buried his face in his hands. "I don't know. I guess I'm trying to come to terms with a few things."

"Like what?" His father's sigh was all sympathy.

He nodded, shook his head, then shrugged. "RJ Malloy's courting Kitty." He shook his head. "And I don't like it."

"Well, now, I imagine you don't." His father sat back. "What are you going to do?"

He looked at his father. "I'm not sure there's anything to do, Dad."

Once again, his father gave him a long, careful look. "You'll figure it out."

Between his conversation with Jensen and his reaction to RJ, he had a whole lot to figure out. There had been a lot of truth in Jensen's words, and he needed to deal with that first. He could start by making peace with this RJ and Kitty thing. If this was what Kitty wanted, he would support her. What his own fool heart might want didn't matter. He'd stopped listening to it years ago, anyway. All it ever did was lead him toward grief and regret. Iris and his own mother had made certain of that.

CHAPTER NINE

KITTY WANTED TO go home. She wanted her bed, the quiet of the ranch, and her privacy. While the outpouring of love and support meant so much, she didn't like being fussed over—she didn't like being the center of attention. As the youngest, she'd been content to stay in her older siblings' shadow. Now, there were no shadows to hide in *and* there was the added delight of greeting half the town while wearing a hospital gown in bed.

"It's like a garden in here." Martha Ziegler walked into her room. "You're so loved, Kitty."

"What's not to love?" her father asked. According to Twyla, he'd arrived at the hospital long before visiting hours started and stayed in the waiting room until they'd let him come up. Now Twyla had gone home to shower and change and her father had been hovering ever since.

"Oh, I agree." Martha approached the foot of the bed. "Kitty's a rare soul."

"That's kind of you." For the fifteenth time this morning, Kitty was blushing and squirming from the praise. "You didn't have to come by. With any luck, I'll be heading home soon." At least, she hoped so.

"We'll see." Her father shook his head. "It'd be fine if he kept you another day—to make sure you get plenty of rest."

"I'd get more rest at home." But she stopped there because arguing with her dad was pointless.

"Isn't that the truth? I never understood it. You can't get a lick of sleep in the hospital." Martha nodded. "Nurses and doctors poking and prodding on you at all hours. I don't know how they expect a person to heal." She smoothed the blanket over Kitty's legs. "But, for your daddy's sake, let's see what the doc says. If they think you need to be watched a bit longer, I'm sure there's a reason for it."

Kitty nodded, watching the look exchanged between her father and Martha. It warmed her through and through to see the honest-to-goodness affection they had for one another.

"How are you feeling?" Martha asked, perching on the side of Kitty's bed.

"Better." Which was the answer she knew everyone wanted to hear. "Just tired." She smiled.

"You look it, too." Martha's gaze swept over her face. "Dwight, didn't you have something you wanted to say to your daughter?"

Her father stood and stretched. "Last night got me thinkin'…" He broke off and rubbed a hand over his face. "About a lot of things but, mostly, about how wrong I've done you and your sister."

"Dad." She sat forward. Seeing her father angry was one thing. Seeing her father upset and emotional was another. "You have—"

"Barked and snapped and sassed the two of you for—well, too long." He cleared his throat. "And, last night, when I saw you like that—" He broke off.

Martha smiled up at him, offering encouragement.

"A father shouldn't see his child like that, Kitty. I thought… I won't tell you what I thought. I don't want to talk about it or think like that ever again. But I didn't like it, not one bit. I couldn't stop worryin' over you. About you being better. About you getting strong and smilin'. And all the things I never said to you and should have. Worrying whether or not you knew that, even as bullheaded and mean as I am, I'm grateful to have you as my daughter."

Kitty's eyes were burning and a rock-hard lump settled in her throat. *Oh, Daddy.*

"I am." He put his hands on his hips, his scowl lines drooping with emotion. "It killed me thinking that you might not know that." He cleared his throat. "I know I ask too much of you—Twyla, too. But, mostly you. I do. The more I ask, the more you give. And that needs to stop. I can't keep dragging you and your sister down."

"Daddy, you don't. I want to take care of you." It was what she did—what she'd always done. "We all do."

"*I* want you to have your own life. What about that? Your daddy, wanting you and your sister to live a good life, doing what you want and being happy. You and Twyla. I want you to go and do and not be beholden to me." He sighed. "I'm old, but I'm not helpless."

"Or alone." Martha stood and went to his side.

"That, too." He took her hand. "How on earth are you going to get this online shop up and running if you're playing nurse and driver to me?"

She didn't have an answer for that. Honestly, she was surprised that he knew about her dream. She blinked, willing herself not to cry. And her father saw it.

"I can't do tears, Kitty." Her father shook his head.

"I know." She waved her hand at him. "I know, I'm trying."

He caught her hand. "I'll try, too. I can't guarantee I won't slip every now and then—"

"I guarantee he will." Martha smiled.

He chuckled, looking a little teary-eyed himself. "Well, that's that and all. I'm going to…"

He sniffed. "I'm gonna take a quick walk and stretch my legs." And he left the room.

Martha watched him go. "He didn't get the half of what he wanted out." She sat on the bed again. "Bottom line is, he loves you and your sister and wants you both to be happy. I know he also wants you to have your own families so he can have more grandbabies but that's a whole other conversation." She shook her head. "He's rough around the edges but his heart is gold."

"I'm glad you see that." Kitty smiled at the older woman. "And that you two have worked things out."

"That man and his temper. Every rose has its thorns, though." She shrugged and looked around the room. "It looks like you've had a lot of visitors."

She nodded. "Dorris and Patsy were here first thing. They brought doughnuts, so Daddy was happy—he knows he won't get those at home. Hazel brought me coffee and a cinnamon muffin from Old Towne Coffee and Books."

"Those muffins are heaven."

"They are and Hazel knows I love them. Brooke stopped by with baby Clara. That's been the highlight. There's nothing like holding a newborn. They're so tiny—so perfect." She shook her head.

"Don't worry, your time will come." Martha's

smile was surprisingly gentle. "And what a lucky baby that will be—to have you for a mother."

The sudden, "Ahem," came from RJ Malloy, standing in the doorway.

"Good morning, RJ." Martha's smile cooled and her expression went frosty. "Come on in."

He entered the room, a massive flower arrangement in hand. "I didn't want to interrupt." He headed straight for the bed. "You look tuckered out, Kitty." He frowned. "You feeling okay? In pain?" His concern was surprisingly sweet.

"Everyone has been taking good care of me, RJ, really." She smiled up at him.

"That's good. So you know, I'd track 'em down and set 'em straight if they weren't." He rested a hand on the railing of her bed. "Didn't sleep last night, myself."

"Oh?" She noticed the dark circles under his eyes.

"Worrying." He grinned, his cheeks going red. "It's a new experience for me." He cleared his throat. "Staying up worrying over someone else."

"Oh." His directness was equal parts unsettling and commendable.

"This was the biggest arrangement in Garrison Gardens." He held up the basket of flowers. "Not big enough, if you ask me."

"RJ, I've never seen a flower arrangement that size. Outside of a wedding or a funeral, that is."

Martha eyed it with an unfathomable expression. "I can put it here, in the window, if you like? That way the flowers get some sun?"

"I'll do it. It's a mite heavy." He hefted the basket and placed it on the wide windowsill amongst the other flowers she'd received. He glanced at each arrangement, then nodded. "I guess it is big enough."

"RJ Malloy." Her father came into the hospital room looking, and sounding, like a thundercloud.

"Mr. Crawley, sir." He shifted from foot to foot. "I stopped by to check on Kitty. I won't stay too long or wear her out."

She braced herself for her father's reaction. RJ's visit was thoughtful and, even though Kitty was still uncertain how to feel about his obvious interest in her, she hoped her father remained civil—at least.

"Well…" Her father took a deep breath. "That is mighty nice."

All Kitty could do was stare, openmouthed at her father.

"You've got more visitors, Kitty. I ran into your brother and Tyson on their way in." Her father stepped aside and waved them forward. "Come on, you two."

If only RJ's name flooded her with excitement, that would make things so simple. But no, it was Tyson. It had always been Tyson. And when he walked in behind her brother, even looking none too happy to be there, she found herself sitting a little straighter and reaching up to carefully smooth her hair.

"You're looking better." Jensen came over and dropped a kiss on her cheek. "Getting a little bruised there." He shook his head.

"Bruising means healing." She smiled up at her brother. "And you're not going to worry or get upset while you're here." She'd caused enough drama for everyone; she wanted to go home and put it behind her. "I'm fine. You're fine. We're all fine."

But Tyson didn't seem fine. He stood in the far corner of the room, all handsome and… Was he mad? He certainly didn't look happy.

"Always looking on the bright side." Her brother chuckled.

"That's Kitty, a ray of sunshine." Martha's unrelenting gaze had yet to let up on RJ.

RJ, however, seemed oblivious. "That she is," he agreed.

Kitty's face was so hot she could only imagine how red she was. "Thank you, but… You can stop, anytime. Please."

"I should be going." Martha patted her arm, then headed for the door. "Don't hesitate to call," she said as she left. "You behave."

"I thought you liked it better when I didn't." Her father winked at Martha. "I'll call you later."

"Dad." Jensen grimaced. "Really?"

"Thank you." Kitty laughed and waved Martha off. "Some of you can sit, if you like. It's awkward with you all standing around, watching me." She tugged her blankets up.

Her father and brother sat, RJ moved to stand at the side of her bed, but Tyson stayed where he was. And, yes, something was bothering him, she could tell. And then she remembered. "How did it go with the girls this morning?" Today was a big day—the girls' first school day. He had a lot going on. It wasn't all about her. "Did they do okay?"

Tyson nodded. "Fine."

That was it? She waited, but he just stood there—tension rolling off of him. "That's nice." She glanced at Jensen. "And Samantha? She wasn't too upset over last night?"

"She's gonna worry about her aunt, Kitty, but she's good. From what I saw of June and July, they were excited about school. And making new friends." He shot Tyson a long-suffering look. "Better than hanging out with that crusty pain-in-the-rear—and his father."

Tyson's sigh was laden with frustration.

"I gotta get." RJ checked his watch. "I'll be

able to focus on my work now that I've seen you're okay."

Kitty opened her mouth but nothing came out—so she smiled.

"I'll check in later." He nodded at her father. "Sir. I appreciate you giving me some time." And, with that, he left.

"He brought you those?" Her father walked over to inspect the oversize flower arrangement. "I bet that cost him a pretty penny."

"Wasn't there a song? 'You Can't Put a Price on Love,' or something like that?" Jensen was grinning.

"You can on flowers." Her father snorted. "And that right there, says he likes you a whole lot, little miss."

"He shouldn't have." She meant it, too. "It's too much."

"That he likes you or that he got you flowers?" This from Tyson. He pushed off the wall and headed to her bedside. When he stared down at her the severity of his gaze had her instantly flustered. "He's showing you he cares about you."

"I… I know." She murmured. "I guess…" His eyes remained steady on her face but a deep crease settled between his brows and his mouth slanted downward. Why? What had upset him? Why was he angry? "It's thoughtful. So was his visit." And still, he stared at her. "But… I feel bad that he wasted his hard-earned money on me."

"Wasted?" His frown deepened. "I guarantee that wasn't how he wanted those flowers to make you feel." His gaze shifted to her hands—currently tightly gripping her sheets—and his jaw clenched tight.

"This is your fault, Dad." Jensen sighed. "There are times sentiment beats practicality. This would be one of those times."

"Well, I agree with Kitty. It is a waste. Flowers die. Might as well take the money from your wallet and toss it in the trash can. It's the same thing."

"Wow, Dad. Do you know what the word *romance* means? Were you always this way? How did me and Twyla and Kitty even get made? It's a mystery." Jensen leaned forward. "Don't listen to Dad. Tyson's right. RJ gave you those to make you smile—to make you feel special. Spending his money on you isn't a waste, it's an investment."

"I said all that?" Tyson grumbled as he eyed the flowers, his jaw more rigid than ever.

Jensen went on to say, "For all you know, he took the time to pick each of those flowers just for you. I didn't know it, but flowers have meaning. Mabel could tell you what they mean when she comes up in a bit."

She dragged her gaze from Tyson to look at the flowers again. "That seems like an awful lot of work."

"If a man's going to pursue you, he should put in the work." Her father glanced at the empty doorway. "I just never thought RJ Malloy would be the one doing the pursuing." He turned back to her. "How... How are you feeling about him?"

She was flustered all over again. Not only was Tyson regarding her with the same unnerving force as before, her brother and father were watching her, too. "I don't know. Are we really having this conversation? I'd rather not. Tyson doesn't want to, either—look at how unhappy he looks." He did, too. So unhappy that she covered her face with her hands. "And...this is none of your concern...let's change the subject." She peered through her fingers. "Please."

"Okay." Jensen pointed at Tyson. "Stop. With that."

Tyson glared at her brother, rolled his neck, and smiled down at her. "Sorry, Kitty. I'm not unhappy. This..." He took a deep breath. "This is all great."

He thought it was great that RJ had brought her flowers? That RJ was courting her? Which was... As it should be. Why would he have a problem with a man showing interest in her?

There was no doubt RJ was interested, either.

She looked back at RJ's massive flower bouquet. Her brother was right, this was a statement piece that left no room for misinterpretation. And if Tyson, her brother, even her father seemed to be okay with RJ's intentions, maybe she should give the man a chance? Why not try, at least? What could it hurt?

WALKING IN TO find RJ in Kitty's hospital room had turned his okay morning into a pile of steaming horse manure. The man was doing everything right. It was like RJ had gone to some "How to Woo a Woman" academy and graduated at the top of his class. The attentiveness. The complimentary and heartfelt words. The flowers. His efforts had been so impressive that even Dwight Crawley had nothing mean to say about the man—and Dwight Crawley *always* had something mean to say about everyone.

Now she was staring at those flowers and, out of nowhere, Tyson wanted to march over, knock the basket of flowers onto the floor, and… And what? What was wrong with him? He wasn't a five-year-old. Tantrums, at his age, weren't okay. Even if he did act like a petulant toddler on a rampage, what was he hoping to gain from it? If Kitty wanted RJ, he'd support it. He would. Or at least he'd try.

Yeah, this wasn't working. He didn't know

where these thoughts were coming from but, at the moment, he didn't like himself all that much. Maybe he wasn't as okay or recovered from what had happened yesterday? Maybe being here, seeing her vulnerable was too much for him? Maybe his heart was already more invested than he wanted it to be? Whatever the reason, he needed to get himself sorted. Until he could stop acting like a jerk, he should give her distance.

"Looks like you're covered here with…flowers and all." He avoided her gaze. "I need to get to work." He needed to get out of here. "Rest and get better." And still, he didn't risk looking at her.

"Good of you to stop by." Dwight followed him to the door. "Tell your dad thanks again for last night. If he feels like making more brisket, I'm sure we could try again."

"I'll let him know." And he walked out—down the hall, around the corner, to the elevator. The rapid thud of his heartbeat echoed in his ears. He pressed the button once, then again. He took a deep breath against the pressure in his chest. Finally the doors opened and a handful of people came off—including Twyla Crawley.

Wonderful.

"Leaving already?" She stepped off the elevator. "What's wrong? You look a little…peeved."

"Morning, Twyla." He brushed past her into the elevator.

"I saw RJ leaving on my way in. Is that why you're…?" She pointed at him, up and down. "Like this?"

The pressure in his chest was getting worse. He mashed the elevator button.

"Tyson, you know—"

"Twyla." He pinched the bridge of his nose. He didn't want to snap at her but, if she picked or teased he feared he would. "I appreciate you taking care of Kitty last night." Thankfully, the elevator doors closed before she could think of some sort of retort.

He spent the day at the stockyards doing a final walk-through with the contractor. He had to sign off on every gate, hinge, fence and corner post for the work to be officially done. Thankfully, the contractor wanted to be just as thorough as he was. After that was done, he picked up some burgers and shakes from Bluebonnet Ice Cream for lunch and headed to Ellis Family Feed & Ranch Supply.

Managing the stockyards for the city wasn't a full-time job and, since his father was a ways from retiring, he wasn't needed at the family store a full eight hours a day, either. He didn't mind juggling two jobs—it kept him busy. Busy was good. Busy kept him from thinking about things he shouldn't. Namely, Kitty.

"How'd it go?" His father took the paper bag he offered.

"Signed off." Tyson sat at one of the tables in the small break room and pulled his burger from his bag. "I know they were a pain in my rear for a good four months, but I don't think the stockyards would be half as safe or half as shiny if the Ladies Guild hadn't gotten involved." He took a big bite of burger.

His father chuckled. "I was talking about your visit at the hospital."

He made a noncommittal noise and kept on chewing.

"That good, huh?" He unwrapped his burger. "So, the stockyards look good?"

He took his father's change of topic and ran with it. There was no further mention of Kitty during lunch, when he inventoried the cattle feed, salt licks, and supplements in the warehouse, or when he covered the first half of a shift for an employee running late. His mind was free and clear to focus—and he was grateful.

It was when he and his father pulled into the elementary school pickup line that he got worried. This time, it had nothing to do with Kitty and everything to do with June and July.

"You think they had a good day?" his father asked, craning his head to try to see around the cars in line before them.

"I guess we'll find out here pretty quick." He wasn't worried about July—having Samantha in her class would help. But June? She was a little thing. Except for monsters, she seemed pretty fearless. He hoped she'd had a good day. Kids could be mean sometimes.

It was a relief to see the girls, smiling and waving, as he pulled up to the curb. He parked and got out, opening the back door to help June up and into his father's older SUV.

"Unca Tyson—" June was breathless as she climbed into the back seat of the car. "I met a boy. He's not stinky. And he's my fwend."

"That's good." Tyson buckled her into her car seat. "Friends are always good. Especially when they're not stinky. What about you, July?"

"I like Mrs. Webber. She's so pretty and sweet." She buckled herself into her booster seat. "And Samantha and Abigail and Kirby are nice, too. We got to eat lunch together."

"An' I saw July in the cafetewia and waved." June bounced her feet. "I waved and waved and July waved back. An' they had sloopy Jims for lunch."

"Sloopy Jims?" His father scratched his head.

"Sloppy Joes." July giggled.

Tyson was still laughing as they drove away from the school.

"Awe we goin' home?" June asked, yawning.

"Not yet, Juney." His father turned to look over his seat. "It's shopping day. How about you two help me pick out what we want to make for dinners this week."

"Macawoni and cheese, please," June sing-songed. "My favowite. Yum yum yummy."

"What else?" his father asked.

"Fish sticks. Chicken fingers. And…macaroni and cheese." July shrugged. "June likes crunchy meat."

"The sloopy joe wasn't. But it was yum." June patted her tummy.

"Sloppy." July shook her head. "You're silly, Juney."

Tyson was grinning through the whole exchange. Was this what it was like to be a parent? A little bit of chaos, a lot of laughter? It was surprisingly enjoyable. And then, for some reason, he remembered what RJ had said about wanting a future with Kitty… *The kids. The dog. All of it.*

The thought of Kitty and RJ sharing this sort of afternoon together, loading up their kids after school and listening to their day, had him white-knuckle gripping the steering wheel.

Their shopping trip was an adventure. His father pushed one cart and filled it full of everything he and Tyson normally ate. Tyson helped the girls push a cart for what they wanted. It was a long, slow process. June didn't ask, she just put things in the cart. July would stop, pick something up and study it for a very long time, then put it back. Or she'd ask a ton of questions about whatever she was looking at—and then put it back.

"Grampa Earl." July stopped in the middle of the bread aisle. "Samantha said her aunt Kitty was still in the hospital."

"She is weally nice." It didn't matter where they were, June would stop and spin every now and then. "She painted my nails and Unca Tyson's nails and bwought ballina skihts to dance in. Does she have a bad booboo?"

There was a slight tug in his chest when he glanced at his nails. He fisted his hand and made a mental note to get nail polish remover while they were there.

"She bonked her head pretty good but she'll be right as rain soon enough." His father patted June on the head.

Tyson nodded. Even with her head all wrapped up, Kitty had looked...good.

"Samantha made her a get-well card. Teacher said it would help her feel better. Can we make one? Me and Juney?" July took a breath and said, "We need colored paper and glue and glitter and scissors and...and markers, though."

Tyson knew they had scissors. Maybe glue. But the rest? He looked at the girls, then his father. "I don't know if we can get all that here, but we can look."

A get-well card from June and July would mean a lot to Kitty. She'd always favored little, thoughtful things… Cards, homemade cookies, spending time together. Big things that drew attention—like a massive flower arrangement—made her uncomfortable. That was why she'd been so rattled over those flowers. That, or maybe it was the flowers and RJ. *Enough already.* He shook his head and steered the cart to the school supplies aisle in hunt of card-making materials.

It took an hour to shop and check out—by the time they were headed home both June and his father dozed off in the car.

Dinner led to a mess. The card making was even worse. His father took bath duty so Jensen could clean, but after thirty minutes of scrubbing, there were still dollops of glue and glitter peppering the kitchen floor. It would all be worth it once Kitty saw the card and lit up like a Christmas tree.

As soon as he thought of Kitty, that pressure in his chest kicked in. He threw the sponge in the sink and leaned against the counter.

Who was he kidding? He cared about Kitty. Like it or not, that was the truth. If it hadn't been for RJ, he'd probably never have realized his feelings for her. But now, no matter how hard he tried, he couldn't ignore them.

And that was...pathetic.

A man would be a fool not to want more with Kitty Crawley. RJ was no fool. He was stepping up and doing his best to stake his claim. At this rate, someone else would be on the receiving end of Kitty's smile and kindness and laughter and love. Could Tyson live with that? He wasn't ready to answer that.

He pressed the heel of his hand over the ache in his chest.

Just because he had feelings for Kitty didn't mean he had to act on them. If he did, everything would change—and there'd be no going back. Was he willing to risk it? Was he willing to open himself up and try again? All the disappointment and heartache and grief had made him bitter, he knew that. Kitty was the kind of person who'd shoulder others' burdens for them. Knowing that, how could he consider pursuing her? No. Knowing how heavy his burdens were, the kindest thing he could do was to keep his mouth shut and do nothing. Eventually, whatever this was would fade and everything would go back to normal. Surely.

CHAPTER TEN

KITTY WAS BORED. Her irritation was only outweighed by her anxiety. Did no one understand the severity of the situation? The Valentine's Festival costumes were not going to magically appear. There were no elves that would sneak into her workroom, work through the night, and leave perfectly assembled tutus for her to discover the next morning. At this rate, the working through the night part of it was sounding good. If everyone was asleep, no one could stop her from doing what needed doing.

They meant well, she knew that. But, somehow, Doc Johnson's offhand comment about avoiding eyestrain for a few days had translated into a ban on sewing.

"You're going to get a crease in the middle of your forehead just like Dad if you keep making that face." Twyla sat, a yard of tulle in her lap, doing what Kitty should be doing.

When it came to sewing, Kitty was twice as fast as her sister. Having to sit here, watching

Twyla moving at a snail's pace, only added insult to injury.

"I want to do something." Kitty sighed.

"Take a nap. Like Dad." Twyla nodded at their father—sound asleep and softly snoring in his recliner.

"I've taken a nap." She'd pretended to nap because her father and Miss Martha had been getting a little too lovey-dovey during lunch. A nap had been a convenient escape.

"Take another one. Isn't that what convalescing means?" Twyla pulled the needle up. "To sleep a lot. Healing through sleep? I'm sure it's something like that." She paused. "You could watch that show Mabel was talking about."

Kitty flipped on the television, not in the least bit interested in watching some melodrama about long-lost lovers who had to fight their way back to each other. But it was better than sitting here doing nothing. After watching the first fifteen minutes, Kitty was far too emotionally invested and panicking about the end.

Would the dog make it out alive? She didn't want to watch it if it didn't. And the love story… They kept collapsing in one another's arms while staying entirely too beautiful. Would the hero or heroine die? Mabel said it had a happy ending, but the more she watched, the harder that was to believe.

Just when it looked like things were going to be fine, the hero's car was hit by a truck. The camera zoomed in on his face. He was unconscious, blood trickling down his temple.

This is bad. Kitty clutched the remote to her chest.

"Wait." Twyla's voice startled her so much she dropped the remote. "But if he doesn't make it to the train station on time, she'll think he didn't wait for her—that he doesn't love her. What if she marries the bad guy. Ohmygosh, wait, could the bad guy have sent the truck to stop him?"

Kitty shushed her. It was torture. The hero didn't make it to the train station. He'd tried, running in slow motion and bleeding and still beautiful, but the train—and the heroine—was gone.

"I can't watch," Twyla moaned. "I can't."

"Twyla." Kitty waved her to be quiet. The last ten minutes of the film was horrible. Beautiful, but heartbreakingly sad. She was sobbing at the end. "Why would Mabel recommend that?" She blew her nose into the tissue. "That was…"

"I know." Twyla was crying, too.

"I don't even know what was happening." Their father, who had woken up at some point, looked a little teary-eyed himself. "That was a three-hanky film, if ever there was one."

Kitty laughed, but her tears were still falling.

"I'm going to see what Mabel recommends next." Twyla pulled out her phone.

"You do that." Kitty handed the remote to her father. "I'm getting some fresh air."

"Don't go far," her father called out. "Don't run or jump or do anything to hurt your head."

"I'll try not to." She pulled open the back door and stepped out onto the back porch. From where she leaned against the porch railing, her family's land stretched in all directions. In the distance, some of their cattle were grazing. It was a peaceful contrast to the emotional roller coaster she'd just watched.

Why had she sat through that? And why was she still crying over it? Everything about the movie had been over-the-top improbability. But that hadn't stopped her from having her heart ripped out over and over again. She sniffed, dabbing at her nose.

The back door opened and she braced herself. If her father or Twyla saw that she was still crying, she'd never hear the end of it. "I just need a minute," she said.

"Okay." That wasn't her father or Twyla.

She spun around. "Tyson?" *No.* She wiped frantically at her tears. *No no no.* This really, *really* wasn't fair.

He was across the porch to her in seconds, concern etching his features. "What's wrong?"

He tilted her chin back to search her eyes. "Are you hurting?"

"No." She shook her head. Well that *did* hurt. So she winced.

"You are." His brows pulled together.

"I wasn't." This close, she could make out at least five beautiful shades of brown in his eyes.

"Kitty…" He shook his head. "You don't have to be strong for me."

It wasn't just that his words were exactly the same words the movie hero had said to the heroine in a superemotional moment that had Kitty blinking back tears. It was also the way he said it. He sounded so concerned and invested and… protective of her.

If she hadn't been so distraught, she wouldn't be crying.

It would also help if he wasn't quite so intense. When he looked at her this way, it felt like he might actually see her. That shook her even when she wasn't on the fragile side.

Pull it together, Kitty. She attempted to take a deep breath—only for her breath to hitch.

His arms were warm around her. Gently, he pulled her close. "I'm being careful so I don't hurt you."

"Tyson." She couldn't breathe. How could she? She was in his arms. And it was for all the wrong reasons. How was she going to explain she was a victim of a romantic melodrama? "It's not my head…"

"No?" His chest reverberated beneath her ear. "Something is wrong. Yesterday, before we went to the hospital, you seemed awful skittish. At the hospital, too. Something's eating at you. You can tell me."

"Yesterday?" He'd picked up on that? She pushed back to look up at him. "You were mad at me in the hospital."

"I said I wasn't." He sighed.

"You said it but you…" She pointed up at him. "That's not what your face said."

He hesitated, then nodded.

"Why were you mad?" She pushed on his chest.

"Why are you out here crying?" His hands slid up, loosely gripping her upper arms.

"You're going to laugh at me." She closed her eyes. "It's embarrassing."

"I've never laughed at you. I might have laughed with you a time or two, but that's not the same thing." There was a smile in his voice.

She opened one eye. He was smiling—and her toes were curling. "This time you will."

He chuckled. "Try me."

"We just watched a movie." She swallowed. "A really bad, really emotional movie."

One eyebrow cocked up.

"I'm serious." She pointed at the back door. "Mabel recommended it. It was… I can't describe it. I was sobbing—I don't even know why, really. Twyla was, too." She leaned closer. "Even my dad." She whispered that. "Other than bad taste in movies, there's no reason for you to worry."

"Oh." His hands slipped from her arms. "That's…a relief." He stepped away from her and shoved his hands into his pockets. "You'll have to give me the name so I can make sure never to watch it."

"Fair enough." She swallowed, getting to the important part. "Your turn."

"I was mad… I am mad at myself." He pulled a hand from his pocket and ran his fingers through his hair. "You…you can always see the upside. A tornado could be headed toward the house, right now, and you'd find some silver lining."

"Mmm, I'm not so sure about that one."

"I bet you could." His eyes swept over her face. "You have hope. You see potential. You have dreams and you go after them."

Oh, Tyson. If you only knew. He was her biggest dream. But she'd never, not even once, considered going after him. The thought of losing his friendship stopped her. They'd been friends forever—there was no changing it now. Putting herself out there and knowing he'd reject her terrified her. No, she'd never recover from that sort of heartbreak. "Twyla would say I'm naive."

He shook his head. "That's because Twyla's a lot like your father. And, probably, she's trying to protect you."

"The last few days it's become very clear everyone thinks I need protecting."

"That's because you got hurt and we all panicked." His attention shifted to the gauze on her head. "All those people showed up to check on you because you bring a lot of light into this world—a lot of hope. Of course, we want to protect you."

We. He said *we* twice. Not that she'd read into it. He panicked when she got hurt because she was his friend. He wanted to protect her because she was Jensen's little sister. "I don't understand why you were mad?"

"Yeah, I'm talking in circles." He blew out a long, slow breath. "The thing is—"

The back door flung open, and June and July came barreling onto the back porch and headed straight for her, squealing and calling her name.

"Miss Kitty." June threw her arms around her knees. "You okay?"

"Yes, Juney." She knelt and hugged the little girl close.

"Pwomise?" Juney looked up at her face, then the bandage.

"Be real gentle, Juney." Tyson's voice was soft. "Small bounces."

"'Kay." Juney clasped her hands behind her back and stepped back, eyeing the gauze. "Is the owie bad?"

"It's not too bad." Kitty reached up to touch the bandage. "This keeps it covered so my owie can heal."

"Oh." June nodded, her eyes still glued to the gauze. "I guess that is okay."

"We came to see you, Miss Kitty." July, who had been waiting her turn, stepped close enough to give Kitty a gentle hug. "Samantha said you were home and we wanted to cheer you up."

"Your hugs are already making me feel better." She smiled at both the girls.

"Come in for a supwise." June grabbed her hand. "Come see."

Kitty let them lead the way, their little voices and excitement filling the house with energy. Samantha and Mabel got home minutes later and the noise level in the house increased so much that she saw her father digging for a cotton ball to plug his ears.

"We got a cake." Samantha pointed at the box Mabel carried. "A welcome-home-get-better cake."

"Because the thing we all need right now is sugar." Twyla burst into laughter. "I'll get plates."

"It's strawberry." Samantha climbed into one of the kitchen chairs to watch Mabel slide the pretty pink cake onto the table. "It's pink."

"And strawberry is Kitty's favorite." Twyla glanced at Mabel. "In case you didn't know that."

"I didn't. But Jensen did. I called him to find out." Mabel glanced at the clock on the wall. "Guess he's still out?"

"Is there daylight?" Kitty's father asked. "Then he's working."

Mabel nodded. "You sound just like my uncle Felix. If the two of you would ever decide to be civil to one another, I think you'd find you have an awful lot in common."

"Not likely." He snorted.

Even though the Briscoe-Crawley feud was over, the two patriarchs of the family weren't exactly on speaking terms. They tolerated one another, just barely. It hadn't helped that they'd been fighting for the same woman. Before her father had realized Martha Zeigler was the woman for him, he and Felix Briscoe were both vying for the hand of Barbara Eldridge. As far as Kitty was concerned, it had worked out for the best. Barbara Eldridge was a lovely woman, but Kitty wasn't so sure her skin was thick enough to endure her father's mood swings long term. Martha Zeigler, however, could hold her own.

"Sit hewe, Miss Kitty." Kitty sat in the chair Juney patted. "Now close ya eyes."

She closed her eyes.

"Where is it?" July whispered. "You had it."

"Nu-uh," June whispered back.

"I have it." Tyson laughed. "Careful of all the glitter."

"Okay," both the girls whispered.

"Open 'em." June clapped her hands.

Kitty opened her eyes. A large construction paper card sat before her. The girls had drawn some stick figures, fluffy clouds, and bunches of flowers—topped off with a liberal coating of glitter.

"It's a little stuck together," Tyson murmured when Kitty struggled to open it. "Too much glue."

Twyla offered her a butter knife and Kitty slid it between the paper halves, working slowly to separate the pages. When she finally opened it, she made sure to ooh and aah over all the artwork. Stickers covered the paper. In the middle, multicolored strips of construction paper overlapped and had been well glued in place. "It's a rainbow. I'll smile every time I look at it."

"Look." July flipped it over, leaving a puddle of glitter on the table. "Even Grampa Earl and Uncle Tyson signed it. And put kisses."

"I told them to." June pointed at herself. "Gotta kiss booboos betta."

Sure enough, both Tyson and his father had signed their names and left a bunch of X mark kisses—in crayon.

"Of all the cards and flowers I've received, yours and Samantha's cards are my favorite." She held her arms out and all three girls ran in for a hug. "Thank you for spending all that time and energy on me."

"Better than the gigantic arrangement from RJ?" Twyla asked.

She didn't even have to think about her answer. "Definitely." She had a hard time imagining there had been a bunch of elementary school craft supplies lying around at the Ellis house. No, he or Earl would have had to go into town for all of this, and that was almost as touching as the card itself. She glanced up at Tyson and mouthed, "Thank you."

Tyson's crooked smile was his only answer. But, like always, it was enough to have her heart rate climbing and tingles filling her stomach.

How Tyson wound up with cake on the back of his elbow, he didn't know. He'd hoped helping June eat would prevent this sort of mess. It hadn't. June's onetime yellow dress was covered in pink cake crumbs and smears of frosting. Her face was no better.

"Here." Kitty handed him a wet towel.

"Wouldn't it be better to take them outside and hose them off?" Jensen sat at the end of the table enjoying his slice of cake.

"It's a little cold, don't you think?" But then Mabel saw June. "Good gravy."

"It's so yummy." June licked the frosting from her fingers. Every finger, too. How she'd managed that, he didn't know—and he'd been sitting beside her the whole time. "I like stwabewwy cake, too, Miss Kitty." June's declaration was so joyful, Tyson had to laugh.

"It is the best." Kitty sat beside June, armed with another wet towel. "Are you done?"

June shook her head. "I wanna eat it *all*."

"I see that," Kitty said, her eyes widening as June shoveled another massive bite into her mouth.

He wasn't sure who was cuter, June or Kitty. Watching Kitty mimic June—opening her mouth superwide when June took a bite—was pretty adorable.

"Wow." Twyla was watching, too. "I've never seen something so small take such a big bite. You're like a snake, Juney, unhinging your jaw to get it all in there."

June grinned, her mouth full of cake.

"Mommy says small bites." July frowned at her sister.

"Your mommy is right. You don't want to choke." Kitty used her fork to cut what was left of June's slice into smaller pieces. "Little bites taste just as good."

June nodded, chewing carefully, then swallowing. "No choking."

Over the top of June's head, Kitty's eyes met his. Seeing her carefree and relaxed was a vast improvement over her being bedridden and fragile. Knowing he'd added to her stress and agitation in the hospital had him feeling like the bad guy once more.

"Someone's at the door," Dwight Crawley yelled but didn't get out of his chair. "Ringing the doorbell."

"We have a doorbell?" Twyla winked, shrugged, and headed for the door.

"Have a lot of people stopped by?" Jensen asked Kitty. "I was hoping things would be quiet so you'd rest."

"It's been quiet." Kitty waited for June to take the last bite of cake before she started wiping the little girl's face. "Too quiet. I can't work or read or it might strain my eyes." She glanced at Mabel. "We ended up watching that movie you suggested—"

"You did?" Mabel grinned. "Did you love it?"

"What was that nonsense? All the slow motion and running and people falling over or crying." Dwight Crawley made a good show of displeasure and, if Kitty hadn't told Tyson her father had cried, he might believe it. Still, it wasn't easy to picture the old man getting emotional.

"I'm not sure I loved it. But I did sob—several times." Kitty kept on wiping June's face. "Goodness. I need to wash the rag out and start again."

"Kitty…" Twyla's voice rang out. "You have a delivery."

Dread took root in the pit of Tyson's stomach. If the delivery was RJ, in the flesh, he'd have to grin and bear it.

"Balloons. And gourmet chocolates."

Tyson stopped holding his breath. RJ wasn't here. It was a relief. But he'd made sure he was well represented. He didn't know how many balloons were in the bouquet Twyla was holding, but it was a lot. Enough to shock Kitty. Her mouth hung open and her eyes were huge.

"It's a little early for Valentine's Day, isn't it?" Dwight asked.

Tyson kept on watching Kitty. Was she deeply moved by RJ's gifts or overwhelmed? It was hard to interpret her expression. Other than she was adorable.

"I think it's the whole sweetheart vibe, Dad. You know…" Twyla tugged the balloons lower, sifted through them, and pulled one large Mylar red balloon forward. "See? It says, 'Will You Be Mine.'"

Once again, Tyson had to give RJ an A for effort. Kitty couldn't doubt his interest.

"That boy just loves throwing his money away," Dwight went on. "That should be a warning sign, Kitty. You don't want to tie yourself to some deadbeat that doesn't respect the dollar."

"Balloons!" June climbed down from her chair and ran to Twyla—July and Samantha running after her.

"Careful, there's so many they might lift you up and into the sky." Twyla grinned. "But I'm sure Kitty will share." She turned to her sister. "Right?"

"Yes. Of course." Kitty nodded.

Twyla untied the balloons and gave the girls two each.

"But not the chocolates," Jensen said. "No more sugar."

"Agreed." Twyla put the large foil-wrapped box on the kitchen counter. "She can share them with me later."

Kitty's phone started ringing. She was so startled, she almost dropped it.

"I'll bet you five dollars it's Balloon Boy." Jensen crossed his arms over his chest. "Any takers?" He looked at Tyson, then Mabel, then Twyla.

"Hello?" Kitty put the ear to her phone. "Yes. They were just delivered. They… They're something." She smiled.

When she smiled, Tyson slumped back in his chair. Better to pretend to be doing something on his phone. That way, it wasn't obvious he was hanging on every word of Kitty's conversation.

"You want to have dinner?" Kitty's voice was more high-pitched than normal.

His eyebrows shot up before he could stop himself. But it looked like Jensen was the only one that noticed. The girls were playing with the balloons, while Mabel, Twyla, and Dwight weren't even pretending they weren't listening in on the phone call.

"I do have an appointment on Friday. And Saturday." She paused. "No. Nothing Sunday."

Twyla waved until Kitty looked at her. She gave Kitty two thumbs-up.

Tyson ran a hand over his face to stop himself from frowning.

"Well…" Kitty swallowed, her cheeks going red. "That's very sweet."

What was very sweet? What had RJ said? Why was she blushing?

This time, Mabel flagged her down to nod vigorously.

Why wouldn't they all be on RJ's team? It was

the only team playing. He sighed and stared up at the ceiling.

"Der Restaurant Von Ludwig?" She opened her mouth, closed it, then looked at the balloons and the box of chocolates and the large flower arrangement that sat on the sideboard in the kitchen.

Tyson closed his eyes and braced himself for her answer.

"Yes. That sounds nice." She was nervous, he could hear it in her voice. "Me, too. Bye." She set her phone down on the counter and leaned forward, covering her face with both hands.

He sucked in a deep breath, hoping the tightness in his chest would ease. The way he was feeling… It wasn't good.

Dwight Crawley got up and out of his recliner. "You're going to dinner with that boy?"

Kitty stayed as she was, bent forward over the counter. "Yes." The word was muffled through her hands.

She'd said yes. She was going on a date with RJ. And he felt like he'd been hit in the chest with a fifty-pound sack of feed.

"Kitty." Twyla was staring at the back of her sister's head. "I can't believe you did it. You actually said yes."

"What do you mean?" Kitty shot up. "You were

all…" She gave Twyla two thumbs-up. "You were. I have witnesses." She pointed around the room.

"I know, but…" Twyla took a deep breath. "Whatever. I get to do your makeup."

"Me. Let me." Samantha jumped up and down. "I did it so pretty last time."

"Aunt Kitty ended up with an eye infection last time." Twyla patted Samantha on the head.

Tyson remembered Kitty's red, swollen eye and her outrageous makeup the day before. Kitty's new look. Samantha had been responsible for that? That explained so much. Kitty would do anything for her niece—including bad makeup and even worse hair. He was grinning when Kitty looked his way.

Her eyes widened, then she blinked and flopped forward on the kitchen counter again.

"It's okay, Samantha." Jensen lifted his daughter onto his lap. "Aunt Kitty's got real sensitive skin so we should probably let Aunt Twyla and Mabel help her out."

"Can I pick out your shoes?" Samantha asked.

"Ask Aunt Kitty when she stops hyperventilating, okay?" Jensen glanced from Mabel to Kitty.

Like Jensen, he was worried. Kitty should be excited, shouldn't she? If she wasn't, why had she agreed to this date?

"Kitty?" Mabel walked over to Kitty and put

her hand on her back. "You look a little shell-shocked."

"I'm great. I'm so happy." Her words were muffled. "I am."

"You don't sound happy." Dwight voiced what he was thinking.

"Is this the ham-some man from the shop?" Samantha asked. "The one needing help with a present for his mommy?"

"That's the one." Twyla took Kitty's hand. "Come on. Come sit down. Eat more cake. Celebrate. You've got a man smitten with you. He's showering you with presents and saying all the right things. I mean, what's not to like?"

Kitty let her sister drag her to the kitchen table and sat, without saying a word. She stayed silent when Mabel slid another piece of cake in front of her, too. She took a deep breath and picked up the fork. "You're right." Even when her smile was forced, she was pretty.

"Maybe he's Prince Charming." Samantha clapped her hands.

June and July both said, "Ooh," excitedly.

That got Kitty laughing. "You never know."

Shouldn't she be ecstatic over this date? Or, at least, seem pleased about it. Instead, she seemed—resigned. Like June when he'd put a couple of carrot sticks on her plate and she, warily, had tried one. Now, June discovered she loved carrot sticks and there was a chance Kitty would end up feeling the same about RJ but, thankfully, it didn't look like she was there yet.

The relief was swift and sure, followed by a sudden drive to act that had him fighting himself. Until then, he hadn't realized just how important this confirmation was to him. If she was sweet on RJ, he would have come to terms with it and been happy for her. But now…well, that wasn't the case. Meaning, she wasn't happy. Meaning, there was a chance that someone else could win her heart. Someone like…him. He closed his eyes, willing himself to stand strong. But his resolve to keep things as they were between them was crumbling and something he'd denied for years was slipping in: Hope.

CHAPTER ELEVEN

KITTY LOVED HER sister dearly but she was getting tired of being asked how she was feeling. Yet, Twyla had asked again, and Kitty replied the same way she had the last hundred and thirty-seven or so times. "I'm feeling much better."

"You're sure you're up for this?" Twyla glanced her way before turning her attention back to the road. Twyla was driving. Twyla didn't drive. It wasn't that she couldn't drive only that sometimes her temper got the best of her when it came to other drivers. Luckily, the roads had been empty so far.

"I am." Kitty was beyond ready. In her family, she was the caretaker. She was the one to make soup or tea, draw warm baths and add mineral salts or essential oils, have cool compresses ready or give pain reliever, offer a light blanket or throw, and generally look after the sick or injured party.

Her father and sister had tried to take care of her—they had. It wasn't their fault that neither of them had an abundance of patience or nurturing genes. It was simply who they were. So, since neither of them knew where anything was and tended to get grumpy when they had to search overlong for something, it was simply easier for Kitty to fend for herself. When she did, however, both her sister and father got their knickers in a twist and groused and whined about it so that Kitty somehow felt guilty for taking care of herself.

Yesterday, Doc Johnson had given her the all clear to resume normal activities. She'd been ecstatic. She was pretty certain Twyla and her father had been, too.

"I just don't want you to overdo." Twyla's gaze kept bouncing to the rearview mirror, her eyes narrowing. "Eighteen-wheelers like to think they own the road."

Kitty glanced over her shoulder at the truck. It was so far down the road, it was hard to see. "We'll be at the Community Center before it catches up to us." She patted her sister on the knee. "I really am fine to drive, you know."

"Hmph." Her sister shook her head, still glaring at the truck. "I am, too."

Kitty turned to look out the window so Twyla wouldn't see her smiling. "Have you heard anything more from the Ladies Guild?" She'd reached out to them to let them know she'd rented the Community Center for an "all hands on deck" day of sewing. Barbara Eldridge, Dorris Kaye, and Patsy Monahan had all promised to be there—their sewing machines in tow.

"Nope." Twyla glanced her way. "It'll be okay, Kitty. Even if we have to order some of the tutus, it will be okay."

Kitty stared at her sister in horror. "I feel bad enough having to ask for help. Now you want me to order premade tutus from…who knows where?"

Twyla snorted. "It won't be the end of the world, I promise. No one will be upset—well, besides you."

Every job she took was something she could use to build her portfolio. Twyla might not understand her desire to expand into an online custom costume shop, but it was her dream. A little dream, maybe, but her dream nonetheless. It was her way of bringing joy into the world—something she felt passionate about.

When they turned off the highway and onto Main Street, Twyla's posture visibly relaxed. Kitty, however, was feeling no less at ease. The sight of the Community Center parking lot nearly full only added to her stress.

"Is something happening today?" She unbuckled her seat belt. "When I called, they said we'd have use of the whole place."

"I don't know, Kitty." Twyla shrugged. "I guess we're about to find out."

Kitty opened the trunk and set up her collapsible wagon. She and Twyla loaded up their sewing machines, boxes of fabric, elastic, sequins, and more, closed the trunk, and started pulling it across the parking lot.

"It's nippy." Twyla shuddered as a surprisingly icy blast of wind hit them.

Kitty was too worried about what was waiting for them inside to give much thought to the temperature. She was so far behind that she was counting on today being productive. Since there were only five of them, they'd fit into one of the smaller classrooms—as long as they still had that as an option.

She opened the door and held it wide until Twyla tugged the wagon inside. As soon as the doors closed, the murmur of voices and laughter was overwhelming.

"Come on." Twyla tugged the wagon. "Stop frowning like that. It'll be fine."

That drew Kitty up short. Her sister was a glass-half-empty sort, so hearing her offer up reassurances was…odd. She wasn't sure whether she should be concerned or touched. But, when she stepped foot inside the hall, all she could feel was gratitude.

"How… When…" She swallowed against the tightening of her throat. "Oh my."

Everyone was there. Well, almost everyone. And they were all smiling at her.

The entire Ladies Guild. Mabel and Hattie Briscoe were there as well as Eloise Green from Garrison Gardens and Gretta Williams from the dance studio, too. There were a few unexpected faces, too. Judy Eldridge, Barbara's mother. Hattie's mom, Gladiola Carmichael. And more.

Inside the large, open hall that served as the main meeting place in the Community Center, several rows of folding tables had been erected—each holding a sewing machine. The floor was covered in a web of cords and powers strips, secured by duct tape.

The pass-through window in the back of the wall that separated the kitchen from the main hall had been opened wide. Hazel and Ryan Diertz, from Old Towne Books and Coffee, were in the kitchen serving pastries and muffins as well as coffee.

"I told you not to worry." Twyla gave her a wink.

"When did…" She wasn't one to get emotional—especially in front of other people—but this was entirely too overwhelming for her. "How did this happen?"

"People seem to like you." Her sister tucked

her arm through hers. "We all made a few phone calls saying my sister needs some help and, *bam*, everyone came running."

"Sorry we're late." RJ Malloy came in, holding a sewing machine under each arm. "My momma and gramma are here, too." He glanced behind him at the two older women slowly making their way inside. "They might move slow as snails but don't let that worry you. They sew fast enough. And so can I."

"Oh, RJ, thank you." She meant it, too. "You didn't have to—"

"Yes, ma'am, I did." He paused beside her—standing a little closer than necessary. His gaze held hers as he said, "If you need something, I'm going to do my best to get it for you."

She was fully aware of the hush that had fallen over the room. And the fact that all eyes were on the two of them. Surely RJ was, too. While she felt color creeping into her cheeks, he kept right on staring at her. It was both unnerving and…sweet.

"People care about you, Kitty."

RJ didn't say this—but RJ turned to see who said it. So did she.

It was Tyson, grinning his crooked grin. "Dad and I might need a little guidance, but we're ready."

She was oh so glad she had her sister's arm to

hold on to. "You…" She swallowed, then cleared her throat. "I can't thank you all enough." She managed not to stare overlong at Tyson—though he looked especially handsome in his pale blue button-down shirt—and include everyone in her smile. "I'm sincerely moved by this. Thank you so much, everyone."

"You're always the first person to offer help, Kitty. Everyone knows that." The warmth in Tyson's voice had Kitty clinging, ever tighter, onto her sister's arm.

"Heart of gold," RJ said.

It was entirely too much for Kitty. All eyes were on her, so her cheeks were flaming. But it was RJ and Tyson, in particular, who had her knees wobbling. RJ was so…sincere. And Tyson? Kitty had never seen that look on his face before—and it flustered her.

"Well… Thank you." Her voice was all breathy and high-pitched—which was probably because she was struggling to breathe.

"What is happening?" Twyla whispered.

Which was exactly what Kitty had been thinking. All she could do was shake her head.

"Let's get you set up." Tyson took the wagon handle. "Any place in particular?" He turned, waiting for her to answer.

Kitty blinked. "Um…no."

"Wherever there's a space." Twyla gave her arm a squeeze.

It took a few minutes for her to hug and thank everyone.

Tyson pulled the wagon to a row of tables with no sewing machines and started unpacking things. "Here, Dad." He nodded at the tables beside those he'd put Kitty and Twyla's machines on.

Earl Ellis nodded and started unpacking his things. "Looks like a good spot to me."

RJ led his mother and grandmother to the same row of tables and took up the two open tables on the opposite side of her and Twyla's workstation.

"Here you go." Mabel Briscoe handed Kitty a coffee. "This is interesting."

"Thank you." Kitty took the coffee. "Isn't it? I'm unbelievably touched that so many of you are here to help out."

"Well, I was talking about… Never mind, there's that, too." Mabel grinned. "I might not be the best at sewing but I'm here to do whatever I can. I'm really handy with a glue gun— so I brought that with me. And a megasize bag of glue sticks, too."

Before long, Martha Zeigler and the rest of the Ladies Guild had converged around her sewing machine to see her designs and take direction.

For someone who was content to blend in and take instruction, handing out instructions didn't come easily to her. She managed, though. Between the tight deadline and the extra hands, this was a chance to get the majority of the costumes done—and she wasn't going to waste a minute of their time.

The Ladies Guild, Bertha and Davida Malloy, and Gladiola Carmichael were in charge of the vests. Between all of them, they should get all seventy cut out and sewn pretty quickly. If they managed that, the pink-and-red-fringed strips could be added along the seams, as well. Later, Kitty would go to the dance studio to do any fittings that might be needed.

She, Twyla, and Eloise were in charge of tutus. Kitty had completed ten already but there were still thirty to go.

Everyone else would work on the seventy heart-bedecked hatbands. Since the felt and sequined hearts were small, they had to be hand-sewn or hot-glued onto the hatbands. It was a time-consuming task. Kitty told them not to worry overmuch about how pretty their stitchwork was—as long as the hearts were secured, she'd be happy.

Once everyone was settled, someone put some music on and the work began.

Kitty was pulling a pleat tight when Tyson sat

in the chair beside her. She was fine until she glanced at him and got caught up in the hard angle of his jaw and the length of his dark lashes. A man shouldn't have such thick lashes. Or be so handsome. If he hadn't been so handsome, she wouldn't have pricked her finger.

She shook her hand and stuck her finger in her mouth, silently chastising herself for letting Tyson Ellis's presence get to her so. Why was it so hard for her stop overthinking and overfeeling when it came to him? She should just get over him. She should try harder to do just that. The alternative, pining for a man that was oblivious to her was both embarrassing and painful to accept.

But then Tyson took her hand in his and held her finger up for inspection. "You okay?" His brows were deeply furrowed when his brown gaze met hers.

She nodded, thankful for the roar of the sewing machines. Without them, there was a chance everyone in the room would hear the telltale thundering of her heart betraying her.

TYSON GRABBED HER hand without thinking. Now that he had a hold of it, he was in no hurry to let it go. "You need some ice or something?"

She shook her head, her light brown gaze bouncing between his face and their joined hands.

"You sure?" His thumb ran along the back of her hand.

She blinked, tugged her hand free from his, and said, "It happens all the time."

"Casualty of sewing, huh?" he nodded. "I'm prepared to bleed for these hatbands." He grinned at her.

And she smiled, that free and easy smile, right back at him. "Hopefully not too much." She shrugged. "But I guess it's okay—since the fabric is pink and red, it won't show too much."

He laughed. "Thanks for the concern."

She rolled her eyes. "Be careful and you'll be fine."

He nodded at her hand. "Should I say the same thing to you?"

"A momentary distraction. It won't happen again." She stared at him for a long moment, then went back to her sewing. "It won't." This was said with an almost steely tenacity.

"I should hope not." He chuckled, wondering what had distracted her to begin with.

"I brought you some water, Kitty." RJ set a tall glass of water on the table in front of her. "You eat something? Miss Hazel's got some pastries, if you like."

Tyson resisted the urge to glare up at the man. He understood what RJ was doing—staking his claim in public was a smart move. And, if Tyson didn't have a problem having his personal business on display for all to know and see, he might consider doing the same. If he ever came to terms with the idea of pursuing Kitty, that is.

Still, he didn't want RJ getting too confident when it came to Kitty. That's why he said, "She likes those cinnamon muffins best, RJ." He turned to smile at Kitty. "Those are your favorite, aren't they, Kitty?"

She nodded but didn't look up from her sewing. "But I'm not hungry."

"I'll get you one and you can save it for later." RJ tipped his hat at Tyson and headed to the back of the room.

"He's determined, no denying that." Tyson heard Kitty's sigh but wasn't sure what to make of it. "Must be nice having someone wait on you hand and foot."

Kitty's horror was comical. "If you're the sort who likes being waited on, I suppose."

"Who doesn't?" It was taking him far too long to thread his needle. Just about the time he thought he'd managed to pull the fine pink thread through the eye of the needle, it'd slip between his thumb and forefinger and he'd have to start all over again.

"I don't especially." She took the thread and needle from him. "I don't like feeling like a burden." She threaded the needle and handed it back to him.

"Thank you. But did you have to make that look so easy?" He liked the little smile of satisfaction on her face. "You shouldn't feel burdened by someone else's choices, Kitty. RJ wouldn't be doing any of this if he didn't want to."

"I'm still trying to figure out why he wants to?" Her question was so soft, he almost didn't hear it.

But it was enough to draw him up short. Did she really not know what a special woman she was? A good person, through and through. RJ had been right when he said she had a heart of gold. And she was just about the prettiest woman he'd ever seen. The sort of pretty that made a man sit up and take notice—now that he'd noticed, he couldn't seem to un-notice.

"Because you're you." He murmured in answer. "Any man would be lucky to have you, Kitty." When he glanced her way, she'd gone perfectly still. "Did I say something wrong?"

She shook her head but wouldn't look at him. "It's just… You don't have to say things like that, Tyson. Jensen's not here and I don't need a stand-in brother to flatter and tease me, okay?"

"Okay." He took a deep breath. He chose his words with care as he said, "I wasn't saying it as a stand-in brother. I was saying it as a man. Any man. And I meant it, too."

"Twenty-plus years and an almost nonexistent love life would say otherwise." She shook her head. "How about less talking, more sewing?"

How long RJ had been standing there, Tyson didn't know. But as soon as his eyes locked with the other man, it was obvious RJ had heard some of what was being said—and he didn't know what to make of it.

"Here you go, Kitty." He set the muffin and water bottle on the table. "Don't get yourself too tired out now, you hear? You've got a room full of people you can call on." He cleared his throat. "Me, especially." He gave Tyson a hard, challenging look.

Tyson's brows rose. "Same."

RJ's brows dipped low, and he cocked his head to one side, his expression all confusion.

Yeah, I get it. I'm an idiot. What am I doing? Tyson had no answer for that question. He shrugged up at RJ.

"Well, alrighty, then." RJ took a deep breath.

"RJ." Twyla was waving him over. "I've got you, Gretta, and Mabel's supplies sorted out. Come on over and let me show you."

"Yes, ma'am." RJ gave Kitty one last, long look, then headed back to his table.

Sewing hearts onto hatbands was tedious work.

Threading the needle was nothing compared to sewing twenty sequined hearts onto each elastic band. If there'd been a sewing machine to spare, Tyson would have figured out a way to make that work. As it was, all the machines were humming away and his fingertips were sore from the amount of needle sticks he'd inflicted on himself.

"You're turning into a pincushion." His father chuckled.

"You don't have to tell me." He rubbed his fingers on his jeans. "But I can't work with a thimble—it slows me down even more."

"I appreciate your hard work." This from Kitty. "Can you both afford to be away from the store this long?"

"Oh sure." Tyson was snipping the threads on the last heart—beyond frustrated that he'd somehow managed to sew this one on upside down. "Ted Barnes has the place well in order. He's sharp as a tack and has a good head for business and numbers. I know he's had some trouble with the law in the past but he's straightened himself out—and become a big help to Dad and me."

"You're awfully bighearted and trusting to give him a chance." Kitty held up the tutu she was working on and gave it a shake.

"Everyone deserves a second chance." His father spoke up. "He doesn't make excuses for himself, either. Keeps up with his parole officer, is never late to work, and does right by his kids. That's all I could ask for."

Tyson glanced down the row of tables at Eloise, Ted's ex-wife, laughing with Mabel over the pile of hatbands they were working on. He knew things hadn't always been easy between the woman and her ex-husband, but he admired how well they'd managed to work things out. Eloise was planning a fall wedding to Mike Woodard. Mike and Ted got along just fine, and they were always on their best behavior in front of the kids: Kirby and Archie. It was nice to see not all divorces ended in bitterness and heartbreak.

"I agree, Mr. Ellis. Whether seen or not, everyone is dealing with their own struggles." Kitty was starting on a new tutu—pink this time.

He watched as she threaded her needle. She had a whole new expression he was now calling her needle-threading face. She'd scrunch up her nose, twist up her lips, and her eyebrows just about disappeared in her hairline. Once the thread was pulled through, she smiled, nodded, and went to work sewing. And every step of it enchanted him—especially the little smile of satisfaction at the end.

"What?" Kitty asked, blinking those big eyes at him.

"Nothing." He was still smiling when he turned

back to his hatband and jabbed the tar out of his finger.

"Tyson." Kitty hissed. "You about hit bone." She set the tulle aside and got up. "I have Band-Aids in my bag. And that—" she pointed at this finger "—is going to need one."

Sure enough, a big bead of blood was forming where he'd stuck his fingertip.

"That's my boy—giving one hundred percent, no matter what he does." His father peered over his reading glasses at Tyson's finger.

"Here." Kitty knelt by his chair, opening the Band-Aid. "Finger."

He held out his finger.

Kitty wrapped the Band-Aid around his finger, shaking her head. "As much as I appreciate the help, maybe it would be safer if you went back to the store?"

If he left, that would give RJ more time with her. "I'd rather stay." He swallowed. "With you." It wasn't easy to get that out, but he had. And he was ready when her eyes darted up to meet his. "If you don't mind?"

She opened her mouth, closed it, and shook her head.

"Good." He grinned. "I'll do my best not to leave here wearing one on each finger."

She rolled her eyes but she smiled, too. And, for that smile, he wouldn't mind leaving here with a Band-Aid on each finger. He wasn't sure when her smile started warming him up on the inside, but it did. And he liked feeling this way, he liked that she worried over him—even if it was something as small as a finger prick.

When it was noon, the Ladies Guild turned off their machines and headed into the kitchen.

"What are they up to, now?" his father asked, continuing to stitch.

Tyson shrugged. He'd made the mistake of checking on RJ's hatband count and was trailing behind—by a lot. Instead of being happy about the man's productivity, he felt a sting of jealousy. All he could do was double his efforts and hope to match the man's productivity.

Not too long after that, lunch was set up in the kitchen pass-through window. Two large pans of chicken spaghetti, a big bowl of salad, and a tray piled high with yeast rolls sat on the counter. Dorris Kaye set up a large tea jug and cups, Patsy Monahan put out paper plates and utensils, and Martha Zeigler whistled so loud, Tyson winced.

"Needles down and come eat." Martha Zeigler waved them all forward. "Once that's done, we can inventory where we are."

"You don't have to move." It was RJ, already hovering beside Kitty's chair. "I can get you something to eat."

"No, that's okay, RJ. It'll do me some good to

get up and move around." Kitty stood, rolling her neck. "If you'll excuse me for a minute?" She headed for the ladies' room.

"You can get me lunch, RJ." Twyla grinned.

"Oh well. Of course, I can." RJ nodded. "I'd be happy to, Miss Twyla." And off he went.

"Are you exploiting your sister's beau for your own purposes?" Mabel asked.

"Am I?" Twyla shrugged. "Is there something wrong with that?"

"Is he her beau?" his father asked. But if he'd meant that question to stay between the two of them, he probably shouldn't have asked so loudly.

"He is doing his best to make it happen." Twyla shrugged. "And since there's no competition, I see it as a foregone conclusion."

Tyson couldn't help but frown after the man. Twyla was only saying it how she saw it—likely, how everyone saw it. If he was hoping to change the narrative, he had a decision to make and a whole lot of work to do.

"Is that so?" His father sighed.

"I don't know about that. You're saying your sister is going to fall for him because he's her only choice?" Tyson shook his head. "You should give her more credit than that. She's not going to settle. And RJ isn't the only one interested in Kitty."

Mabel's, Gretta's, and Twyla's heads all swiveled his way.

"Why, Mr. Tyson Ellis, what do you know, and why am I just hearing about this?" Twyla was up and out of her chair, leaning in close to him with her eyes narrowed and a grin that had him taking a step back. "You better spill the tea."

"Someone else likes Kitty?" Mabel's voice lowered. "Does she know?"

No. Why had he said that? Because Twyla's comment had rubbed him the wrong way?

"Who is it?" Eloise was also whispering. "Does RJ know? Poor guy really is pulling out the stops to impress Kitty." She shook her head. "But I agree with Tyson. Just because RJ is pursuing her doesn't mean Kitty will reciprocate his feelings. She's under no obligation to feel anything for the man—no matter how many flowers or balloons he sends to her."

Tyson nodded. "Feeling obliged isn't the same as feeling…feelings."

"You're really not going to say who has *feeling feelings* for my sister?" Twyla stabbed her finger in the middle of his chest. "That's not cool, Tyson. Why bring it up?"

Why, indeed?

"Well, isn't this an interesting turn of events?" His father was chuckling. "I'll be."

"Do you know, Mr. Ellis?" Mabel asked.

His father shook his head and held up both hands in mock surrender. "Nope. And I'm gonna skedaddle before the food's gone." He headed to the kitchen, still chuckling.

"He totally knows." Mabel sighed. "If Mr. Ellis knows and Tyson knows, then…" She blew out a slow breath. "That doesn't really help because everyone knows you and your dad."

Which was a relief. He'd said too much, too fast. He was still working through what to do. But he'd rather make his intentions known to Kitty before the rest of Garrison got wind of it. It was, he thought, the right thing to do. "It'll all come out eventually." And, hopefully, it would lead to a happy ending—for Kitty. Even if it didn't include him, her happy ending would be enough.

CHAPTER TWELVE

KITTY CAME OUT of the washroom to find her sister poking Tyson in the chest. Whatever they were saying, it was intense. Twyla was sort of glaring up at him, and he was laughing down at her. He had a nice laugh but, since his divorce, he didn't laugh as much.

"Now, Kitty." Davida Malloy, RJ's grandmother, stepped right into her path. The woman was barely five feet tall and, likely, weighed less than a hundred pounds soaking wet. Her energy, and the slight tick of her right eye, reminded Kitty of an elderly Chihuahua. "There are a few things I need to know before I'm gonna let you steal my grandson."

She was speechless. *Steal* her grandson? What on earth?

"Now, Momma, you leave her be." Bertha Malloy tucked the woman's arm through hers. "I think Kitty is a doll, just a doll." She patted Kitty's cheek. "You and RJ are going to make the prettiest babies, too. Goodness sakes, I can't wait."

Babies? With RJ? She'd just agreed to have dinner with him—

"You do have good birthing hips." Davida nodded. "That'll make things easier. You're lucky that way."

She had *what*? Was that a compliment? She swallowed.

"Isn't that the truth?" Bertha sighed. "I was in labor with RJ for forty-six hours. Forty-six. It was agony. They gave me something for the pain, but it didn't work. I felt it all. He was a big baby, too. Ten pounds. I swear, I've never felt such pain." She shook her head. "You know how they say you forget about the pain of childbirth once they put your baby in your arms?"

She didn't wait for Kitty's answer. "It's not true. I remember. Why do you think I didn't have any other children? I didn't want to feel like I was being split apart again."

"You think you had it bad?" Davida put her hands on her hips. "I did it five times. Each time was different from the last."

Kitty glanced around her, eager for any possible escape.

"And don't forget, RJ's daddy was breech. That was a whole other thing. The doc and nurses pushing and pushing on my stomach to turn the baby—"

Bertha cut off her mother-in-law with a gentle pat on her hand. "We shouldn't carry on so. Don't you fret, Kitty. You're built for childbearing. You won't have any problems having lots of little RJs and Kittys—all of 'em cute as can be."

"Don't you wait too long. I want to meet my great-grandchildren before I kick the bucket, don't you know?" Davida gave Kitty another head-to-toe. "You're not getting any younger, either. Having babies is easier when you're young."

"Kitty?" Martha Zeigler called from across the room. "You need to come eat and check everyone's progress."

"Yes. You're right. If you'll excuse me." She all but ran away from the two women. As far as conversations went, that had been one of the top five most uncomfortable she'd ever had. She barely knew either woman—nothing beyond the normal well-wishes and small talk she'd exchange with anyone she passed on the street. How they'd jumped to her birthing hips and age, she didn't know.

"You all right?" Tyson was serving himself some chicken spaghetti. "You look a little pale."

"Is it a good thing to have birthing hips?" The words were out before she realized what she'd asked. Of course she'd have to ask Tyson. Because, so far, she hadn't humiliated herself in front of him today. "Forget it."

He held the serving spoon, piled high with chicken spaghetti, but wasn't moving. Instead, he was staring at her. So far, he was staring at her face and not her hips.

"Really, forget it." She grabbed a roll.

"Are we talking cattle?" He served the scoop of chicken spaghetti onto her plate, not his.

She laughed. "Thank you. And, no, not cattle."

He served himself two scoops of chicken spaghetti and reached for three rolls. "I feel like there might be more information required to answer this question."

She shook her head. "It's not important." At this point, she'd rather forget the whole awkward conversation. Besides, her stomach was grumbling and the food smelled delicious.

"I saved you a seat, Kitty." RJ patted the chair beside him. "Got you some tea, too."

Considering most of the round tables that had been set up for lunch were full, there weren't a lot of alternatives. It wouldn't have been too bad if it was just RJ. But no, the seat was between RJ and Davida Malloy—who did, indeed, seem to be reassessing Kitty's birthing hips as she nibbled on a roll.

"Thank you." Kitty sat.

"Of course." He slid the tea in front of her. "You feeling better? That bruise is almost gone."

"Doc Johnson gave me a clean bill of health." She lay her napkin on her lap.

"Glad to hear it." His gaze lingered on her face. "Well, eat up. You've been working hard."

Tyson stopped behind the last empty chair at her table. His gaze met hers and she shook her head, looking pointedly at the table behind him. The one without Davida and Bertha Malloy *and* Dorris Kaye and Patsy Monahan. Why anyone would choose to sit here was a mystery. But he was all smiles as he sat across from her and said his hellos.

"You know, watching you just now, I'm not so sure anymore." Davida crossed her arms over her chest. "You don't have as much meat on your bones as I thought. You've just got a round face, I s'pose. Kinda chubby. In the face, anyway."

Tyson started coughing.

"Gramma, behave." RJ leaned behind Kitty. "You keep that up and you'll scare her off. I mean it now, be nice."

"What? When did speaking the truth get to be mean?" Davida was clearly offended. "I've got a right to my opinion, don't I? You keep saying she's going to be family soon and all. Well, if that's the case, then I'll be eating my meals across from her for the rest of my days. Nothing wrong with me wantin' to get to know this girl, since you're talkin' about marryin' her. I should have some say-so in that, being that it's my house and all."

Tyson was coughing harder now.

"You good?" RJ asked him. "You choking? Need me to do the Heimlich maneuver? I'm certified in CPR, by the way." He said this to Kitty, smiling proudly.

She was too worried about Tyson to know how to respond.

"Good." Tyson took a long sip of tea. "Just… caught off guard."

"Davida, you're putting the cart before the horses," Dorris Kaye said. "You need to let the young people come to an understanding, make things official, before you start acting like this. That way Kitty can't get out of it." She burst into laughter.

RJ started laughing, too. Soon, everyone at the table was laughing—except her and Tyson.

Kitty poked at her chicken spaghetti.

"She does have a point." Bertha Malloy patted her mother-in-law on the shoulder. "You're wanting great-grandkids so you best play nice."

That had Tyson coughing all over again.

Poor Tyson. He had no idea what he was getting himself into when he sat here.

"Good gracious." Patsy turned to Tyson. "You

sound just like my brother. He's always choking, too. 'Course he's a might older than you and suffers from GERD something fierce. You don't have that, do you, Tyson?"

Tyson shook his head. "No, ma'am."

"GERD?" Bertha asked. "My second cousin, Karen, has the same."

"It's not Karen, it's Janice," Davida corrected her daughter-in-law. "I swear, Bertha, you need to get your memory checked next time we go see the doctor. Your own father had Alzheimer's and it can be genetic."

Tyson's dark eyes met hers.

She mouthed, *I'm sorry* his way.

His brow furrowed and he shook his head—making a point of looking at each of the four women around the table—then RJ. *It's not you*, he mouthed back.

She smiled at him, he smiled back, and her chest felt heavy and tight. While she'd be all too happy to sit here and smile at Tyson for the next thirty minutes, it probably wasn't the best idea. Eventually the four busybodies at the table would stop talking about their own medical maladies and notice the staring. Interestingly enough, it wasn't just her staring...

Tyson was, very definitely, staring at her.

"You should eat," RJ whispered, right by her ear.

It startled Kitty so, she tossed her roll and almost knocked heads with the man.

"Land sakes, what was that?" Davida pressed a hand to her chest. "You about stopped my heart, young lady."

Her roll landed in the middle of the table then rolled to the edge—where Tyson caught it. The whole thing was so absurd, she wanted to laugh. All of it. From RJ to his family to fooling herself into thinking Tyson was really, truly seeing her to her flying roll.

"I'm guessing you'd rather have a new one?" Tyson asked.

"I'll get it." RJ was up before she could stop him.

She stared after the man, wishing she could transfer her feelings from Tyson to him. RJ was trying—not just with her but turning his life around, too. Of course, now that she'd met his grandmother, she had some concerns she hadn't before. She could deal with crotchety— she'd years of practice courtesy of her father, but her father loved her. And he didn't see her as a grandbaby maker. Or, if he did, he'd never said as much. It stood out that the only conversation she'd had with either Bertha or Davida revolved around her potential child birthing abilities.

When she turned back, Tyson was watching her again. There was such warmth in his gaze.

Likely, because he felt sorry for her. This whole lunch had been excruciating. His steady gaze was offering support, nothing more. She had to stop looking for what she wanted to see and start seeing things the way they were: RJ Malloy was romantically interested in her. Tyson was not.

HE'D MET HIS fair share of characters over time, but Davida Malloy was something else. He couldn't decide whether to be amused by her alarmingly outspoken observations or irritated. Either would work. But getting irritated over someone else's bad behavior was a choice and he was choosing not to go there.

Instead, he sat and watched Kitty. There'd been a certain wistfulness to the way she'd stared after RJ. Was she sad he'd left her? Granted, she had every right to be sad he'd left her to fend for herself with his grandmother. Talk about a trial by fire. But she was holding up, smiling and being… Kitty.

And each and every time their eyes met, he smiled. Like instinct.

But he wasn't smiling so much when RJ came back with a plateful of rolls.

"Oh, RJ." Kitty's eyes widened at the number of rolls piled high on the plate. "I can't… That's a lot."

"Well, next time you can try juggling 'em versus throwing them." Davida Malloy thought this was hilarious. Her cackle of a laugh was loud and bracing.

"Gramma." RJ shook his head.

"Don't you 'Gramma' me, boy." She got up. "I don't need to sit here and let you shush me. We're only here because of her." She pointed at Kitty. "Because you said she needed help and she was important to you and all that other nonsense. So here I am. For you—for her. And you're going to shush me for having some fun?"

"Don't go getting all puffed up." RJ's hands settled on the old woman's shoulders. "I appreciate you lending a hand. Kitty does, too."

Davida turned to Kitty. "Is that so?"

Kitty, who had finally taken a bite of food, swallowed. "Yes. I do. Thank you."

"See?" RJ patted the old woman's shoulders again. "I know you're just looking out for me and wanting what's best for me."

"Is that asking too much?" Davida peered up at him. "Now that you've got yourself pulled together, you need someone to look after you. That's all." She lowered her voice but not a single person at the table had to strain to hear her say, "And I'm not so sure this Miss is that person, RJ. You need someone with a little starch in her backbone. You know, like her sister over there."

Tyson was awfully glad he didn't have something in his mouth or he'd have been choking all over again. The woman was shameless. She had to know everyone could hear what she was saying—but went ahead and said it anyway. For a woman that professed to want her grandson's happiness, her behavior suggested the exact opposite. Not that he cared a whole lot about RJ or his family.

But Kitty…

Kitty's discomfort was palpable. She sat, staring at her mostly untouched lunch, blinking rapidly. And he couldn't bear it.

"Kitty, you got a second?" He stood and came around the table. "I need a fresh set of eyes." He helped her out of the chair and away from the crowded lunch table before RJ could stop them. And, from the noises he was making, he was seriously thinking about stopping them.

"You good?" Tyson murmured, resting his hand on Kitty's back and steering her back to their workstation. "As far as lunch conversation, I'd give that a…seven out of ten."

"Is ten good or bad?"

"Bad. Definitely bad." He grinned down at her.

"Only a seven?" She shook her head.

"What would you give it?" Now that they were standing by her workstation, he had no reason to keep his hand on her back.

"You know my dad." She sighed. "If he and Martha don't work out, maybe I could fix him up with Davida?"

That had Tyson laughing.

"Did you really need a fresh set of eyes?" She smiled up at him, the corners of her eyes creasing. She looked prettier than ever.

"I didn't think it'd be appropriate to ask if you needed rescuing." He lifted one of the hatbands he'd been working on. "But I should go on and apologize, because I know this isn't up to Kitty Crawley standards."

Kitty took the hatband. She ran her fingers over the hearts and looked back up at him. "No complaints. Those hearts aren't going anywhere—that's what matters most. I do appreciate you doing this, Tyson. You didn't have to, you know."

"I didn't have to. But I wanted to." He swallowed.

"You did?" Her smile dimmed. "I wouldn't have expected you to be here, Tyson. I know this isn't your thing… Or your responsibility."

"Well…" He swallowed again. Words rose up and spilled out before he could stop them. "I wanted to… I wanted to ask you if you…" He was tripping over his tongue like a high-schooler. What was he hoping to accomplish here? So far, it wasn't working.

She nodded. "You can ask." A V formed between her brows.

"Everything okay?" RJ was headed their way, his smile forced. "You two look awful serious."

"If it's serious, maybe you should give them a minute?" Twyla grabbed onto RJ's arm. "You know, I'd love some more tea. And a cookie."

RJ was torn—it was all over his face. The man was trying to reform his image, and turning Twyla down wouldn't help with that. But it might be that he was picking up on Tyson's intentions, because he kept glancing, nervously between him and Kitty.

"Will do, Miss Twyla." Not that RJ was happy about it. "What kind of cookie you wantin'?"

"Well, I don't know, Mr. RJ. Why don't you take me to check out the choices." Twyla tucked her arm through his.

"You see?" This from Davida. "Feisty." A long cackle followed.

Tyson turned so no one would see him laughing.

"I can hear you, you know." Kitty nudged him. "Should I save my sister?"

"She can handle herself." With any luck, RJ would take his grandmother's advice and go after Twyla. "She's feisty."

Kitty nodded. "That she is." Her light brown

gaze swiveled back to him. "What were you going to ask?"

Right. He swallowed. "I was thinking about…" Spending time with her. Having a picnic under erste Baum tree, the oldest tree in Texas and a proud Garrison landmark, in the park. Admitting he'd been a fool for far too long. But saying any of those things would put them on a path there was no coming back from. Instead, he asked, "I was thinking about bringing the girls out to go horseback riding? Try talking to your dad again about the calves?"

"Oh." Kitty blinked, her smile returning. "Of course. I know Samantha would love that, too."

Coward. He was, too. She didn't know it, but he did. He'd chickened out—big-time. But horseback riding with three tiny chaperones wasn't the worst way to spend time with her. He would still be spending time with her. That was something. That was a start. But there was so much more he wanted to say. "I'm not doing it for the girls."

"No?" She sat at her worktable, already threading a needle. "Oh, the calves." She glanced up at him. "I'm sorry. I forgot to talk to Daddy about it. But I will before you come out. It's the least I can do." She shook her head. "After everything you've done for me the last couple of days, I owe you."

"You don't owe me anything." He didn't want her thinking or feeling that way.

"I do. I know how busy you are—more so now that you've got the girls to look after." Her movements were sure and steady as the needle flew through the tulle.

"Kitty." He took a steadying deep breath. "Busy or not, I'll always make time for you. You're…you." *I can do better than that*. He cleared his throat. "You're special. To me."

She kept right on sewing. "Being your honorary little sister isn't so bad."

What? No. "Little sister?" Was that how she saw him? A big brother? He sure hoped not. That would be even worse than being put in the friend zone. "I've never thought of you that way."

She stared up at him, then. "You haven't?"

"No," he whispered. The ache in his chest wasn't a surprise. It wasn't the first time he'd felt something inside him shift, but now it was so strong there was no ignoring what it was. All the bits and pieces that once made up his heart were waking up and wanting to be whole again—for Kitty.

CHAPTER THIRTEEN

KITTY PULLED HER brown hair up and braided it back, taking extra care to avoid the still tender spot from her collision with the door. She smoothed the wisps of hair that framed her faced and added a touch of lip gloss—before reaching for a tissue and wiping it off.

I've never thought of you that way.

She stared at her reflection. "Stop." She shook her head. "Stop setting yourself up for…disappointment." Any minute, Tyson, June, and July would arrive to go horseback riding. Now was not the time to get caught up in a fantasy of her own making.

"Why are you making that face?" Twyla leaned against the doorway, watching her sister's reflection.

"What face?" Kitty avoided her sister's all-too-knowing gaze.

"That face." She sighed and pushed off the door frame. "Why are you trying to hide things from me? You know I'll figure it out, so you might as well just tell me."

"There's nothing to tell." It was true. Seconds after Tyson's cryptic announcement, Martha Zeigler had stepped in and insisted she take stock of everyone's progress. After that, she was too busy to touch base with Tyson again—let alone ask him what, exactly, he'd meant. Instead, she'd spent far too many hours pondering what, exactly, he'd meant.

Twyla perched on her bed. "So…nothing happened with Tyson?"

"No." Her laughter was forced.

"Yeah, I'm not buying that." Of course, Twyla would pick up on that right away. "He said something to you. I saw your face. You got all wide-eyed and turned pink."

"I did?" That was embarrassing.

Twyla nodded. "What did he say?"

She turned to face her sister. "Nothing. Really…" She rolled her eyes. "Why are you determined to make nothing into something?"

"Because." Her sister's sigh was long and drawn out. "I guess I'm trying to figure out what my baby sister wants, so I can encourage her to go after it. You know, do the big sister thing—and all that."

"I want the costumes to make Gretta and Martha happy." She smiled at her sister. "I want Daddy to take his medicine without complaining." She paused, then added, "And I really want Samantha to do well on her dance—she's been working so hard on getting the footwork just right."

"Kitty Crawley, you are a pain in the rear, you know that." She blinked. "None of those things have a thing to do with what *you* want. I asked you what *you* wanted."

"What's wrong with wanting other people to be happy?" She shrugged. "I have everything I could ever need—and then some."

"There are times you're as obstinate as Daddy, you know that?" Twyla stood. "I give up. Go on being a martyr, then. I don't know why you're so set against being happy or doing something for yourself every once in a while, but I can't make you do it, so…" She shrugged.

Kitty stood and hugged her sister. "I am happy."

Twyla snorted.

"But I love you all the more for worrying over me." She let go of her sister. "Are you going riding with us? It is Samantha Sunday, after all."

"She's thrilled to be going horseback riding with her new little friends." Twyla waved aside the offer.

Was it her imagination or did her sister sound a little jealous? "You know she'd love you to be there, too, Twyla."

"I prefer our Samantha Sundays to be a little less crowded, thank you very much. Tyson, June and July, *and* Mabel and Jensen. I won't be missed." She sniffed. "Besides, I have a book to finish." She headed back to the door. "Don't be too late. You've got your big date tonight, don't you?"

She nodded. When she hadn't been pondering Tyson's words, she'd been worrying over tonight's date. Not about RJ, he'd been nothing but a gentleman toward her, but how to act or feel. Or, more accurately, how she wasn't feeling.

"And he's taking you to Der Restaurant Von Ludwig?" Twyla shook her head. "That means he's got to wear a coat. You definitely don't want to go smelling like a horse."

She nodded again.

"It's a night out. The food there is great. You're going with a nice, good-looking man who's going to hang on every word you say. It's *just* dinner, Kitty, so try to enjoy yourself, won't you? If he says something about eloping, say no." Twyla waited for her to laugh, then left the bedroom.

Her sister was right. She couldn't remember the last time she'd gone out with someone that wasn't family. And while she had yet to develop any romantic feelings toward RJ, he was nice enough and they got along well.

She finished getting dressed, tugged on her cowboy boots, and headed into the living room.

The moment she came around the corner, Samantha started jumping up and down, saying, "They're here. They're here."

Samantha yanked open the front door and hurried out onto the porch, her voice carrying as she called out. "Hi, June! Hi, July! Come on, come see the horses."

"There's no missing her enthusiasm." Mabel hooked her arm through Jensen's.

"Nope." He grinned. "You ready, Kitty?"

"I'll be right out." She paused and looked at her father. As usual, he sat in his recliner, working on one of his puzzle books. "Dad, did you take your medicine this morning?"

"Mmm-hmm." He peered over his reading glasses at her.

"After about thirty minutes of arguing this time." Twyla was in the kitchen, pouring herself a glass of iced tea. "Before long, I'll have to mash them into powder and put it in pudding."

"Now I know not to eat pudding." Her father snorted.

"It was a joke, Dad." Twyla carried the glass around the large island that separated the kitchen from the living room and sat on the end of the couch. "I'll just use a funnel."

The startled laugh that escaped their father ended with an abrupt throat-clearing.

"We're fine." Twyla picked up her book. "You go have fun with the girls…and Tyson."

"It's about time for that boy to act," her father grumbled.

"Dad," Twyla hissed.

Her father looked ready to fire something back Twyla's way when he saw Kitty and closed his mouth.

"What was that, Dad?" she asked.

He looked up, the picture of innocence. "I didn't say a thing." His gaze darted to Twyla, then back to his puzzle book. "Not a thing."

She didn't know what her father had been talking about, but neither her sister nor her father seemed inclined to clear anything up. Twyla appeared to be lost in her book and her father was intently focused on his puzzles—both clearly avoiding eye contact with her. "Okay, then. Bye." She pulled the front door closed behind her and went down the porch steps to greet their guests.

The first thing she noticed was Tyson. Because…he was too handsome not to notice. Tall and fit and exactly the way a man should look. Strong. Capable. One of the girls said something that had him smiling, and Kitty slowed her step to give herself time to recover. If there was a way to teach her heart not to trip over itself or her lungs to continue breathing as usual, life would be so much easier. She did manage to tear her eyes from his before he noticed her ogling—so that was a mini-win.

The girls were gathered together, their little voices overlapping and their excitement building. Listening to them made it easier to pretend Tyson wasn't there.

"I have a hawsie and I bwaid its tail," June was saying. "It has a poiple tail."

"None of these are purple." Mabel smiled down at the little girl.

"Oh." June took a minute to process this before regaining her enthusiasm. "Any pink ones? Pink is pwetty."

"We have a spotted one." Samantha held up her pointer finger. "Not pink, though."

"That's okay." June patted Samantha on the shoulder.

"I've never ridden a horse." July was holding Samantha's hand.

"It's okay." Samantha was swinging their arms. "I have a secret." She leaned forward. "Mabel is a princess and she can talk to the horses, so she makes sure they're nice."

Kitty watched all three little girls stare up at Mabel in awe. A year ago, Samantha had determined that, since Mabel could "talk" to animals, she must be a princess—because all the princesses in her storybooks or movies could talk to animals. It was five-year-old logic but, in a way, oddly irrefutable logic.

"My daddy is also the bestest rider." Samantha pointed at her father.

"I am." Jensen nodded.

She and Mabel laughed then. To be fair, they'd all grown up in the saddle.

"Modest about it, too." Tyson shook his head.

"Did you know your uncle Tyson used to ride in the rodeo?" Jensen nodded at Tyson. "He did. He rode the big horses—the ones that didn't want to be ridden."

"You did?" June's eyes were wider than ever.

"That was a long time ago." Tyson's smile dimmed. "I'm a lot older and wiser now."

"I agree about the older part." Jensen clapped Tyson on the shoulder and grinned. "Wiser? I'm not so sure on that one."

"Yeah, well, maybe not." Tyson's deep brown eyes met hers. "I'm still figuring things out." His crooked grin had the usual devastating effect on her.

"Don't take too long," Jensen murmured, nudging Tyson in the side.

Tyson nodded, but his eyes remained on her.

What did that mean? Kitty sighed. First her sister and dad, now Tyson and Jensen. She didn't like feeling left out of conversations—especially when the conversations might have something to do with her.

The three little girls bounced and squealed all the way to the barn. When they got inside the barn, there was more bouncing and squealing over the four saddled horses waiting for them. It was only when June was standing beside the horse that the enthusiasm dipped.

"It's a big big hawsie," June whispered, grabbing Tyson's hand.

"It's not so big." Tyson squatted by her side.

"It's okay, Juney. This is my horse." Kitty ran her hand along the horse's neck. "Her name is Clover. Isn't she pretty?"

June was still studying the horse. "It's a girl hawsie?"

"Yep. A girl horsie is called a mare." Tyson scooped June up and settled the little girl on his hip. "And Clover here has been friends with Miss Kitty since she was little."

Kitty pressed a kiss against Clover's nose. "Clover is sweet and patient and loves carrots."

"Me, too." June leaned back into Tyson when he stepped closer to the horse.

Kitty swung herself up and into the saddle. "See, you're destined to be friends."

Tyson nodded, smiling up at her. "You want to sit up there with Miss Kitty? I don't trust a whole lotta people, but Miss Kitty is one of them." His gaze swept over her face. "With her, you're safe."

The longer he stared at her, the harder and faster her heart was thumping. He was trying to make June feel comfortable, that was all. He didn't know how his words affected her—that they amplified the ache pressing in on her chest and made her yearn for more.

TYSON COULDN'T HELP HIMSELF. He was staring at Kitty Crawley. It was plain and simple. He wanted to, so he was. She was…beautiful. Every little thing about her seemed new and fascinating and held his attention. The way her long hair was braided and draped over her shoulder. She sat in the saddle like she was born for it. The knot of her straw cowboy hat's leather chin strap rested in the hollow of her throat so her hat hung low between her shoulder blades. And her eyes…

The confusion on her face said it all. He was giving off all sorts of mixed signals. She probably thought he was teasing her. He'd given her zero reasons for her to suspect he had feelings for her or that he was hoping she felt the same way.

"Let's go, Daddy." Samantha was already up and sitting in front of her father on a horse.

"Yes, ma'am." Jensen gave the horse a nudge with his knees and they headed through the gate into the covered corral adjacent to the barn.

"Mabel can show you how to steer, July," Samantha called back over her shoulder.

July was sitting on the horse, Firefly, with Mabel. Both of her little hands gripped the saddle horn while she squished up her nose and closed her eyes.

"You ready?" he asked her.

July nodded. "Okay." Slowly, she opened her eyes. "Okay," she said again.

"Don't you worry, July." Mabel clicked her tongue and Firefly took a step. "We'll go slow a few times."

"And have fun." Tyson gave the little girl a thumbs-up. "You can tell your momma all about it when we talk to her later tonight."

"Okay," July repeated a third time, her grip tightening as the horse walked on.

"Bye, July." June waved at her sister. "July's riding a hawsie, Uncle Tyson."

"You can, too, Junebug." Tyson kept his voice low and calm. He wanted the girls' first ride to be a positive experience. "Want to ride with me or Miss Kitty?"

June reached for Kitty. "Miss Kitty."

Kitty lifted one arm as he set the little girl in front of her. "You lean back into me like I'm a comfy chair." She slipped one arm around June's waist.

"I wanna wide with you 'cuz Uncle Tyson's

hawsie is even biggah." June had one hand on the pommel and one hand gripping Kitty's forearm.

Tyson swung up into the saddle and winked at June. "You look like a real cowgirl. Just like Miss Kitty."

June smiled at his praise. Kitty, however, rolled her eyes.

"What?" He laughed. "You *are* a real cowgirl, Kitty. It's a compliment."

Kitty steered the horse through the gate and into the corral. "How are you doing, Juney?"

"Okay." June was relaxing enough to lean forward. "What's Samantha's hawse called? It's pwetty."

"That's Stardust." Kitty pointed at the horse. "She's a paint horse."

"See how she's got lots of little spots all over her hindquarters? Like someone shook out a paintbrush and spattered paint all over her?" Tyson kept Boomer alongside Clover.

"Yep." June nodded, her hold tightening on Kitty's arm when the horse started to trot.

"That's why she's called a paint horse." Tyson kept talking, hoping to alleviate the little girl's fear. "Is Clover called Clover because that's what she likes to eat?" he asked Kitty.

"That's part of it." Kitty turned in the saddle and pointed at the horse's left thigh. "And she has a lighter colored spot, here, that kind of looks like a four-leaf clover."

Tyson eyed the horse's thigh. He could distinguish no particular shape to the grayish smudge. "If you say so."

Kitty smiled. "It did, when she was younger. Really."

"Uh-huh." He shook his head, teasing her. "Might need to get those pretty eyes of yours checked." Yep, he'd just said that out loud. It was fine. It was true. He'd always thought so.

Kitty's cheeks were turning a soft shade of pink.

"You like Miss Kitty, Uncle Tyson?"

June's question gave him the opportunity he'd been looking for. "I do, Junebug. Very much. I always have." *More than she knows.*

Kitty's cheeks had gone from pink to red and those pretty eyes were staring at him like he'd grown a second head.

All he could do was smile at her.

She didn't smile back. In fact, she did her best to avoid his gaze for the next hour as they rode around and around the corral.

Eventually, Jensen drew Stardust to a stop and turned back to face them. "How about we take the girls onto the trail?"

"Yes." Samantha gave a thumbs-up.

"We can go down to the creek, see if there

are any ducks hanging around." Jensen looked to Mabel for her nod.

"I brought bread so we can feed them, just in case." Mabel patted the saddlebag.

"I love duckies." June clapped her hands together. "Let's go."

"I don't see why not." Tyson was all too happy to keep the girls busy. Added bonus was spending time with Kitty, too. She'd kept up a constant stream of conversation with June the entire ride—mostly about horses and cows and ranch life. She'd asked how the girls were enjoying dance lessons and clogging, which June was all too happy to talk about. Kitty had an answer for every one of June's questions, and that sweet smile of hers had never wavered. He was getting awfully fond of that smile.

"Juney, do you think you could ride with your uncle?" Kitty peered down at the little girl. "I'll have to feed the ducks with you next time."

"Okay." But June's gaze widened as she assessed the larger horse he was sitting on.

"Tonight's the night? The big dinner date." Jensen shot Tyson a not-so-subtle look. "You gotta give the guy credit. He's pulling out all the stops to win your heart, little sister."

Yeah, thanks for the reminder. Tyson's stomach sank, then twisted.

"You're having dinner with the flower man?" Samantha asked.

Flower man? Tyson wasn't sure whether to be jealous RJ had a nickname or laugh that his nickname was flower man.

"Ooh." July leaned forward to see Kitty. "Is the flower man your Valentine, Miss Kitty?"

He glanced at Kitty. A first date was bad enough.

"Make him a cawd." June patted Kitty's arm. "With glittah and hawts? Make it so pwetty."

"Valentine's cards are love notes." Samantha looked up at her father. "My daddy says Mabel is his Valentine, right, Daddy?" She grinned when Jensen nodded.

"Who is yaw Valentine, Uncle Tyson?" June frowned at him.

He resisted the urge to tug at his collar and forced a laugh. "Well, now… I don't have one yet." But there was still time—if he stepped up the pace and Kitty's date didn't go so great, that is.

"How 'bout Aunt Twyla." Samantha's whole face lit up. "She needs a Valentine."

He didn't have to force a laugh this time. "Twyla?" Twyla was a little too strong-willed and opinionated for his taste. Plus, she didn't make everything in him sit up and take notice the way Kitty did.

"Daddy and Mabel. Aunt Kitty and the flower

man. Mr. Tyson and Aunt Twyla." Samantha listed off the couples on her fingers. "Everyone is happy."

July cocked her head to one side. "What do you think, Uncle Tyson?"

All eyes were on him, now. That included Kitty's—not that he could figure out what was going on in that head of hers. He wished he could. It'd help steer him in the right direction. "Your Aunt Twyla might have someone she likes. If she does, it wouldn't be right for her to be my Valentine now, would it?"

All three girls shook their heads.

"If you like her, ask her." June shrugged. "Easy-peasy."

He laughed again. "Easy, huh?" Then why was he having such a hard time with it. In theory, it *should* be easy. He should say, *Kitty, I like you. I want to date you. I want you to go out with me, not RJ.* Say it and be done.

It was Kitty. He knew Kitty. Knew that, even if she rejected him, she'd be gentle about it. She was a good person. Loyal. Honest. She didn't put on airs or make a fuss. She was one hundred per-cent genuine. A beautiful woman with an even more beautiful heart.

All the reasons he'd kept his heart locked away didn't apply to her.

Unlike his mother, she wouldn't drop in when

she needed something only to disappear weeks later and stay gone for years at a time—without sending a word until she showed up needing something else. And she was no Iris, wanting him to be a part of the rodeo community and have bragging rights to his accolades.

Kitty was Kitty. If she loved him, she would love *him*.

But that was a pretty big *if*. Until now, that word had never scared him. Now? There was no scarier word.

He glanced Kitty's way to find her staring back at him. He was glad June was riding with Kitty or the little girl would have likely been deafened by the pounding of his heart. And, knowing June, everyone else would have heard about it.

"Samantha, did Cupid ask you, July, and June to help out making couples this year?" Jensen tickled Samantha's side, earning a peal of giggles.

"No," she said, amidst giggling.

"Cupid is the flying baby in a diaper that shoots people with arrows and makes them fall in love?" July asked.

"He shoots people with awwows?" June looked and sounded horrified. "That's not nice."

That had everyone laughing.

"I agree," Tyson managed to say. "Falling in love is the last thing I'd be thinking about if someone shot me with an arrow."

"How about we all go potty and wash up, before we go feed the ducks?" Mabel turned to Jensen.

They all steered their horses back to the gate. While Kitty and Mabel helped the girls down and led them to the bathroom, he and Jensen tied the horses' reins to the pipe fence.

Seconds later, Kitty came out and waved. "I hope you find the duckies."

It took effort for him to watch her walk away—knowing where she was going. He was on the verge of taking a step when Jensen stopped him.

"You need to think this through," Jensen murmured. "Are you going after her to tell her you like her? And, if so, why now—all of a sudden? Is it because you needed her to know, right this second, you have feelings for her? Or are you hoping to stop her from going out with RJ?" He sighed. "You're my friend, Tyson, and I can tell you're working through things. That's good. Figure it out. But figure it out so you know how you feel and what you want before you go after her." He gave Tyson a long, hard look. "Friend or not, I won't stand by and let you mess around with my little sister."

He wasn't offended. Jensen was being a good big brother. And yet, "You give RJ the same talk?"

Jensen's gaze narrowed. "There's no mistaking his motivation or intentions. Right now, I'm not so sure about yours."

That stung a bit—but it wasn't wrong. He'd spent so long ignoring his feelings, it was hard to give in to them. To feel. To act. It went against years of self-discipline and distancing himself from potential hurt. "That's fair." He swallowed, scanning the trail for Kitty but not finding her. "You're right about RJ." He sighed. "I don't want her going out with him. I don't…like it."

"Duly noted." Jensen shrugged. "But he seems to be getting his life sorted, so…"

"Good for him. Doesn't mean she needs to be a part of it." He broke off, his throat going tight.

"That's Kitty's choice, isn't it?" Jensen's tone was unyielding. "I don't care if she chooses RJ or you or someone else. All I care is she chooses the man willing to put his everything on the line for her—into loving her." He met Tyson's gaze again. "She deserves nothing less."

He knew that. He did. Hearing it from Jensen only reminded him how selfish he was being to even think about pursuing Kitty. That was why he'd held his peace. He didn't know if he could be that man for her, but he wanted to be. Life, however, had no guarantees, only plenty of chances for regret. If he didn't try, this was the sort of regret that would haunt him until the end of his days. He didn't want to live with that. He didn't know if he could.

CHAPTER FOURTEEN

KITTY RAN THE brush through her hair again.
Then set it down. Her sister had already checked
in on her once—and made a huge fuss over how
nice she looked. RJ was taking her to the fan-
ciest restaurant in the whole county—shouldn't
she look nice?

RJ Malloy was in a suit. And, according to
Twyla, he was looking every bit the gentleman. Kitty had yet to see for herself because
she was, sort of, hiding in her bedroom. She was
dressed. Her hair was done. She was even wearing makeup. There was absolutely no reason for
her to stay in her room—but here she was.

"Are you coming?" Twyla came back into the
bedroom and closed the door behind her. "Dad
is grilling him, so if you wait too much longer
RJ might run for the hills."

"I'm coming." But she stayed where she was,
perched on the cushion-topped stool before her
vanity.

"Uh-huh." Twyla flopped onto her bed. "I see

that." She propped her elbows on the bed and rested her chin in her folded hands. "What's up? Your complexion is an odd shade of pea green at the moment. Not exactly your color."

She glanced at her reflection. *Pale* was more like it. So much so that the blush on her cheeks was far too bold. She pulled a tissue from the box and wiped.

"Stop." Twyla threw a small pillow at her. "I was kidding. You look gorgeous. Honestly. You do."

"I do?" She ran a hand over the soft-as-butter tan suede shirtdress.

"Yep." Twyla nodded. "What's the holdup, Kitty? I'm serious. Is it RJ? Do you not like him? I mean, if you don't, why are you doing this?"

"It's not that I don't like him…" She nibbled on the inside of her lower lip. "He's been so nice and considerate. I honestly don't know how I feel about him. I'm hoping tonight will help me figure that out."

"In case you didn't know, a guy being nice isn't a reason to go out with him. You're under no obligation to him."

"I know." She frowned. "That's not what I meant, exactly. I appreciate that he's trying so hard. With me and—with life. I don't want him to feel discouraged or give up."

Twyla snorted. "You've got to stop worrying

about everyone except yourself. Are you going to marry the guy simply because he asks you?"

"Of course not." She shot her sister a look.

Twyla didn't flinch away. Instead, her eyes narrowed as she asked, "Is it that there's no room inside? Because Tyson is taking up too much space." She poked her own chest. "In here." She sat up and sighed. "You know what you should do? Forget him. I mean it. Tonight I want you to forget about everyone and everything else and *enjoy* yourself."

Kitty reached up to check the backs of her hoop earrings. "Okay." She'd try. She really would. She'd love to have a nice evening, too.

"You could have an amazing time." Twyla stood up and leaned forward so she was nose-to-nose with her sister. "You might even come home swooning over RJ Malloy." She pretended to fan herself. "If you don't, maybe I will." She winked. "Now, come on." She grabbed her sister's hand and tugged her up. "Let's go."

Kitty let her sister lead her from her room, down the hall, and into the great room. She'd been prepared for RJ and her father, she had not been prepared for Mabel, Jensen, Tyson, and the girls to be there, too. The collective *ooh*s from the girls, followed by squeals of excitement did nothing to ease her nerves.

It's fine. As long as she didn't look at Tyson

or Jensen, she'd be fine. The two of them would tease and poke and make things ten times more awkward than they already were.

"Oh, Aunt Kitty, you look pretty." Samantha hurried to her, then circled her. "I like your shoes. They have bows."

"I like bows." June ran over and crouched, staring at her shoes.

"Me too." Kitty had only had one occasion to wear the pretty lace-up wedge sandals. Tonight seemed as good a time as any to wear them again.

"Miss Kitty." RJ stepped forward, a bouquet of flowers in his hands. "You look... You are..." He cleared his throat. "You're as pretty as a peach."

The way his voice wobbled told her he was feeling just as nervous as she was—which was a huge relief. "Thank you." She took the flowers. "For the flowers, too."

RJ had a nice smile. And, Twyla was right, he'd dressed for their date. Suit, tie, high-polished shoes and all.

"I don't think I've ever seen you without a cowboy hat." She'd never noticed how thick and curly his black hair was.

"It takes some getting used to." He reached up to pat his hair. "It's in the truck." He grinned.

"You look good." Twyla pointed at him, up and down. "You do."

RJ went beet red. "Thank you kindly."

"Flowa man." June peered up from where she was crouching. "Bwought flowas."

"It's proper." Her father stood, his gaze bouncing between Kitty and RJ. "I expect you home by midnight."

"Dad." Kitty was mortified. "I'm a little old for a curfew."

"Midnight is fine, sir." RJ nodded.

Her father chuckled. "Respecting the father. Good choice."

"You look lovely, Kitty. I remember when we bought that dress—thinking how pretty you looked in it." This, from Mabel. "You two are going to get a few looks tonight."

"I don't know about me, but Kitty here? I'm thinkin' you're right." RJ's admiration was obvious. "We should get. Reservation's coming up."

Kitty nodded and followed him to the front door and down the steps. His truck was parked beyond the lush green lawn her father watered every single morning.

"Bye, Aunt Kitty." Samantha ran out onto the front porch.

"Bye, flowah man." June's little voice rang out.

"That's not his name," July said.

"I don't cawe. I like it." June waved after them.

"They're cute," RJ said, holding open the passenger door for her. "And, boy howdy, do they have a lot to say."

"They do." Kitty smiled, climbing into the truck when she realized. "I left my purse."

"You stay put." RJ smiled. "I'll ask Miss Twyla to get it." He headed back up the path and to the porch.

The porch. Where everyone that had been inside the house was now standing... *Really?* Kitty covered her face with her hands. This was worse than her high school prom. Her father had waved her off that night, scowling and shooting daggers at her nervous date the whole time.

But this, this was worse. She was an adult. This was a first date, a simple get-to-know-you dinner date. That was all. Why had they all felt the need to follow them outside? This sort of attention was unnecessary, and it made her deeply uncomfortable—her family knew that.

She smoothed her skirt over her knees and, blushing, waved at the three little girls who kept waving madly from the front porch. Luckily, it looked like Tyson had gone back inside with Twyla and RJ.

But the longer RJ stayed gone, the more she began to second-guess things. She shouldn't have sent him back inside with her father. He had seemed to be on his best behavior but there was no telling how long that might last. That, plus the audience they'd been forced to endure, was asking a lot of any man.

She was on the verge of going back inside when the door opened and RJ hurried out, her purse in hand. He trotted down the steps and walked toward the truck—the set of his shoulders off somehow. When he closed the driver door and offered her the purse, there was a tension about his mouth that hadn't been there before.

"I should apologize for my dad." She took a deep breath. "He can be a bit...much. Okay, a lot. He's nosy and grumpy but he means well—"

"Your daddy is being a daddy, that's all." RJ's easygoing smile was back in place. "I'd wonder if he wasn't being overprotective of you."

"Oh." She paused to study his face. "You seemed... I thought he'd said something."

RJ chuckled. "Your daddy didn't say anything a father shouldn't say to the man taking his daughter out to dinner."

Was it her imagination or had there been a certain emphasis on the word *daddy*? Had someone else said something? Twyla, maybe? Jensen hadn't gone back inside, so it wasn't her brother.

"Nice to see you've got so many people that care about you, Kitty." He glanced her way before turning onto the highway. "Of course, you're easy to care about."

"Family is family. Some days you love them to pieces, some days you can't get away from them fast enough." She tucked her hair behind her ear.

"I guess Tyson is family?" He was looking at her now.

"Tyson?" Her throat went tight and her mouth felt dry.

"Sorta like a big brother." He kept right on looking at her, like he was looking for something.

"Well…" *No.* He'd always been Tyson. Separate and yet, somehow, hers. "He is my big brother's best friend." It took effort to swallow. "Did he say something?" Surely not.

"Yes, ma'am. He did." RJ chuckled and shook his head. "But I'll leave it to him to tell you himself. I don't think he'd appreciate me speaking for him."

She wasn't sure how to respond to that. She wanted to know what Tyson had said, of course. But she was on a date with RJ—she should at least try to focus on the man she was with. Otherwise, what was she doing?

The drive into town was fine. He kept the radio on and sang along, his voice pleasant.

He continued being the perfect gentleman by helping her out of his truck, holding open the door to the restaurant, and pulling out her chair.

"So, Kitty, you always liked sewing? Or is it something you sort of…fell into?" He hung his hat off the chair back and gave her his full attention.

"I love it." It was easier to relax if she was talking about something she enjoyed. "Ranch life, as you know, is very practical. Being able to repair and sew clothes from scratch helped me feel like I'm doing my part. If that makes sense?" She took a deep breath. "But, what I really want to do is get into custom costumes. For dance or theater or cosplay—anything along those lines. Samantha has shown me how magical a costume can be. It can make a person feel confident or lift their spirits or boost their creativity." She shrugged. "I'd love to give people that little extra spark."

"Costumes, huh? Well, that's something." He smiled. "I admit, the only costume I've ever worn was some plastic mask for Halloween a long time ago. It smelled funny and I couldn't see a darn thing but I remember coming home with a bucketful of candy."

Kitty laughed. "Sounds like it turned out in the end."

"It did." He shook his head. "Lost a filling to a caramel, though. Back then, just about nothing scared me more than a trip to the dentist." He shuddered. "Come to think of it, I'm still not all that fond of the dentist."

She was surprised at how easy it was to talk to RJ. He seemed different here—like he wasn't trying so hard. "How do you like working on the Briscoe place?"

"It's a big spread, Kitty." He shook his head.

"You could ride all day and still not get from one side to the other. It's hard to wrap my mind around owning that much land. But you know all about that, don't you?"

"It's a lot of work."

"It's a lifestyle, isn't it?" He nodded. "But I don't mind the hard work or the long hours. It keeps me focused and out of trouble. Time to grow up and all that." His gaze met hers.

"What does that look like for you?" She paused. "What do you see in your future?"

"Being foreman on the Briscoe place. Finding myself a wife and starting a family. Puttin' in good, honest work to live a good, honest life." He shrugged.

By the time they'd finished their schnitzel and were working through their cherry pie, Kitty found she liked RJ Malloy. While she liked the idea of being the man's friend, that was all. He didn't cause a single tingle or make her knees go remotely weak. Not once.

Once he'd turned on his truck to drive her home, she knew what she needed to do.

"RJ, I had a great time." She smiled at him in the dimly lit truck cab.

"Me, too, Kitty." He nodded.

"I believe honesty is important in any relationship, so I'm going to be honest with you." She took a deep breath, knowing she needed to get it all out there before she could overthink and second-guess and say all the wrong things. "It's just...my heart's taken. It's one-sided and ridiculous, but that's the truth. All I can offer you is friendship. But I do, sincerely, offer that. And hope you'll accept it."

"I appreciate that, Kitty. And if we're being honest here, then I'll go ahead and admit I'm kinda relieved." He shook his head. "Don't get me wrong, you're a fine woman. But, I think, too fine for me. Audy was the one that said you'd be the best mother and wife in Garrison—after Brooke, that is. And that sounded good to me. Plus, you're kind and pretty and all. And you are." He sighed. "But, you see, my whole life, I've had loud, bossy, and short-tempered women in my life. They've kept me in check, most of the time. I need that. And you... You're about as sweet-tempered and gentle a person as I've ever met. Too good and sweet for me." He let out a long slow breath.

"I'm glad you're relieved." She was, too. "It means we're on the same page and no one is getting hurt. But I'm not too good for you, RJ. We're just not the right fit."

"Yes, ma'am." He chuckled. "I'm guessing I know who's got a hold of your heart."

She stared at RJ, his features too shadowed to read in the near dark. "You...do?"

"Well now, if it's Tyson Ellis and there's ever anything I can do to help with that fool, you just let me know." He chuckled again.

"You would?" She shook her head. Was she really that transparent? At this point, she was starting to feel like everyone in Garrison *except* Tyson knew how she felt.

"That's what friends do, isn't it? Help each other out."

"They do." She was so surprised by the turn this conversation had taken, she found herself laughing. "You are going to make one lucky lady very happy someday."

"I'll do my best. But you feel free to point me in the right direction if you find someone that might suit me."

"It's a deal." She shook his hand before sitting back, against the seat, fully relaxed. Even if things hadn't gone the way she'd expected, she'd had fun. RJ might not make her heart kick into overdrive or cause full-body tingles, but it had been nice to spend time with someone who'd been interested in spending time with her. Not as someone's aunt or sister or daughter or friend, but as a woman worthy of time and attention.

TYSON POKED AT the eggs on his plate. He was bleary-eyed from all the tossing and turning he'd done last night. Ever since he'd watched

RJ's pickup truck drive away from the Crawley ranch the night before, he'd been out of sorts. He couldn't seem to shake it.

"Glad you had fun." His father spread some strawberry jam on a piece of toast and handed it to June.

"The hawsies were so big." June stood in her chair and held her hand up, over her head. "Like this."

"Were they, now?" His father chuckled. "That's something. Now, have a seat so you don't fall or hurt yourself."

June nodded and sat. "We wode wound and wound."

"And we fed ducks." July grinned. "But only for a little while 'cuz Juney had to go potty again."

"Can't help it." June shrugged.

"When you gotta go, you gotta go." His father laughed, then glanced over at Tyson. "You're not saying much this morning."

Tyson leaned back in his chair and ran a hand across the back of his neck. "Tired is all." He could tell from his father's expression he wasn't buying it but, thankfully, he didn't push it. "I was thinking after school, maybe we could get some ice cream."

"Yay!" July clapped her hands.

"Well, I can't think of a thing that'll make a Monday a good day better than ice cream." His father glanced at the clock on the wall. "Finish up your breakfast, girlies. It's about time to head into town for school.

"I love ice cweam." June took a too-big bite of toast.

"Me, too." July leaned forward, eyes wide. "Chocolate chip cookie dough is yummy."

"What do you like, Unca Tyson?" June's grin was made even bigger by the smear of straw-berry jam on each cheek.

"I like plain ol' strawberry." Tyson stood and ran the washcloth under some warm tap water. "Hold still. Gotta see if it's still Junebug under all that jam."

June looked up at him and giggled. "It's me. It's me."

It hadn't been long since the girls arrived, but just about everything had changed. Before their arrival, he and his father had a quiet cup of cof-fee at the kitchen table. Some mornings, he'd fry some bacon and eggs, others he'd make them oat-meal. The girls didn't know how to be quiet— but they bounced into the room with such energy he didn't mind. The girls didn't like bacon or eggs or oatmeal—they liked waffles or toast, fresh fruit, and yogurt. For the first time in his life they had yogurt in the house. Yogurt drinks, tubes of yogurt for the lunch box, and large tubs of vanilla yogurt they'd add fruit and granola to for breakfast and snacks. His frugal father was tickled pink over the tubs since he could wash them out and reuse them for leftovers.

His father loaded the dishwasher while Tyson checked lunch boxes, made sure shoes were tied and backpacks were ready to go. Of course, June announced she had to go potty as soon as he'd locked the front door behind them—but he'd rather they go again now than be in panic mode all the way into town.

The drive into town had changed, too. There was no more morning agriculture report on the radio. Instead, the girls sang all sorts of songs. Some he knew, some he felt certain they'd made up between the two of them. They pulled up into the drop-off line at the elementary school and the girls' excitement mounted. It was a relief that they both loved school, their teachers, and new friends. If not—well, he didn't want to think about that.

They exchanged morning pleasantries with Mrs. Webber, Samantha and July's teacher, as she helped the girls from the car. The girls called out a final, "Bye!" and Mrs. Webber slammed the door, holding the girls' hands as she led them to the front door of the school.

"Ever notice how quiet it is after we drop the little rug rats off?" his father asked as they left the parking lot.

"Kinda hard not to, Dad." Tyson grinned.

"They're like a whole pot of coffee, aren't they? Giving me that boost to wake me up." His father chuckled.

"Agree." He nodded, pulling up to the four-way stop that led into downtown. "Speaking of which, you want some coffee?"

"I'll never turn down coffee, son, you know that."

Tyson drove to Old Towne Books and Coffee, bought two to-go coffees, two blueberry muffins, and one cinnamon muffin, then climbed back into the SUV. "A snack for later." He handed the brown paper bag to his dad.

His father peered inside the bag. "Don't mind if I do. I'm guessing we're dropping one of these off?"

"Yep." It was a Monday. Everyone could use a little something to get their week started off right. Kitty loved cinnamon muffins so...

His father sighed. "You still out of sorts because you saw RJ taking Kitty out last night?"

He nodded. No point denying it. "I talked to RJ." Not that he'd planned to. It'd come out—unexpectedly. He wasn't sure who'd been more surprised, RJ, Twyla, or himself.

His father made a startled sound. "You did what, now?"

He cleared his throat. "I told him I was interested in Kitty." As soon as he'd opened his fool mouth, guilt had him by the throat. He might not have planned to say anything but there was no arguing why he had. He'd wanted to rattle RJ's confidence. He'd no idea if Kitty would return his feelings but he was already trying to undermine RJ? It'd been an entirely self-serving thing to do. Until now, he hadn't thought of himself as selfish.

"And what did he say to that?" His father chuckled.

"He said I'd had plenty of time to do something before now, so why hadn't I? And he asked whether I wanted her because someone else did." RJ's questions were valid, so there was no point getting angry over them. And if he was going to get angry, the only person to be angry at was himself.

His father nodded. "Did you have an answer?"

"I blamed him. Told him watching him pursue her gave me a wake-up call." *I can't ignore how I feel anymore, even if I want to.* His fingers tightened on the steering wheel. By the time the two of them were done talking, he'd felt worse than he had before. "You don't need to say anything. I acted like a jerk—I know it." *I am a jerk.*

"Hmm." His father's tone didn't help.

"I know I need to talk to her." For all he knew, RJ had already told her everything. "I figure you can drop me off at the Calico Pig and I'll make my way to the shop in a bit."

"Fine. You've got a plan?" His father lifted up the paper bag. "Or is this it?"

Tyson looked at his father and frowned. "It's a start, isn't it?" He wasn't one for grand gestures. He'd never done one in his life. None of his previous relationships had ever become serious, and Iris had pretty much thrown herself at him. Not only was he having to come to terms with having feelings for Kitty, he was having to figure out what to *do* with them. All he knew was not doing something was no longer an option. "And don't start giving me any advice, either."

"Me? No worries there." His father chuckled. "I'm no Casanova. Never claimed to be." He shrugged. "Not saying I won't get there, though. I've still got plenty of time."

"Oh really?" Tyson was so surprised, he laughed. "I like your confidence, Dad."

"I read in some magazine that women find it an attractive quality." His father waited until Tyson had parked the SUV in front of the Calico Pig, then handed over the bag. "So go in there and be confident, son."

Tyson took the bag, handed his father the keys, and climbed out of the SUV.

"Tyson?" It was Twyla, leaning out the front

door. "What brings you by bright and early this Monday morning?"

"I was in the neighborhood." Which wasn't true. Ellis Family Feed and Ranch Supplies was on the edge of town. The Calico Pig was right on Main Street.

"Oh really?" She laughed, then pointed at the small brown paper bag. "Is that for me?"

"Oh…" He glanced at the bag. "I feel real bad now—"

"I'm kidding." She rolled her eyes. "I'm assuming you're here to see my sister?" She waved him inside. "She's not here. Dad has an appointment with Doc Johnson this morning. He behaves for her. Sort of." She shrugged. "What can I say? My little sister is a saint."

He grinned.

"Yeah, yeah, you know. I was there last night, remember? What on earth were you thinking?" She leaned against the door. "Telling RJ you like Kitty? When is my sister going to know? I feel like she's the first person you should have told."

He ran a hand along the back of his neck. "Why do you think I'm here?"

"Oh?" Twyla pushed off the door frame. "In that case, you might as well go sit at Olde Towne Books and Coffee. She and dad have a snack before she takes him home—since it's so close to Doc's office."

"Is that so?" He held out the bag. "Muffin?"

"Aw, thanks, you shouldn't have." She took the bag. "So…good luck?"

He touched the brim of his hat. "Thank you." With that, he headed down the sidewalk to Olde Towne Books and Coffee. When he walked past Doc Johnson's place to get to the coffee shop, he hadn't expected to find Kitty and Dwight Crawley parked in front. Dwight was sitting in the passenger seat, scowling as fiercely as ever, while Kitty stood by the open passenger door. From the looks of it, they were in the midst of a not so pleasant conversation.

"I don't see the point in coming in every couple of weeks so that leech of a nurse can poke me full of needles and take more blood." Dwight's tone was snippier than ever.

"It's so we can keep you healthy, Dad." Kitty rested a hand on his shoulder. "You know I'm not a fan of needles. I get it, I do—"

"You do not." The old man shrugged her hand away. "You're talking to me like I'm five years old. Trying to get me to do what you want. You think I don't see through what you're doing here? Before long, you'll be getting the good doctor here to write up the paperwork so you can put me in one of those homes."

"Dad." Kitty looked horrified. "We would never do that."

"If I get too sick and decrepit that might change." He pointed at her. "You'll go off with that Malloy boy, Jensen'll have Mabel and Samantha—you think Twyla's going to take care of me? She'd probably sneak into my room and smother me with a pillow."

Tyson was glad they hadn't spotted him yet or they'd see how he was struggling not to laugh. The old guy was really pulling out all the stops. Here he was accusing Kitty of emotionally manipulating him but, really, it was the other way around. It was clear they were at a standstill, so Tyson pulled out his phone and called Doc Johnson's office.

"This is Tyson Ellis. I'm out front with Kitty Crawley. She's trying to get her father inside but it's not going so hot."

"Tyson? Morning. It's Aurelia. I was wondering why they weren't here yet." Doc Johnson's longtime nurse, Aurelia Vega, was the sort of no-nonsense person that was needed when it came to prickly patients like Dwight Crawley. "I'll send Doc out." And she hung up.

"Daddy, be nice. You know we all love you." Kitty reached for his hand. "The sooner we go in, the sooner we can go home."

"We're going home, now." Dwight reached forward, grabbed the door and pulled it shut, clipping Kitty's shoulder in the process.

Before Tyson knew it, he was by Kitty's side. "You okay?"

"Oh. Yes. Hi, Tyson." Her smile appeared, then instantly began to fade. "Fine. Just... Dad's not all that keen on seeing Doc Johnson today."

"I'm picking up on that." He turned and waved at Dwight through the window.

Dwight did not wave back.

He thanked the stars his father wasn't a bitter old man. Every once in a while he and his father would butt heads, but his father had never pulled an out-and-out tantrum like this. "What can I do to help?"

Kitty shook her head. "I'm not sure. He's never been quite this obstinate before."

"I can hear you." Dwight Crawley's voice boomed.

"I'm not saying anything you can't hear, Dad." She frowned at her father.

"And *you* should be on your way." Dwight Crawley leveled him with a pretty intimidating glare. "Mind your own business and stay out of my family affairs. Especially if you want those calves for the rodeo."

"Daddy!" Kitty looked like she wanted the ground to swallow her up.

But Tyson laughed. "Well, sir, this is a public place." He gestured to where they were parked and the good people of Garrison all up and down the street, going about their business. "Seems to me, this is becoming everyone's business." He crossed his arms over his chest and held the man's gaze. "How can I help?"

"Keep on walking." Dwight all but spat the words out.

Thankfully, Doc Johnson chose that moment to come out. "Dwight, now, come on. Don't be ridiculous. What do you think Martha will do if she hears about this?"

"There's nothing wrong with me—you just want more of my money, that's all this is." Dwight slapped the dashboard.

"All you're doing is getting your blood pressure high. If you don't calm down, you'll end up in the hospital. You really want that to happen?" Doc Johnson opened the passenger door.

"Fine. But I'm not going to any hospital." Dwight stepped out of the truck. "You best not call Martha."

"We'll see how the rest of your appointment goes." Doc Johnson shook his head.

"Thank you, Dad." Kitty stepped forward and offered her father her arm. *Thank you* she mouthed to Tyson.

He grinned and tipped his hat her way. It was only after she'd disappeared into Doc Johnson's office with her father that Tyson realized he hadn't done what he'd set out to do: talk to her.

278 HER COWBOY CUPID

Once he'd assessed the situation, all he'd wanted to do was help her. But it was okay. There was time. Later, after lunch, he'd circle back around to the Calico Pig and try again. Today was the day—today was the day he'd take that first step and find the words to, finally, start courting Kitty Crawley. It'd been a long time since he'd been this happy.

CHAPTER FIFTEEN

"His blood pressure was out of whack." Kitty stirred the pot of low-fat, low-sodium minestrone soup that was on her father's approved food list. Her father didn't like it but, after the visit they'd had today, she knew more changes were going to have to be made to keep her father healthy. "Doc said part of that was how worked up he'd gotten, but still. He didn't tell me he's had a headache for a couple of days."

"Me neither." Twyla pulled the fresh baked rolls from the baking sheet and put them into a basket. "For a man who likes to complain, he's been keeping us in the dark about a lot."

"It's his pride." Jensen was chopping cucumbers to put in the salad. "The man has more pride than good sense."

Their father had been diagnosed with coronary heart disease the year before and, despite their best efforts to implement small changes, he'd pushed back on everything. He didn't want to eat healthy foods—he especially didn't want to give up fried foods or bacon. He'd worked hard every day of his life so why did he have to go walk every day? When Mabel had suggested getting him a dog to take on walks, her father had refused, saying he didn't want "a dirty animal in the house and in the way." The only regular *exercise* he got was going from his bedroom to the living room recliner and back again. It wasn't enough. Doc Johnson had been pretty candid with them today. If her father didn't start taking his health seriously, it was only a matter of time before he had a heart attack or a stroke.

"I don't know what to do." She kept stirring.

"Kitty." Twyla came to her side and slid an arm around her waist. "You know there's nothing *you* can do, right? He is a grown man. An ornery one at that."

"But he's our dad. We can't give up on him." She refused to give up on him.

"All right." Jensen stopped chopping. "It's not like we haven't all tried to talk to him about this. We have—and we've all gotten told to mind our own business, too. I'm all ears, Kitty-cat. What should we do?"

She shrugged. "I'm thinking." So far, she hadn't come up with a single idea to boost her father's interest in his own health.

"At least Martha gets him out of the house more often. Dance classes, seminars at the Community Center, and gardening club." Twyla shrugged. "And he never misses any of Samantha's dances or class parties or clubs. Doc Johnson said those sorts of activities are helpful, too."

"Maybe we should get Miss Martha into the loop?" Jensen asked.

She and Twyla stared at her brother.

"No?" He held his hands up.

"I don't know how Dad would take that. They seem to be doing pretty well at the moment and I'd rather not strain their relationship. That should be a last resort." Kitty waited for them to nod before going on. "How about we all brainstorm some, and we can talk tomorrow? Anyway, dinner is ready now."

If it hadn't been for Samantha, their evening meal would have been a quiet affair. As it was, they got to hear all about Samantha's day at school—every single minute of it.

"And it was Carson's birthday so his gramma brought us heart-shaped cookies and they were so good. And then, we started making our Valentine's boxes." Samantha grinned. "For our class Valentine's party."

"When is that?" Jensen asked. "We need to make sure to get valentines for the class."

"It's next Friday," Mabel answered.

"That's going to be a big day." Twyla reached

for the salad bowl. "A Valentine's party at school and the Sweethearts Rodeo that night."

"I hope Juney will be better then." Samantha tore her roll in half, frowning. "She got a bug in her tummy and got sick."

Kitty's spoon paused halfway to her mouth. "She did?" Poor June. Poor Tyson and Mr. Ellis. Likely, a tummy bug wasn't something they'd planned for. Would they have children's medicine? Electrolyte drinks? Or crackers?

"Teacher says they have to steribilize all the rooms 'cuz lots of kids have it." Samantha wrinkled up her nose. "Eddie threw up *all* over in the hallway."

"Eddie's in your class, isn't he?" Jensen was frowning now.

Samantha nodded. "I like this soup, Aunt Kitty."

"I made it special for Grandpa." She smiled at her dad.

"Hmph." But her father kept on eating his soup.

"It's delicious." Samantha dipped her roll into the soup. "Can we get Valentine's cards for my class, Daddy?"

"Might not hurt to stock up on some tummy bug stuff—just in case," Kitty added. "I wonder if they have what they need to care for June and July?"

"I was thinking the same thing." Jensen nodded. "I'll call him when we're done eating."

"That's our Kitty, always thinking of others." Twyla popped a cherry tomato into her mouth.

"There is something extra mischievous about that smile." Kitty pointed at her sister. "Should I worry?"

"Did you talk to Tyson today?" Twyla asked, poking around in her salad bowl.

"Yes." She frowned. "He was outside Doc Johnson's this morning."

"Sticking his nose into things that are none of his business." Her father grumbled.

"He meant well, Dad. He was trying to help. That's what friends do." Kitty suspected Tyson was the reason Doc Johnson had come out to collect her father.

"Yeah, Grampa. Mr. Tyson is nice, I think." Samantha nodded. "He's Daddy's friend, he's taking care of Juney and July, *and* Aunt Kitty thinks he's ham-some."

Kitty's face went hot. She'd mentioned it one time—one time—and Samantha had never forgotten. She stared into her bowl of soup to avoid making contact with any of the people now staring at her.

"Is that so?" her father asked.

"Does Aunt Kitty still think he's ham-some?" Jensen, in typical big brother teasing mode, sounded tickled pink. "From the color of your face, it would appear so. I wonder if RJ stands a chance."

Kitty covered her cheeks with her hands. "I'm...warm. Overheated." She fanned herself, still having a hard time making eye contact with anyone.

"Eating soup will do that." Twyla giggled.

"He is ham-some." Samantha shrugged. "Not as ham-some as Daddy, though."

"I agree." Mabel winked at the little girl.

"Oh, please." Twyla rolled her eyes.

"Is something going on between you two?" her father asked. "Is that why he showed up this morning? Was he looking for you?"

It had been a happy coincidence. "No—"

"Yes." Twyla cut her off. "He stopped by the shop and I told him where you were."

Kitty blinked. "Oh." Why hadn't Twyla said he'd stopped by? Then again, she'd been so worried about their father since his appointment, Twyla could have said something and she might have missed it?

"Did he say why he was looking for Kitty?" Jensen was watching her now.

She was grateful her brother had asked the question so she didn't have to.

"Oh, I know why he was looking for her." Twyla looked like the cat that had eaten the canary—all self-satisfied. "But I'm not at liberty to divulge that information."

"There are no secrets in this household." Her father was not happy. "You can't start something and then not finish it."

"You were the one that just said people should mind their own business. Well, this business is between my sweet sister and ham-some Tyson Ellis." Twyla shrugged. "I'm sure you'll hear about it once it's said and done."

"Once what is said and done?" Her father used his roll to point at Twyla.

What on earth was Twyla going on about? What needed to be said and done? And why had Tyson come looking for her?

Twyla only smiled and batted her eyes, feigning innocence. "And how did your date with RJ go?" She spooned up some soup.

That was a sudden shift in conversation. She took a bite of roll and smiled. Did she really want to share *everything* with her family?

"Now who's not minding their own business?" her father snapped.

"Did you have fun with flower man?" Samantha asked. "Did he hold your hand?"

The table went silent.

She tried to swallow but the roll seemed to stick in her throat. She took a long sip of her iced tea, set the glass down, to find all eyes still on her. "It was nice. We did not hold hands."

"That's it?" Jensen asked, looking dissatisfied.

If someone had told her five years ago that she'd become friends with RJ Malloy, she'd never have believed it. But, by the time he'd dropped her off, she felt like they were on their way to becoming friends. He was surprisingly self-deprecating, insightful, and funny. And she was so glad she hadn't hurt him. If anything, she was sad he'd felt she was too good for him. She hoped he believed her when she'd said that wasn't true. "We're going to stay friends." Kitty said this to no one in particular. "Nothing more."

"Because of Tyson Ellis?" her father asked.

"Now who's being nosy?" Twyla laughed.

"No, not because of Tyson." Kitty shook her head. "I don't think of RJ that way. It wouldn't be fair to him to string him along. There's no reason for him to waste his time on me instead of finding the woman he's meant to be with."

"You don't think, in time, something more could develop? A relationship based on friendship is often stronger for it." Mabel's voice was soft.

"You're right but…no." Kitty shook her head. "We get along but we don't…click. You know? He was fine with it. He said he felt relieved."

"He said that? Relieved?" Her father was scowling again. "That's downright rude."

Kitty sighed. She should have kept her mouth shut. "No, Dad, it's all good—"

"What you're saying is he's not brokenhearted?" Twyla sighed. "And there's no reason why I can't ask him out?"

All Kitty could do was stare at her sister. Twyla and RJ? She remembered RJ's comments about needing a loud, bossy, and short-tempered woman to keep him in check and smiled. *Twyla and RJ.*

"Twyla Crawley." Their father sighed. "What sort of example are you setting for your niece?"

"Um, a good one?" Twyla forked up some salad. "A woman should go after what she wants—just like any man. Who knows, maybe this Valentine's Day, everyone will get hit by one of Cupid's arrows."

Kitty knew better. Everyone but her, that is. She was perfectly content to receive cards from her family—again.

"No." Samantha shook her head frantically. "I don't want to."

"Don't you worry, sugar, your daddy won't let Cupid or his arrows get anywhere close to you. He'd likely throw himself in the line of fire, if need be." For the first time since they got home, their father was laughing. It was enough to drain all the tension from the room.

"Did RJ say anything else?" Twyla asked, her gaze searching Kitty's. "Anything at all?"

"Not really." What was that look for?

"Good man." Twyla sighed, smiling brightly.

Kitty wasn't sure what her sister was up to, but she was glad that conversation moved back to the upcoming festivities—and the rodeo. Which reminded her. "Daddy, you need to let Tyson know about the calves for the rodeo. He'll need time to find another sponsor if we're not going to do it this year."

"You *do* like that boy." Her father set his fork down and leaned back in his chair.

Kitty sighed. "I don't want our family to be responsible for the rodeo not having a calf-scramble this year."

"She's right, Dad. It *is* tradition." Jensen nodded. "How about I take care of it?"

"Fine," their father snapped. "I'm just going to sit here and eat my bland soup while you all decide everything."

FOR THREE DAYS, Tyson had been cleaning nonstop. He'd never been a fan of horror movies, so experiencing two kids with a stomach virus was way outside of his comfort zone. He'd never realized how much a tiny person could throw up. Or how one minute, they were smiling and laughing and sipping juice and the next they were sobbing and he was running for a bucket. It didn't stop at bedtime, either. It didn't seem to matter if it was three in the afternoon, or three in the morning—throw-up didn't care.

"Unca Tyson." June sat in his lap.

"What's up, Junebug? You okay? You need to throw up?" He eyed the bucket across the room.

"I'm okay." June yawned. "No tummy wumbles."

"Good." He relaxed some. "You let me know if that changes."

"Yep." She bounced one foot.

"I'm glad you girls are going to be all better in time for the rodeo and Valentine's party. You don't want to miss out on that. It's real special."

"Why, Grampa Earl?" July was resting against a pillow against the arm of the couch. She rolled just enough to peer over the arm at his father.

"Well, now, it just is." Earl closed his magazine and laid it on his lap. "The rodeo's good fun. Horses, cows, cowboys, rodeo clowns—your momma said you'd never been to one before so you're in for a real treat. Uncle Tyson here helps out with that, too. You girls could even try mutton bustin' if you want?"

"What's that?" June was all wide-eyed. "Bustin' who?"

"It's a fancy way of saying you can ride a sheep." His father chuckled.

"A sheep?" June and July exchanged a surprised look.

"And then the next day is the Valentine's party. There are booths, games and rides, a dance showcase, and arts and crafts. And everyone who makes a valentine hangs it on a streamer and ties it on one of the branches of erste Baum."

"Why?" June asked.

"It's tradition." His father smiled. "It's mighty nice to find a valentine tied there with your name on it. It lets everyone else know you're cared about."

Unfortunately, thoughts of RJ tying some blinking, sparkled-up, singing valentine for Kitty to erste Baum filled his mind. It was possible. So far, RJ had done nothing on a small scale. Why would he change now?

"I hope I get one." July smiled.

"Me, too." June clapped her hands.

He and his father exchanged a look and a wink. They'd make sure both girls got their very own valentine on erste Baum.

June peered up at him. "Can we watch the princess movie again?"

"If that's what you want." He rifled through the blankets the girls had been burrowing under for the remote control.

"I like that one, too." July rested her head

against the arm of the couch, a ragdoll tucked under her arm. "I like the songs."

"They are catchy." Tyson knew all the songs. By now, he could probably perform a one-man version of the movie. His father had been humming one of the songs, over and over, since they'd watched the movie the first time—which was at least twenty viewings ago now. He didn't mind, though. What else was there to do when every little move could cause significant stomach distress.

"My favowit is the kitty." June smiled up at him.

"The one that wears the big hat or the one that plays the piano?" he asked. Finally, he found the remote.

"The one that wears the hat is called Pierre. The one that plays the piano is Hubert." His father sat in his recliner, flipping through a wholesale feed supply catalog. "Don't forget there's another one that dances the flamenco. He's named Ramondo."

"Thanks for the clarification, Dad." Tyson grinned as he pressed Play.

"Who do you like, Uncle Tyson?" July asked.

"I like the snail." He pulled the blanket over June.

"Fwancisco?" June giggled. "He's funny."

"Just like your uncle Tyson." His father chuckled. "Though I think Uncle Tyson might be a little faster than Francisco."

Tyson shrugged. The last three days had taken all of his energy reserves. He was pretty sure he and Francisco would be neck and neck in a race. That thought had him shaking his head. A couple of weeks ago, he had no knowledge of cartoon films and he'd been just fine. Now? He was content to watch them. Heck, he'd even found himself analyzing one or two of the movies' lessons. Which should be concerning, shouldn't it? It was a sign he needed to get out of the house, at the very least.

"I'm thinking of running to the store." He glanced at his father.

"We need more crackers and electrolyte drink." His father nodded. "And some of the Popsicles, too."

It had been eight hours since the last vomit-related incident, but he and his father weren't going to take any chances.

"Anything else?" Tyson asked, smiling as both girls giggled over part of the movie.

"I'll call Lorraine and see if she can make up some of that chicken noodle soup?" His dad set the magazine aside and reached for his phone.

"Yummy." June nodded.

"I'm so hungry." July agreed.

Tyson shifted June against the couch cushions

and made sure to tuck them both under the blanket. "Maybe a little bit. I don't want either one of you getting sick again."

"Me neitha." June shook her head, leaning around him to see the television screen.

"Didn't mean to get in your way, Junebug." Tyson stood.

"Look, look!" June pointed at the television. "It's Fwancisco."

Tyson turned in time to see the snail—trailing behind the parade of singing animals. "There he is."

"I'll call you if we need something else." His father nodded at him. Since the girls' arrival, his father's emergency-only phone usage policy had gone out the window. If the girls needed or wanted something, he let Tyson know, and Tyson took care of it right away.

"You're good?" A twinge of guilt washed over him.

"They're fine." His father nodded. "We're over the worst of it."

Tyson grabbed his hat off the coat tree by the front door and headed out. It was surprisingly chilly. By now, the temps were normally climbing into the eighties. They were nowhere near that today.

His phone started ringing as he climbed into

his truck. He pressed the button so it connected to his Bluetooth and answered, "Hello?"

"Tyson." It was Jensen. "Wanted to make sure you're all still alive."

"It was pretty touch-and-go for a while, but the worst is behind us." He chuckled. "At least, I hope it is. Who knew something so small could produce such quantities of gross."

"And you had two of them. Samantha had a real mild case and it was nasty." Jensen sighed.

"She okay? Anyone else get sick?" Was Kitty okay? He knew she still had a few tutus and some finishing touches to do for the costumes. Getting sick would get in the way of that.

"Dad's started making noises this morning about feeling poorly, so Kitty is keeping an eye on him. She's about the only one he'll tolerate when he's under the weather."

Tyson took a deep breath. *Poor Kitty.* Twyla had called her sister a saint and she wasn't wrong. Dwight Crawley healthy was hard to handle. He could only imagine how difficult the man could get when he was sick. It was a good thing Kitty had more patience in her little finger than most people had in their whole body. "Sorry to hear that."

"Yeah, me, too. I'm hoping he just woke up on the wrong side of the bed this morning and not sick." Jensen sighed. "I'd love for this virus to be behind us."

"I hear you." He didn't know how he and his father had managed to escape unscathed. Probably because the two of them had disinfected and washed and disinfected again several times a day. He had the chapped knuckles to prove it. "I was getting ready to call you and thank you for dropping off all the supplies. Dad and I didn't have any of that sort of thing on hand." He rolled to a stop at the end of the long, gravel driveway.

"Figured as much. Well, Kitty did. She suggested it."

Tyson was grinning. "Then I'll make sure to thank her when I see her next." He'd been planning on stopping by the Calico Pig anyway. Not for any particular reason. He wanted to see her—that was reason enough.

"I've got another reason for calling, though."

"Oh?" He turned onto the highway. "What's up?"

"I talked to Dad about the calves and it's a go. I can deliver them to the stockyards next week. Just tell me when."

"Oh really? That is good news." And a huge relief, since he'd been having a dickens of a time finding a replacement. "I was waiting, in case he changed his mind—"

"I didn't really do anything. You can thank my

sister for that, too. If she hadn't brought it up, I would have forgotten."

"She did?" He couldn't stop grinning. "Good to know." He'd liked knowing that Kitty was thinking of him. He'd be a fool to believe it meant something more—she'd always been considerate of others. It was one of the things he loved about her. He paused. Even thinking the word *love* was hard. Until now, *love* had been code for a sort of game full of tricks and lies. Now, love was something entirely different. And he wanted to experience it all with Kitty.

CHAPTER SIXTEEN

IT WAS THE night of the Sweethearts Rodeo and Kitty had never been so happy to be out and about. Samantha's bout with the tummy bug had been a breeze compared to her father's illness. For five days, he'd been so miserable he'd barely let Kitty out of his sight. If Martha hadn't shown up and chased her out of his room, she'd likely have collapsed into a heap. But the woman had swooped in, taken charge, and put her father—gently—in his place.

Kitty had stood by and listened, more in awe of Martha Zeigler than ever before.

"Land sakes, Dwight Crawley." Martha had taken one look at him and shaken her head. "Why did you wait so long to call me?"

"I didn't want to burden you, Martha."

"So you'll burden your daughters? You keep saying you want Kitty to do more for herself. You keep saying you feel like you were holding her back." She'd put her hands on her hips. "Or did I hear you wrong?"

"No, you didn't." Her father had glanced her way. "You're right."

"I normally am." Martha had no problem agreeing with him. "It's not right. That's why you should have called me. And another reason you should move in with me. I never get sick and I have nothing but you to worry about. You hear me?"

"Yes, ma'am." And he'd held out his hand for the woman.

"Mmm-hmm." Her tone was impatient, but she'd taken his hand in hers. "Foolish man."

"*Your* foolish man." His smile took years off his expression.

"I know it." She sighed, but her affection was obvious. "You go on, Kitty. You take care of yourself now, you hear?"

After that, Kitty had left them alone—and crawled in bed. There'd been plenty of time to consider what she'd heard. Martha Zeigler wanted her father to move in with her so she could take care of him? It'd been quite the revelation. Who knew if her father would actually consider such a thing?

She'd done her best to stay healthy but hadn't succeeded. Almost forty-eight hours later, she was feeling human again and full of possibilities. For the first time in weeks, she had the energy boost she needed to focus on the online store.

Last night, she'd worked on updating the website for hours. It'd turned out even better than she'd expected.

Tonight, she wasn't going to think about her father or the online store or RJ or Tyson or anything else. She was going to have fun with her niece and enjoy the rodeo. She held Samantha's hand as they climbed up the steps of the new shiny bleachers. "How high do you want to go?"

"*Way* up." She pointed at the top of the new bleachers.

"You sure?"

"Not too high." Jensen pointed at a row in the middle. "That way, you won't get a bug up your nose or buzzed by a bat."

"Daddy." She giggled. "Okay."

Kitty led them down the row and sat, Samantha, Mabel, and Jensen filing in after her. "Save room for Aunt Twyla." Her sister was getting cotton candy and lemonade for them.

"Grampa, too?" Samantha asked.

"Grampa is sitting with Miss Martha." Mabel patted Samantha's knee.

Her father was getting the VIP treatment. Thanks to Miss Martha, he was sitting in a box seat right up front with her. He'd been pleased as punch about it, too. Since her arrival at the ranch to take care of her father, they'd been closer than ever.

"Look!" Samantha took off her cowboy hat and used it to wave. "It's Juney and July."

Sure enough, the two little girls stood at the bottom of the bleachers with Earl Ellis. They looked more adorable than ever in their plaid shirts, straw cowboy hats, and jeans—little cowgirls through and through. The minute they saw Samantha, they started jumping up and down and squealing with glee.

Earl led them to the steps and let them run up until they'd reached them, following close behind. "Mind if we sit with you?" he asked.

"Of course not." Kitty hugged each of the girls.

"I like your hats." Samantha pointed at her own. "We're all cowgirls."

"Uncle Tyson says we have to be." July nodded, holding up one foot. "See."

"Boots, too." June pointed at her feet.

Earl sat on the bleacher before them. "Never took two little girls clothes shopping before."

"I'm betting it was an adventure." Jensen chuckled. "At least, it is when I take Samantha shopping. It doesn't matter if it's a folder for school or a new pair of boots, it's going to take a while."

Earl chuckled. "You don't say? Makes me feel better. It might have taken the better part of the afternoon to get them outfitted just right."

Rodeo had always been part of Kitty's world,

but watching it with June and July was like see-ing it for the first time. Their wide-eyed wonder as the flag girls galloped into the arena, the flags unfurling to wave in the wind as they rode, was precious. When everyone stood to sing the na-tional anthem, they did, too—their little voices ringing out with excitement.

"Look, look, it's Unca Tyson," June squealed.

Sure enough, Tyson rode into the ring on his big buckskin horse. He rode the fence line to the far side of the arena and stopped.

"What's he doing?" July asked.

"He's a pick-up man," Earl explained. "If a cowboy gets hurt or falls or needs help, Tyson rides up and gets that cowboy out of there."

"He does?" June blinked. "He wescues them?"

"Yes, ma'am." Earl was clearly proud of his son.

"Uncle Tyson is neat." July sighed.

Kitty didn't bother pretending the sight of him didn't have her heart rate skyrocketing. How could it not? He was so handsome. The way he sat tall in his saddle, one hand resting on his thigh, eyes alert and focused—he was the epit-ome of a cowboy. Ready to ride into danger, if needed. A protector, through and through.

As the announcer was introducing the bull riding event, Tyson's gaze shifted to the stands.

"I think he's looking for you," Earl whispered. "Give him a wave."

Both girls stood up and waved like mad.

Tyson's smile was instantaneous. He lifted the hand from his thigh to wave—and tipped his hat, too.

Oh, my heart. She took a deep, wavering breath. If she did her usual staring, there was the potential for half of Garrison to witness it. Better to avoid looking at him for the remainder of the rodeo. Considering how much was going on, it shouldn't be too hard.

"Miss Kitty." June grabbed her hand. "That bull is so scawy."

Sure enough the first bull—and his rider—had erupted from the chute and were flying all over the place. Kitty wound up with June in her lap while July and Samantha huddled together between her and Mabel. Bull riding wasn't their favorite. In fact, both June and July covered their faces for most of the main event.

They loved barrel racing. As soon as a new rider came racing into the arena, all three of the girls were on their feet, cheering and clapping until the horse and rider had exited the arena.

"It's that time of the night. Mutton bustin' time," the announcer was saying. "Let's get all the little cowboys and cowgirls down here for a chance at a belt buckle. Then we'll go right into the calf scramble."

"Are you going to do it?" Jensen asked Samantha. "Your call."

"Nah." Samantha smoothed her hands over her jeans. "I don't want to get all dirty."

Jensen chuckled. "Fair enough."

"You want to try?" Earl turned to June and July. "If you hold on longest, you get a big belt buckle and bragging rights."

"What's bwagging wights?" June looked confused.

"You get to tell everyone about it." He winked.

"I don't want to." July shook her head. "I'm gonna stay with Samantha."

"I do!" June hopped up. "Let's go!" She grabbed Kitty's hand and started tugging her to the stairs. "Come on."

"I guess I'll take you, then." Kitty laughed as she followed after the little girl.

There was a crowd assembled by the time they got to the sign-up table but June was too excited to care.

"I'm widin' a sheep." She smiled up at her.

"Yes, ma'am." Kitty nodded. "I've got a secret, too." She crouched. "If you listen to me, I'll give you the best way to hold on."

"Okay," June whispered. "I won't tell." She

pressed a finger to her lips. "No shawing sec-wets."

"I came to cheer you on." Tyson crouched beside them, grinning. "But we're telling secrets?"

"Hi, Unca Tyson." June's excitement gave way to exasperation. "You can't hewa. It's Kitty's *sec-wet*."

He laughed, long and loud. "Okay." He covered his ears. "Go on."

By the time it was June's turn, the little girl was hyperfocused. Instead of getting nervous from watching the other riders, she seemed to be taking notes. She shook her head or nodded or clapped when a ride was over.

"Looks like she's in the zone." Tyson stood at the fence beside Kitty.

"That face is intense." Kitty nodded, smiling at June as one of the rodeo workers led her to her sheep. "Remember what I told you," she called out.

June gave her two thumbs-up and climbed onto the sheep. She rested her cheek on the sheep's hindquarters, slid her arms around right in front of the sheep's back legs, and wrapped her legs around the sheep's neck.

"I seem to recall a little Kitty Crawley riding that way." Tyson glanced her way.

"I won the belt buckle that year." Kitty had

been so proud, too. "Maybe Juney will have the same luck."

"Was this your secret?" he asked, gesturing to June.

"If it's a secret, I can't tell you." She smiled up at him—and was instantly aware of him standing beside her. She leaned more heavily against the pipe fence and struggled to control her heart rate.

She was grateful when the horn went off, and June and her sheep started running to the other end of the arena.

"Hold on, Juney!" she called out.

"You can do it, Junebug!" Tyson yelled.

It was over in seconds. June held on until the buzzer went off—and kept right on holding on. It took both of them and one of the volunteer judges to convince June she'd won and it was okay to let go.

June's shirtfront and jeans had a coating of dust and there was a smudge of dirt on her cheek, but the little girl was downright euphoric when they handed her the belt buckle. "I did it," she breathed, staring at the silver belt buckle as if it was a true treasure.

"I knew you would." Kitty hugged her close. "You fought hard."

"I wanted it weal bad." June hugged the belt buckle close.

"That's what you do when you want something, Junebug. You fight for it, with everything you've got." Tyson patted the little girl's head. "You hold on tight and don't let go."

Kitty was surprised to find Tyson staring at her as he said this, not June. It wasn't just the words he said that had her lungs deflating and her heart ping-ponging inside her chest. It was the look on his face as he said it. It was the same focus and determination she'd seen on June's face right before the little girl had walked into the arena to win her mutton bustin' belt buckle.

TYSON GLANCED DOWN at June, who sat on the saddle in front of him. She'd asked for a ride around the arena and, now that the rodeo was over, he saw no reason not to. He'd take any opportunity to foster her newfound love of horses. And, apparently, sheep.

"That belt buckle is almost as big as you are." He tapped the large metal buckle. At some point during the rodeo, his father had found June a real leather belt at one of the craftsman's booths and had the shiny new belt buckle attached. "It's not going to make you fall over?"

"You awe silly, Unca Tyson." June giggled. "I'm a weal cowgirl now. Widin' sheep and hawsies, too." She leaned forward to pat the horse's neck. "What's his name?"

"This is Stryder."

"Hi, Stwyder." Juney patted the horse again. "Nice to meet you."

Tyson smiled, steering Stryder to the gate of the large arena, where his father was waiting. "Let me get Stryder taken care of and I'll meet you at the fairgrounds."

"We'll be over by the funnel cakes." His father reached up for June. "Rodeo's not complete without one."

"What's that?" June asked.

"Yummy, Juney. It is yummy." Tyson lifted June from the saddle and handed her to his father.

"Yay!" She slipped her arms around his father's neck. "Let's go, Grampa Earl. I'm hungwy."

"Yes, ma'am." His father carried June into the crowd, talking to her the whole time.

"You're looking downright domesticated." RJ Malloy was leaning against the fence, his cowboy hat pushed back on his head, and a smile on his face.

"I don't know about that." Tyson slid off Stryder. "Good riding tonight."

RJ nodded. "Not too shabby." RJ was a solid bronc rider and calf roper. "Amazing how much easier it is when you're sober."

Tyson chuckled. "Go figure."

"Kitty around?" RJ was watching him.

He stared at the other man. "I was surprised

the two of you weren't sitting together." And more than a little happy, too.

RJ's brows dipped. "You were?" He laughed then. "So you don't…" He broke off.

"What was that?"

"Oh, nothing." RJ stuck his thumbs through his belt loops. "I guess I'll go find her, try to fill up her dance card before you get there." He tipped his hat and headed off toward the dance pavilion.

Tyson stared after the man, struggling to keep his irritation in check. "Let's go," he murmured to Stryder. He got Stryder unsaddled and settled in before heading back to the fairgrounds. His official duties for the evening were over, now he could spend time with his dad, the girls, and, hopefully, Kitty.

The last week had gotten away from him. There'd been a shipment mix-up at the shop, the girls had twice as many dance rehearsals to make up for the classes they'd missed, and the new sound system at the stockyards had stopped working. It wasn't easy to find someone capable of fixing the latest, greatest technology in these parts. Calling someone in from Austin had been costly, but necessary—otherwise tonight would have been a catastrophe instead of a success.

But the thing that weighed most on him was Kitty. Specifically, trying to win her heart. The

Valentine's Festival was the perfect place to confess his love to her. Once he'd decided how he wanted to, hopefully, sweep Kitty off of her feet, he'd enlisted the girls help. He'd sworn them to secrecy—with a pinkie-promise—before he and the girls had made two dozen Valentine's cards just for Kitty. They'd insisted on lots of glitter, stickers, and white paper lace trim for every one of them and, in the end, he thought they looked just about perfect. Waiting until the Valentine's party to tell her how he felt was…romantic. He'd never done romantic before, but he'd try—for Kitty. For Kitty, he'd try just about anything.

He'd only found out Kitty had gotten sick yesterday, when he'd had lunch with Jensen. While he'd been putting out fires at work, she'd been nursing her father and herself back to health. That was the sort of thing he should've known. If he had, he'd have sent her soup or flowers or something to try to cheer her up. If she was struggling with something, he should be there for her. That's what he should do… It's what he wanted to do.

The fairgrounds were bustling. Before long, the booths would close down and everyone would move to the dance pavilion. The Ladies Guild had brought in a live band that played classic country hits, all made for two-stepping.

There was no way around it, he was nervous.

His only plan was to ask her to dance but… He was nervous, all the same. He'd spent so long convincing himself he was better off alone. Opening himself up, letting people in—even acknowledging he had a heart—went against everything he'd spent years resisting. And, if it wasn't Kitty, he'd keep on resisting.

But it was Kitty. She'd changed everything.

He nodded as he passed the Schneider family, murmured, "Evening," and kept on walking.

"Tyson." Rusty Woodard flagged him down. "We're headed to Buck's in a bit. Play some pool. You're welcome to join us."

"Maybe." He hoped he'd be with Kitty but… He might need a few beers with friends if things went south.

"Got it." Rusty clapped him on the shoulder. "Figured you might need a break from the whole kids thing."

"I appreciate it." Strange as it was, he'd gotten kinda partial to having the girls underfoot. If anything, it was going to be hard to go back to normal when he put them on a plane in two weeks.

When he finally got to the funnel cake booth, he found his father, the girls, and the Crawley family sitting at one of the large picnic tables.

"There you are." He sat—then started laughing. "I guess you girls like funnel cakes? If you didn't, you two wouldn't be covered in powdered sugar."

"Is there a way to eat funnel cake without getting covered in powdered sugar?" Kitty asked, shaking out the front of her pink polka-dot blouse. "I thought that was part of the experience." Her gaze bounced his way as she talked.

He nodded, taking in just how pretty she was. And she was. Sweet, too. Sweeter than any funnel cake could ever be. He cleared his throat. "I guess it is." He broke off a piece of the fried dough covered in sugar and popped it into his mouth. "All I know is, it's delicious."

While the girls filled him in on their thoughts about the rodeo, he tried to concentrate. Really, all he wanted was a minute alone with Kitty.

"Kitty." Where had RJ Malloy come from? It was like the man could read Tyson's thoughts and knew just when to swoop in and mess up his plans. "Would you be willing to take a turn around the dance floor with me?"

"Me?" Kitty stopped wiping powdered sugar from Juney's face.

"Yes, you." RJ winked and held out his hand.

"But you can't, Miss Kitty." June shook her head. "You hafta dance with Unc—"

"Go on, Kitty." Earl covered June's mouth with the tissue—saving Tyson from an all-out heart attack. "I've got Juney."

Kitty glanced at her sister—who waved her away. "Sure."

Tyson watched as Kitty took RJ's hand and let him lead her to the dance pavilion.

"Sowwy." June whispered. "I fogot about Unca Tyson's secwet."

"It's okay, Junebug. Tomorrow, it won't be a secret." His father winked at her.

"Ooh, can we dance, too?" July asked.

"I don't see why not." His father was still trying to de-sugar June's face and hair. "It's been a while since I've taken a turn around the dance floor. Your uncle's a pretty good dancer, too. Not as good as me, but close."

"Thanks, Dad." Tyson rolled his eyes.

"You can dance, Tyson? I don't believe you." Twyla called from the end of the table. "I think I'll need a demonstration. Come on, let's dance."

"Yay!" June clapped her hands. "You can do it, Unca Tyson!"

Tyson didn't resist when Twyla grabbed his hand and tugged him after her. He liked dancing well enough—even if she wasn't exactly the partner he'd been aiming for.

"What's got you wound up so tight?" Twyla asked once they were on the dance floor. "You seem mighty distracted."

"Nope." He shook his head. "Are you leading or am I?"

"Oh, please." She rolled her eyes. "You're not fooling anyone, Tyson Ellis. Well, except for Kitty. She has no clue how you feel about her."

That caught Tyson's full attention. "And you do?"

"I was there when you told RJ, remember? Not like I didn't already know before that." She was definitely leading—the dance and the conversation. "That's why we're going to make our way across the dance floor so you can swoop her out of RJ's arms and stare into her eyes and confess your undying love for her."

All he could do was stare at the woman.

"We're almost there." Twyla was heading toward Kitty and RJ without an ounce of subtlety. "Ready?"

No, he wasn't. Not tonight. He'd worked it out in his head—

"We're cutting in—" Twyla disentangled herself from him and shoved Kitty at him. "Bye. Have fun now." She smiled up at RJ and let him spin her away.

"Hi. Sorry." Kitty's cheeks were red. "My sister…"

"She's an original." He sighed, then stared down at the woman in his arms. This was what he'd wanted. Now that he had it, he wasn't going to think about anything else. Beneath the strands of white lights and lanterns, Kitty's eyes were near copper. Her long, dark lashes fluttered against her cheeks as she took a deep breath. "Having fun?"

She nodded, her gaze locked with his.

"And how's it going with RJ?" Why had he asked about RJ?

"We're friends. Just friends. It… We decided… That's all." The words poured out.

He knew he was smiling like an idiot, but there was no way to stop it. "Is that so?" He even sounded giddy.

"It didn't feel right." Her hand seemed to tighten on his. "Not when I have feelings for someone else."

His smile evaporated. "You… What?" His heart froze up—but not before pain sliced through it. "You do?"

She nodded. "I have, for a long time. But I know it's one-sided, so I haven't said anything because I don't want anyone to get hurt or things to get awkward or to cause drama." Her words came out all at once—without pause. "I don't like causing problems or doing anything that draws attention my way."

"I know." He swallowed, the urge to pull up his defenses and shut down overwhelming.

"But if I don't tell him, I'll regret it, won't I?" She seemed to be waiting for his answer.

"I…don't know." Why was she telling him this? He didn't want to know.

"Oh." She frowned, then took a deep breath. "I think I will. No, I know I will. As far back as I can remember, my heart has been his. I want to be with him. I want him to be happy. When he's been hurt, I hurt, too. He's been through so much, lost loved ones and been betrayed. It's harder to see the person you love go through that than it is to endure it yourself, I think." She took another deep breath. "I… I know I'm not what he wants, but there's nothing I can do to stop loving him." Those eyes were so warm, so beautiful.

"Kitty." He was having a hard time breathing. Everything she said, he wanted her to feel for him. He wanted her unconditional love and support. Him, not someone else.

"I need to get it all out, Tyson. I… I love you." Her voice was trembling. "I love you so much."

I love you. Tyson shook his head, stunned. Everything she'd said was for him?

She nodded, a sad smile on her lips. "It's okay. I expected this. I have no expectations. None."

"But, Kitty…" He was reeling. She loved him? *Him.* And his heart was full to bursting. All this time, he'd been terrified she'd reject him and she'd been feeling the same about him? He was a fool for letting fear steal so much time from them.

"You don't have to say anything." The music

had stopped at some point and she was stepping away from him.

"No... I... Kitty, I..." He swallowed—so many words rushed up to force their way out that everything else stuck. He swallowed again but it was no use. "I care about you."

"I know." She patted his shoulder. "And that's enough. Thank you for the dance." She turned and ran away before he could set the record straight.

CHAPTER SEVENTEEN

KITTY HADN'T BOTHERED to dress up. The only reason her dress was pink was because Samantha had picked it out for her. Samantha was excited about today—about the dance showcase. That was why she was sitting here, in erste Baum Park, surrounded by balloon hearts, pink and red streamers, and garlands of pink and red and white flowers strung from the branches of the massive tree overhead. She was surrounded by love—from decorations to the people of Garrison themselves. Brooke and Audy. Mike and Eloise. Jensen and Mabel. Hattie and Forrest. Even Twyla was being wide-eyed and flirty with RJ while the two of them stood in front of the lemonade stand.

She didn't begrudge any of them. Love and family and happiness were what most people wanted—it's what she wanted. And, even if she wound up alone, she wasn't willing to settle for anything else.

"You look pretty." Her father sat beside her.

"Thanks, Dad." She didn't buy it. Her reflection had revealed puffy eyes with dark circles.

"You'd look prettier if you smiled." He reached over and patted her knee.

She smiled. At least, she tried to smile. From her father's expression it was possible her efforts were in vain.

"What's eating you, Kitty?" This from Martha Zeigler, who sat on her father's other side. "I thought, after last night, you'd be smiling ear to ear."

"Well, now…" Her father gave Martha a stern look and a headshake.

Everyone had seen Tyson smile and tip his hat at her. Everyone had seen them on the dance floor together. But the two of them were the only ones who knew what had been said. She'd like to keep it that way. Her family, however, had been present to watch her run to her room. And later, when Twyla had come to check on her, she'd been crying. Knowing Twyla, that information had been relayed to the rest of the family. She was surprised her father hadn't shared that bit of information with Martha.

"I get it. It's none of my business." Martha nodded. "That's fine by me." She gave Kitty a smile and sat back.

Kitty pressed her hands against her knees, eager to get the performance over with. The sooner they were done, the sooner she could help clean up and head home. She'd always known the risk she was taking in telling him how she'd felt. But she'd had no idea how much his rejection would hurt. It hurt—a lot.

So much so that sitting here pretending that all was right with the world was physically exhausting. That she hadn't slept much last night probably didn't help her exhaustion, either.

It was temporary. In a couple of days, it wouldn't hurt so much. And, honestly, she'd rather live with heartbreak than regret. At least she'd tried. He knew she loved him.

"Kitty." Twyla nudged her.

"When did you sit?" Kitty frowned at her sister—now sitting on the other side of her.

"I walked right past you to sit." Twyla's eyes swept over her face. "You were staring straight ahead, all dead eyed, so I guess you didn't see me." She handed her a glass. "Lemonade. Maybe some sugar will perk you up."

Kitty took the glass. "Thank you."

Gretta Willams came out a few minutes later. "Good afternoon, ladies and gentlemen, moms and dads, aunts, uncles, and doting grandparents. We have a fun Valentine's showcase for you today. I want to give a very special thanks to Kitty Crawley for taking on the costumes. And to all her helpers."

Kitty shook her head.

"Stand up, Kitty." Gretta was all smiles.

She stood, mortified. The only reason the costumes had been completed was because of the help she'd received. Taking credit for it—at least being the only one named—felt wrong. So did the audience's applause.

"Now, on to the show. First up, our little Cupids take flight." Gretta stepped aside as an adorable troupe of three- and four-year-olds walked onto the stage.

The best thing about adorable children? They wholly distracted her. She was caught up by the little ones hopping across the stage in their tutus. Next came a group of older kids, middle or high school probably. Their dance was an actual dance—with choreography and a cohesive performance. As impressive as they were, Kitty favored the little guys bumping into each other, falling down, or waving out into the audience.

"Let's hear it for our cloggers." Gretta stepped aside.

"It's Samantha. It's Samantha." Her father doted on Samantha. As far as he was concerned, his granddaughter was the most talented dancer in all of Garrison.

Sure enough, Samantha, July, and June came out with five other dancers. They were fully decked out in their tutus, fringe-and-sparkle vests, and cowboy hats with equally sparkly hat-bands.

She found herself scouring the crowd for Tyson and Mr. Ellis. This was probably just as big a deal for them as it was for the girls. When she saw Mr. Ellis, grinning from ear to ear, she smiled. Tyson, who stood next to his father, was holding up his phone. She figured he was either recording the performance for Samantha's parents or live streaming it.

"Kitty." Twyla nudged her. "They're about to start."

She turned back, gave Samantha two thumbs-up, and waited.

Samantha had put a whole bunch of hours into practicing. She wanted to move up to the older kids' class and said she couldn't miss a single step. Not only did she want to keep clogging, she wanted to try ballet, too.

"Look at her sparkle," her father whispered to Martha.

Kitty nodded. She wished she'd had the chance to give Gretta a list of everyone that had helped—all the extra work had been worth it. Every step and stomp had the sequins moving under the floodlights they'd set up to illuminate the stage.

"She is as cute as a button." Martha patted his arm. "The cutest button that ever there was."

"Isn't that the truth?" her father agreed.

Samantha was one of the two lead dancers. June and July were behind her, watching every move she made and mirroring it to the best of their ability. Gretta had been kind enough to let June dance with her sister's class but it was obvious the little girl was struggling to keep up.

At one point, June tripped on her clog and went down. Her lower lip flipped out and her eyes went round but July slipped her arm around her sister and helped her back up.

This earned a round of applause from the audience—and put a great big smile back on little June's face.

"She is so cute," Twyla whispered to her. "I mean, I know she's not Samantha but, come on, look at that little face. And I don't even especially like kids."

"She is precious," Kitty agreed, laughing when June spotted her and waved like mad. "And you do, too. You'll probably wind up having the most kids out of all of us."

Twyla shot her an overly offended look and snorted.

The clogging got louder and louder until it stopped. All the dancers were red cheeked and breathing hard, and all the parents were clapping.

"Now, that was something." Her father whistled loudly. "That's my girl. Way to go, Samantha."

He pointed and waved, making sure everyone knew who she was.

There were two more performance groups before Samantha's class came back onstage for another dance. After that, all the students squeezed onto the stage so parents could take pictures.

"Here you go." Jensen held out a bouquet of flowers for Samantha. "You did a great job."

"Thank you, Daddy." She spun around. "It was fun."

From the corner of her eye, Kitty saw June and July with Tyson. They each had bouquets and were smiling and waving at the phone he was holding out. They were too far away for her to hear what they were saying, but both their faces were animated and their hands were moving and pointing, too.

Tyson handed over his phone and tipped his hat back on his head. That smile of his… She took a deep breath and tried to rein in her typical Tyson reaction. She might have succeeded if he didn't choose that moment to look her way. Then she was swimming in those dark brown eyes and all the memories she'd managed to keep at bay through the dance recital came rushing in on her.

I...care about you, Kitty. He'd scrambled to say those words—his startled expression like salt in a paper cut.

She knew he cared about her. They'd known

each other forever. At least it seemed that way. He was a fixture in her life. That wouldn't change. In time, she'd be okay with that. Again. When she really thought about it, nothing had changed. And, knowing Tyson, nothing would. It was a sort of comfort.

He took a step in her direction and Kitty's heart took a nosedive. She wasn't ready to talk to him or act like she hadn't poured her heart and soul out to him. She had no regrets about telling him what was in her heart, but that didn't mean she wasn't embarrassed by his response.

She didn't realize she'd been holding her breath until June grabbed his arm and stopped him. Next thing she knew, he was scooping the little girl up and heading across the park.

"Let's go enjoy some snacks and see if we've got any valentines on erste Baum, shall we?" Twyla took Samantha's hand. "Do you have a secret admirer?"

"Just Daddy." Samantha skipped along. "That's not a secret."

Jensen laughed.

"And what about me?" Kitty's father asked.

"You're not a secret admirer, Grandpa." Samantha grinned up at him.

"She's right, Dad. There was nothing secret about your abundant pride today." Twyla took Samantha's hand.

"But you can be my valentine, too, Grandpa." Samantha led Twyla to erste Baum.

"Before long, the boys in her class will be the ones hanging valentines for her in that tree." Her father's comment had Jensen scowling. "What? It's true."

"I'm not ready to hear things like that, Dad." Jensen stared after his daughter. "She's not even seven yet."

"You young people think time drags on. I'm here to tell you it flies by. Before you know it, she'll be sixteen or twenty-three, dating some hairy-legged boy and sneaking out at night." Her father shook his head.

Mabel grabbed hold of Jensen's hand. "How about we go get some lemonade before that vein in your forehead ruptures."

"Good idea." Jensen draped an arm over her shoulders and steered her to the lemonade stand.

"You were laying it on a little thick, there, weren't you, Dwight, dear?" But Martha was smiling.

"It's my job, isn't it? Keep my kids on their toes." Her father winked at Martha, then her.

"Dad, you're terrible." Kitty shook her head. But her father was making eyes at Martha Zeigler, and Kitty felt the need to make herself scarce—immediately. "I'm going after Saman-tha," she murmured, already walking away.

She loved erste Baum Park. Growing up, she'd made so many memories here. On days like today, when families were gathered and everyone was celebrating, she couldn't help but feel a twinge of wistfulness. No. Stop it. Better to count her blessings and focus on all the good things she had in her life. There were so many. A loving family, lifelong friends, her shop, and, now, online custom orders. Even if she never married and had children of her own, she'd have a full life. Her heart hurt now—and seeing Tyson was hard—but time would take the sting off, and she'd make peace with things the way they were. More than that, she'd be happy.

Tyson helped fold up the wooden chairs and carried them to the long flatbed trailer. "I appreciate the help." He handed the chairs up to RJ.

"Not a problem." RJ nodded. "Twyla told me I had to take her to get ice cream anyway, so I figure I should make myself busy until she's done."

Tyson chuckled.

"She's something else, isn't she?" RJ shrugged.

"She is." Jensen hopped up on the trailer, adding more chairs to the stack. "She can take care of herself. But that doesn't mean I won't come after you if you take one single step out of line."

RJ held up his hands. "Got it."

"Like she'd let him." Tyson laughed then.

Jensen laughed, too. "Yeah, you know what. Good luck, RJ."

RJ looked back and forth between the two of them and shrugged before jumping off the trailer and going for more chairs.

"I'll be clearing out soon. Kitty's gonna watch Samantha while Mabel and I go and have a date. Do the whole Valentine's thing." Jensen turned, his features smoothing out when he spied Mabel and Samantha under erst Baum.

"You might need to find someone else." Tyson cleared his throat. "I've got plans with Kitty."

Jensen turned back to him, his brows high. "Does she know this?"

"She's about to." He took a deep breath. "I was waiting for the crowd to thin out a little."

"Go on." Jensen pointed in Kitty's direction. "Last night she went home, went to her room, and cried. I have a feeling that's on you."

He'd made her cry? He'd done that to Kitty. Hurt her. "I'll fix it. I'll make it up to her." He jumped off the trailer and headed straight for her.

But the closer he got to her, the more determined he got. His heart was near pounding its way out of his chest and all the words he wanted to say were bouncing around inside his head— too scrambled to make much sense but he wasn't going to let that stop him.

"Kitty." The word was gruffer than he'd intended, making her jump. "Kitty."

"Oh, hi." She swallowed, her gaze dodging his. "I'm just getting the last of the cards down. It's sad when people don't get their Valentine's cards, don't you think?"

He nodded.

"But…" She frowned and nodded at a stack of valentines on the ground. "I'm guessing the girls had a hand in this?"

"They love doing arts and crafts." He nodded.

"You could have made some for other people. I don't normally get valentines on erste Baum." Kitty's laugh was nervous. "But I keep taking new cards down and they're for me."

He took his hat off. "I imagine most of the rest of these are, too." He pointed at the remaining streamers. The handmade construction paper cards taped to the ends blowing in the spring breeze. "Did you read any of them?"

"It's getting late and we need to get everything packed up." She shook her head.

"Read one. They all say the same thing." He stood, his hat in his hands, to keep himself from reaching for her. There were things that had to be said—he had to say them. All he could do was hope she'd listen. But the way she was looking at him, rather the way she wouldn't look at him, made him curse himself all over again.

She grabbed one of the valentines still hanging from the tree. "'Will you be my valentine?' Good handwriting, too." She smiled. "Is this from Juney or July?"

"Well, they're from me." He cleared his throat. "I've got some explaining to do."

"You really don't." She pulled down the valentine's card and streamer. "It's okay, Tyson. I'm a big girl. I'm fine. We're fine. Okay?"

"No." He stepped forward. "It's not okay. What I've done? None of it's okay."

She drew in a wavering breath, her faze fixed on the card she held.

"I'm sorry I hurt you last night." *Sorry* wasn't a big enough word. "I would never hurt you, Kitty."

She waved away his words. "Can we please just let this go?" She sniffed. "Let's pretend yesterday didn't happen. I think that's best for both of us."

"I don't want to forget about yesterday." He swallowed. "I don't ever want to forget what you said."

Her eyes met his.

"You know my history. You know about… Mom and Iris." No, that was the coward's way out of this. Making excuses. Blaming someone else. This was on him. All of it.

"I do." She nodded, her gaze falling from his.

"You don't have to talk about that. We don't have to talk about this."

"Kitty." He stepped forward. "We do." He reached out and caught her hand in his. "Please, give me a minute. If you don't like what I have to say, you can send me on my way." Even though the very idea had his heart in knots. "Love... Love is a tricky thing. It's always come with strings for me. Saying it costs something—something that'll hurt in the long run. You said you loved me and I... I panicked. My brain locked up."

She looked up at him then, nothing but sympathy on her face. Of course that's how she'd respond—hurting for him even when he'd hurt her. "You've had more than your fair share of hurt, Tyson. It's not fair."

He nodded. "My mom made it so love was when she needed something. She'd come back full of sweet words and bright smiles and leave as soon as she'd gotten what she wanted from Dad. She didn't just leave me, she left him, too. I saw him open his arms to her, open his heart to her, only to have her toss him aside like he was nothing. I do have memories of her when I was little. I'd like to think she was happy to be my mother then." He shook his head. "I vowed I wouldn't do that. I'd never let myself be used as a doormat. Or a meal ticket. But then Iris came along and that's just what happened. She pursued me, said she loved me, and was at my side at every rodeo event. But after I had my accident and retired, she left. It wasn't me so much as the lifestyle. If I wasn't going to rodeo anymore, what did I have to offer her? A family feedstore? Nights and weekends managing the stockyards or organizing the rodeo—that I wouldn't ride in. I went from feeling like a man to feeling like dirt. It broke me inside. My pride, more than anything."

"Tyson, you know none of that is your fault, don't you?" She shook her head. "It breaks my heart that your mother didn't show you what unconditional love was."

"She didn't. But my father did." He sighed. "It's a shame I chose to let the two people that left me influence my choices over the person that's always been there for me." He shook his head again. "No, that's not right. He's one of the people that's always been there for me." Kitty had been there, too. Quietly, yes, that was her way. But she'd never wavered. "If only I'd gotten out of my own way to see things this clearly."

"We all heal differently. It takes time." She gave his hand an encouraging squeeze.

"The thing is, Kitty, none of that was really love. Not my mother or Iris. They might have said it, but those were words—not what was in their heart. What they said and did has nothing to do with you." He had to get it all out. "That's not how you love. I know you, Kitty Crawley. I know there's not an insincere bone in your body. I know you put everyone else before yourself without thinking. I know you'd drop everything if someone you cared about was in need." He took a deep breath and kept on going. "I know that it can be storming outside but you being in the room brings out the sun. I know I smile when I see you—and I look for you when I don't. I know I'm the luckiest man on the whole planet to have your love. And I promise I won't take it, or you, for granted." He pulled her closer to him. "I love you. I always have."

She was stunned. "But you—"

"I didn't suddenly fall for you because RJ was going after you. But him going after you made me realize I could lose you. And that, I can't do. I can't lose you. So it's a good thing you love me."

She was openmouthed now. The hand he held was shaking—all of her was shaking.

"I am sorry it took me so long to sort myself out." He swallowed. "But I promise fear won't get the upper hand again. I won't let it. I'm used to doing things on my own. I'm not anymore. Whatever comes up—"

"We will handle it together." There was so much love in her smile.

He saw it and knew what it was. More importantly, he felt it—as real as when she slid her arms around his waist. "Yes, ma'am." He put his hat on his head so he could wrap her up and hold her close against him. Only then could he really breathe. All the worry and stress dropped away.

"I love you, Tyson." She breathed against his chest.

He closed his eyes and let her words sink in. There was no doubt or hesitation in her voice. And no disbelief or wariness in his heart. Only peace and happiness. Oh, so much happiness. He turned to press a kiss to her temple. "I'll try to step up my game a little. Flowers, chocolates, jewelry—whatever you want. Tell me what you need to know that I mean what I'm saying." Whatever she needed, whatever she wanted, he wanted to give to her.

She took the slightest step back and looked up at him. "You said you know me."

He nodded.

"Then you know I don't want any of that. I certainly don't need it." She pressed a hand to his cheek. "I don't need anything other than this. You. Taking my hand. Holding me. Telling me you love me." Her smile grew when he leaned into her touch. "This is enough."

"I can do this." He grinned. "And this." He

bent his head, his lips brushing hers in the lightest whisper of a kiss. "I'd like to do that again."

"Yes, please." She stood on tiptoe to greet him.

He kissed her gently. Slowly. There was no need to hurry. "I promise a day won't go by when I don't do this." He pressed another kiss to her lips.

"That's a big promise, Mr. Ellis." She was just a little breathless.

"One I intend to keep." He ran his fingers along the side of her face. "Now that I've got you, I don't want to miss out on anything. I want to take time with you—spend time with you—and build a future together."

She nodded, and that made him so happy he had no choice but to smile.

"As long as I make you happy, I'm happy." His words were a whisper.

"As long as you love me, I will be happy."

"I like the sound of that." And, just because he could, he kissed her again and again.

* * * * *

HARLEQUIN
Reader Service

Enjoyed your book?

Try the perfect subscription for Romance readers and get more great books like this delivered right to your door.

See why over 10+ million readers have tried Harlequin Reader Service.

Start with a Free Welcome Collection with free books and a gift—valued over $20.

Choose any series in print or ebook.
See website for details and order today:

   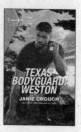

TryReaderService.com/subscriptions